The Admiral

One of Scotland's best-loved authors, Nigel Tranter wrote over ninety novels on Scottish history. He died at the age of ninety in January 2000.

'Fishing and hawking, porridge and game, the smell of peat and bitter cold Highland nights: a page from any of Nigel Tranter's Scottish historical novels evokes the lie of the land better than a library of history books'

The Times

'Through his imaginative dialogue, he provides a voice for Scotland's heroes'

Scotland on Sunday

'He has a burning respect for the spirit of history and deploys his characters with mastery'

Observer

'A magnificent teller of tales'

Glasgow Herald

'Tranter's popularity lies in his knack of making historical events immediate and exciting'

Historical Novels Review

The Admiral

Nigel Tranter

CORONET BOOKS
Hodder & Stoughton

Copyright © 2001 by the estate of Nigel Tranter

First published in Great Britain in 2001
by Hodder and Stoughton
First published in paperback in 2001
by Hodder and Stoughton
A division of Hodder Headline

The right of Nigel Tranter to be identified as the
Author of the Work has been asserted by him in accordance
with the Copyright, Designs and Patents Act 1988.

A Coronet paperback

10 9 8 7 6 5 4 3 2 1

A CIP catalogue record for this title
is available from the British Library.

ISBN 0 340 77015 5

Typeset in Imprint by Hewer Text Ltd, Edinburgh
Printed and bound in Great Britain by
Clays Ltd, St Ives plc

Hodder and Stoughton
A division of Hodder Headline
338 Euston Road
London NW1 3BH

Principal Characters in order of appearance

Andrew Wood: Small laird of Largoshire, in East Fife, of the family of Wood of Bonnytoun.

Janet Lindsay or Wood: Mother of above.

Sir John Lindsay of Pitcruvie: Kinsman of Janet.

Henry Lindsay: Son of above, merchant-trader at Leith and shipowner.

James Barton: Experienced shipmaster and trader.

James the Third: King of Scots.

James, Duke of Rothesay: Son of above, heir to the throne.

John Stewart, Lord Darnley, Earl of Lennox: Kinsman of the monarch.

John Laing, Bishop of Glasgow: Chancellor of the Realm.

Elizabeth Lundie: Daughter of Lundie of Balgony, notable Fife family.

Robert Lundie: Sheriff of Fife, and brother of Elizabeth.

Andrew Forman, Prior of Pittenweem: Later Bishop of Moray.

Hans Poppenruyter: Brass-founder and maker of cannon, at Antwerp.

John, Lord of the Isles, Earl of Ross: Great Highland leader.

Robert Cochrane: Mason and builder, favourite of the king.

Archibald Douglas, Earl of Angus: Great Scots noble.

Stephen Bull: English privateer.

William Elphinstone, Bishop of Aberdeen: Chancellor of the Realm.

Robert Keith: Earl Marischal.

Patrick Hepburn, Earl of Bothwell: Master of the King's Household.

Robert Blackadder: Bishop of Glasgow.

Mariota Hepburn: Wife of Bothwell.

Charles the Eighth: King of France.

Manuel: King of Portugal.

Queen Joan: Widow of King Alfonso of Portugal and aunt of Manuel.

Donald, Lord of the Isles: Highland leader, grandson of John, Lord of the Isles.

Mary Gunn: mother of Donald, above.

Margaret Tudor: daughter of Henry the Seventh of England and wife of James the Fourth.

John of Denmark: King, uncle of James the Fourth.

Henry the Seventh: King of England.

Henry, Prince of Wales: Son of above, heir to the throne.

De la Motte: French ambassador to Scotland.

James the Fifth: Infant King of Scots.

John Stewart, Duke of Albany: heir presumptive to James the Fifth.

Antoine de la Bastie: Noted soldier, friend of Albany and his envoy to Scotland.

James Hamilton, Earl of Arran: Friend of Albany, also envoy to Scotland.

Alexander Home, Lord Home: High Justiciar South of the Forth.

Archbishop Beaton of Glasgow: Chancellor of the Realm.

Prince Henry: Dauphin of France.

Marie de Guise, Duchess of Longueville: Second wife of James the Fifth.

1

The young man gazed out from the eastern horn of Largo Bay, as so often he did. Great was the prospect, south, east and west, across the Forth estuary, to the mighty rock-stack of the Craig of Bass sixteen miles off, rising out of the sea backed by the conical hill of North Berwick Law, westwards to the distant heights of Arthur's Seat, Edinburgh Castle and the Pentland Hills, and much further. But it was rather nearer where his regard was fixed, a mere ten miles, this on the cliffs of the Isle of May, that mile-long island at the very mouth of the firth. For it was there, within a hidden inlet at its south end that the English pirates, or privateers as they called themselves, claiming their government's permission, were apt to lurk, to issue out and attack any vessels that were unwise enough to sail the seas singly rather than in safe convoy. That trap of an island, holy as it might be, former hermitage of St Ethernan, one of Columba's disciples, and seat of a little Benedictine monastery, was very much on Andrew Wood's mind, always was, for there his father had been slain and his ship captured four years before, and he, his elder son, had vowed to avenge him one day.

He would do so, indeed.

Frequently Andrew came here to gaze, however much his good mother declared that he should be doing other things more useful, tending and herding their sheep on Largo Law, aiding her brother at La'hill Mill, working for their kinsman, Sir John Lindsay at nearby Pitcruvie Castle – or even spearing flukies, or flounders, in the shallows of the sands. This last was what he had come to do now; but as so often he got distracted by that Isle of May and its challenge – for that is what it was for him, where one day he would pay the debt to his father.

He well recognised, of course, that this might be quite a long way off. At eighteen years he could scarcely hope to be in any position to carry out his vow very soon. But he would, somehow.

He kicked off his boots, rolled his breeches higher, and picked up his pronged fork on its pole, to wade into the shallows. He quite enjoyed flukie-spearing however cold the water on his feet, this when the tide was right. The flatfish lay hidden just below the surface of sand and water, but they could be felt to wriggle when stood upon by bare feet. Then the spear had to be plunged down into them – with care not to spear the toes in the process, easily done. Then the fish had to be jerked up and caught before it could twist itself off the hook, fall back into the water and swim away free. Care also had to be taken not to make a splashing of the feet, which could warn the creatures, and they could slither away before they were reached.

Andrew had to wade that day for quite some distance through the shallows of the great six-mile-wide bay before he felt movement under his left foot, and he stepped aside and stabbed. But the flukie was too quick for him, and he missed it. However another wriggle quickly followed, and this time his point struck and penetrated. Expertly he hoisted the flapping catch up so as to keep it transfixed until he could grab it with the other hand, detach it, and stow it, still squirming, in the satchel slung from his left shoulder.

There were quite a number of flounders thereabouts, and before long he had as many as to fill his bag.

Before he turned for home, he gave another stare at the May island. That place preoccupied him, he admitted. Were there any English pirates hiding behind it now?

He had some distance to walk to his home. Largo community was odd in being divided between Upper and Lower, half a mile apart. His late father's house stood between the two, as the ground began to rise towards the foot of Largo Law, the highest hill in what was known as the East Neuk of Fife, no mountain as it was. Largostone, as the house was named, after a standing stone in the grounds, was not what could be called a mansion, rather a medium-sized hallhouse, but a suitable and roomy establishment for folk who were not lairds but of lairdly background. His father had come of the Woods of Bonnytoun, in Angus, of which Sir Henry was the present head; and his mother was a Lindsay, kin to Sir John nearby at Pitcruvie Castle. So although his sire, another Andrew, had been a merchant-trader, with his own ship, he was well enough connected.

His mother, Janet, welcomed the flukies, even though she was apt to be critical of his frequent spearings, with her own ideas as to how her elder son should spend his time; while his young brother Jamie, aged ten, was reproachful that he had not been taken along to share in it. Andrew was fond of him, but found him no help at the fishing, for he ran about splashing and shouting, and thus warned the flounders so that they swam away.

Janet Wood had word for Andrew. Sir John Lindsay, at the castle, wanted him to call for some reason.

So, after a hasty meal, he set off on the mile northwards to Pitcruvie Castle.

This was no great fortalice but a fairly simple square tower-house within a barmekin or curtain wall, this containing the usual courtyard, with stabling, byre, brewhouse and storage sheds. Sir John was a younger son of the sixth Lord Lindsay of the Byres, in Lothian.

Now elderly and a widower, his family grown and fled the nest as it were, he was always glad to see young Andrew, who was a frequent visitor and whom he quite often took hawking up the Boghall Burn and on to Norries Law, a lesser height. But this time he had a different proposal for the young man. One of his three sons was a merchant-trader based on Leith, the port of Edinburgh, as indeed Andrew's father had been, a quite common activity for the younger sons of lairdly families. It seemed that this son had recently bought a second ship, this to take part in the increasing trade with the Baltic Hanseatic League, an ever-growing merchanting syndicate, and he wondered whether his far-out young kinsman would consider joining him in this venture, possibly as aide and companion? Andrew's father had suggested a partnership with this Henry Lindsay when he had started up his enterprise at Leith, and been helpful. Now he might demonstrate his appreciation to the son.

Needless to say, Andrew was well pleased to hear of this, and said so. Better than herding sheep, milling and farm work. When did Henry Lindsay want him? He was told whenever he cared to go, the sooner the better probably.

Back at Largostone, his mother was in two minds over this suggestion for her son. She recognised the possibilities of it, but would miss Andrew's company and assistance. Jamie was too young to go herding sheep on Largo Law, and a man about the house was always to be valued. But it could be the sort of start for his son that his father would have wanted. So be it.

A few days later, then, Andrew boarded one of the small vessels that frequently sailed over to Dunbar, North Berwick, Musselburgh or Leith with goods to be exported in larger ships to France, the Netherlands and the German dukedoms, this from Leven, Lower Largo haven being only capable of mooring fishing-boats. Across the Forth they went the fifteen miles, well west of the May, to Leith, with no sign of pirates, passing near the isle of Inchkeith.

At the mouth of the quite wide water of Leith, the port for Edinburgh, Scotland's capital, they entered a major harbour, lining both sides of the river with docks, shipyards, warehouses, granaries, rope-works and sheds, backed by the premises of merchants, shipowners and craftsmen. The harbour was lengthy, half a mile of it along the riverside, but tidal, with its complications for docking, and the necessary "roads", as they were called, offshore, for vessels having to wait for higher water. Their small craft, however, with shallow draught, did not have to linger.

Enquiries led Andrew across the river from where their vessel had docked, by one of the wooden bridges, to the eastern bank, he noting the three-arched stone bridge being built, he was told, by the Abbot of Holyrood, the churchmen ever foremost in encouraging trade. He found the house and merchant establishment of Henry Lindsay at the corner of Tolbooth Wynd and the Shore, the actual residence a tall gabled building of no fewer than five storeys.

Lindsay proved to be a cheerful bulky man of early middle years, who welcomed Andrew heartily, declaring that he was growing not unlike his father in looks. Was he interested in this of trading and shipping? Assured that he was, the position was explained. He, Lindsay, had long had a two-hundred-and-fifty-ton vessel, the *Goshawk*, with which he traded to the Netherlands, carrying wool and hides and spirits. But, for a year or two, the growing commerce of the Hansa merchants of Lübeck and Hamburg and the Baltic had been preoccupying them at Leith with its opportunities, and he had had a new ship built, which he was calling the *Merlin*, of three hundred tons, for this new Baltic traffic; and he was assembling a crew to man it. He would go with it himself for the first voyage to Lübeck; but with his other vessel and his established trading links with Veere and Rotterdam in the Low Countries, he would require a representative to sail in it for the Baltic venture, or so he intended if the Hansa merchanting proved worth while for him, as seemed likely, with the Baltic lands of Danzig, Riga, Latvia, Estonia, Finland and all the Russias hopefully to exploit. So it had occurred to him to approach the son of Andrew

Wood, who had so greatly aided him to establish himself at Leith.

Andrew assured him that he certainly was interested. What was proposed?

Lindsay said that after his first visit to the Baltic in under a month's time, with Andrew possibly accompanying him, to discover the situation and prospects there, if it all proved worthy, would *he* go again thereafter as his representative, and so initiate a trading arrangement with those eastern parts; for as well as the Baltic lands there were Denmark, Norway and Sweden to consider, providing surely great opportunities for commerce.

Andrew declared that he was ready to co-operate, and grateful for having been thus considered. How soon would he be required?

If he could come back to Leith in, say, two weeks' time, to become acquainted with the trading matters, the cargoes, and the shipmaster and crew, that would be best. And they would sail thereafter.

This all very much commended itself to Andrew. Staying the night with the Lindsays, he found a vessel next day to take him back to Fife, not to Leven but to Buckhaven, this only a five-mile trudge from Largo.

His mother learned of it all with an odd admixture of doubts, concern and approval. She recognised that her elder son had reached an age when he demanded more of life than house-dwelling and tending a few sheep, and would wish to follow in his father's footsteps. But she was going to miss him, and was unsure about him venturing to that outlandish and possibly heathenish country among Russkies and even worse. She hoped that he would take great care, and not be away for overlong. He could give her no indication as to when he would be back, but promised that he would bring her some gifts from foreign lands.

He took Jamie up on to Largo Law to instruct him in shepherding, how to pick out their sheep from those of others by the coloured markings on their fleeces, and urged

6

his mother to obtain a trained dog from some shepherd or farmer, which he himself had always meant to get.

There would be no flukie-spearing for some time.

Two weeks later, then, he said his goodbyes, and sailed from Leven back to Leith. Still no sign of pirates or privateers in the estuary.

Henry Lindsay, whom he was now to call Harry, took him to inspect the *Merlin*, and meet the shipmaster, one Gavin Muir by name. It was a fine new three-master, high of forecastle and poop, with ample cabin space, and already laden with coal – which was apparently much sought after in the Baltic lands – ironware, salted mutton and whisky casks. Just what would be the best goods to take to these lands they would have to discover when they got there. This was to be a more or less exploratory expedition, with much to learn.

They were ready to sail the following morning, but had to wait for other ships, to form the necessary convoy as protection from the English attackers, those scourges of the seas. These tended to operate in pairs, so groups of five or six Scots or foreign vessels were advisable, their crews armed and on the alert.

It was learned that one other vessel was heading for Lübeck, the others for the Low Countries. So the *Merlin* would have company, which was always helpful for safety.

Andrew was able to go up to Edinburgh, as they waited, and visit the great fortress-castle on its rock, and the famous abbey of the Holy Rood. He also saw his father's former quayside mooring place at Leith, and the warehouse behind it, now in the hands of strangers.

At length, with six ships assembled and ready, and the tide right, it was casting off, and heading out into the firth, Andrew interested especially in the piloting necessary when a group of craft were sailing in close formation, and the skippers had to work in careful harmony. He was eager to learn.

2

All aboard the ships were fairly confident that they would not be assailed, six of them, as they headed for the open sea. They had to pass near that Isle of May, but so far as they could see no pirates lurked there presently – although the southern end of the island did lend itself to craft wishing to remain hidden. At any rate, nothing emerged therefrom.

With the prevailing south-west wind they were able to make good headway, with a minimum of tacking necessary. The six would remain together for as long as was possible, due eastwards for fully one hundred miles, whereafter the two for the Baltic would have to swing off east-north-east while the others turned south. The privateers seldom operated that far out into the Norse Sea, preferring to work from their respective bases of Newcastle and Sunderland, Hartlepool and Scarborough, Grimsby and the Wash. There was a known rivalry between these various Englishry, their craft having fairly clearly defined areas to harry. The seas between Newcastle to Grimsby and the great Dogger Bank, that extensive shoaling where the water reached its shallowest at no more than a depth of fifty feet, and a menace to pirates as well as their intended victims, were the most perilous as to assault. Fortunately Baltic-bound craft did not have to go that far south, heading off to pass between the other navigational hazards of the Devil's Hole and the Fisher Bank.

With the fairly favourable breezes they were able to cover the distance out to the parting area in a day and night's sailing. They did see other vessels, single and in pairs, some of which looked suspiciously like privateers; but six ships sailing together were practically safe from attack, and only one other vessel approached them, this coming out from Berwick-upon-Tweed, and joining them for its own protection.

Andrew took much heed of all this, making only a short night of it in his bunk.

Lindsay and his shipmaster, Gavin Muir, reckoned that they were safe by the following midday; and with the other Lübeck-bound vessel, just south of the Devil's Hole, they left the others to make for the Skagerrak, another one hundred and fifty miles eastwards.

Fascinated by all the shipboard work, especially the navigation and compass-bearing, Andrew sought to aid as well as learn. This was the life for him, ships and the sea. To be a merchant-trader, as had been his father, was well enough; but it was this of the ocean and great waters that drew him: the spread, the far-flung vastnesses of it, the endless surge and power of the waves. When storms came, of course, it could be testing; but that would make the greater challenge.

Harry Lindsay was amused at his young friend's enthusiasm.

In just over a day's further sailing they descried land ahead. This, Muir told them, was what he called the Skaw, the most northerly point of Denmark. They had to round that to reach the Kattegat from the Skagerrak, which they were now entering.

Andrew had heard of these channels or straits. Now he was to see them both, these the access to the all but inland sea of the Baltic.

The first seemed to be lengthy, over one hundred miles altogether and perhaps half that in width, with Norway on the left and Denmark on the right, the former a more rugged coastline, with cliffs and mountains and islets, not unlike Scotland's own west coast, the Danish side more level, but with some spurs and hillocks, atop one such what was pointed out as Frederikshavn Slot, a seat of the King of Denmark. Lindsay had been to Copenhagen, the capital and greatest port, but not beyond. He would be interested to see what lay further.

The Kattegat was merely a right-angled extension of the Skagerrak, heading southwards down the coast of the province of Jutland, with Sweden now at the other side. Andrew had heard of Jutland, whence came the Jutes, who with the Saxons and Angles had invaded and colonised what was now England, part of ancient Britain. Here was Jutland, and he knew approximately where Saxony was. But where was the country of the Angles, who gave name to England, Angle-land? Lindsay said that there was a district of Jutland known as Angeln, in Schleswig, further south; presumably that must have been their homeland, small and unimportant as it now was. It seemed strange that *its* folk should have given name to the invaded land rather than the Jutes and Saxons.

The Kattegat divided into two channels eventually, the area between the great island of Zealand, on which lay Copenhagen. Even Gavin Muir had never been further. They must be almost entering the Baltic. Would they need a pilot in these narrow waters?

Still southwards they sailed, along the shoreline of what must be Schleswig. Lübeck must be not far ahead. The Norse Sea now seemed far off.

Muir decided that they should pick up a pilot to guide them among the scatter of Danish islands. This they did at Svendborg. The pilot told them that Lübeck lay another seventy miles due south, after the last of the Danish isles, and across the huge bay of Keil, with the likewise great bay of Lübecker Bucht itself, this cutting a score of miles into the Germanic province of Hamburg, and narrowing into the Trave River.

They indeed needed a pilot, for now they found themselves having to navigate among and past a seeming legion of ships instead of the islands. Something of the mercantile importance of Lübeck was becoming very evident. Andrew was kept busy noting all the various types and sizes of the vessels.

Their pilot led them into the Trave, not so much an estuary as a very wide river-mouth, where the shipping had to marshal itself in disciplined fashion, so many were the craft coming and going. Here the wind was easterly, coming from the vast hinterland of all the Russias; sails were lowered to a minimum for slow and ordered progress. They had to go quite a long way upstream before docks began to line the riversides, and they could see ahead of them a vast array, a forest, of spires and steeples, of towers and domes, all rising from a slight upthrust of ground on the east side of the river. They were reaching their destination at long last.

The pilot, a Dane but speaking fair English – and no doubt many another tongue – told them that, as well as being the focal point of the Hanseatic League, this had been the capital of a Slovak principality formed eight hundred years before by Count Adolf the Second of Holstein, but taken over by Henry the Lion, the great Duke of Saxony, who largely built the city to regular planning centred round a spacious market-place. It later had become subject to the Holy Roman Emperor, but was granted self-government and was able to make most of its own laws. The emperor's Order of Teutonic Knights co-operated with other Slavik, Polish and Baltic rulers, and spread its influence far and wide as its trading importance grew; so that now the laws of Lübeck applied to over one hundred cities, several of them larger than Lübeck itself, such as Danzig and Kolberg in Poland, Königsberg and Memel in Lithuania, and Riga in Latvia. At the end of the last century a long and wide canal had been constructed, mainly to bring vital salt from the mines of Lauenburg for the preservation of meat and fish, the Baltic being all but a freshwater sea. Now, next to Cologne, Lübeck was the largest city in all northern Germany, with a resident population of well over a score of thousands.

Finding a mooring place for the *Merlin* was quite difficult, so numerous were the ships of all nations. There were two harbour basins on the lower course of the Trave, but both were full. Their pilot had to take them further inland towards the adjoining community of Travemünde.

Lindsay and Andrew wondered where first to go to discover where the goods they had brought were to be sold advantageously and where they could learn the details they sought as to the imports to take back to Scotland. The central market-place, presumably?

Creeping along, as it seemed, in all the traffic, and that easterly breeze to cope with, the passengers could at least admire the architectural splendour spread around them. There seemed to be not one but three cathedrals, huge steepled minsters in the Gothic design, which their pilot named as the Marienkirche, the Petrikirche and the Jahns-kirche, spires soaring to over four hundred feet. He pointed out the Rathaus or town hall, another magnificent structure, and the mighty towered gates, the Burgtor and the Holstentor, all indications of enormous wealth. On the summit of a modest hillock stood the castle built by Henry the Lion of Saxony. Less lofty but still impressive were the multitude of fine houses, the ceramic factories, the metal foundries, the timberyards and shipyards, the mints and arsenals, the loom-houses and the mills, all laid out in planned wide streets and squares. The Scots had never seen the like.

Lindsay reckoned that the Rathaus was probably the best place to make their first enquiries. Landed, there they found that the Lübeckers were great linguists – they had to be, no doubt – and they had no problems in being directed to various merchant notabilities, dealers, master crafts-men, and trade guildsmen, as well as the city officials. They would find out all they needed to know here, un-doubtedly.

Andrew listened and looked and learned.

Lindsay and he had assumed that, apart from the

Germanic states and dukedoms nearby, the vast Russian Muscovy lands would be the most important for trade, with Estonia, Lithuania, Latvia and Finland. But they now gathered that Poland was considered more profitable, and that Lübeck was the entry place to that nation. Lindsay had never heard of any Scots dealings with the Poles. Here could be a possible market to exploit.

They found the Polish representatives in a large establishment in a central position, and were received with interest, almost as envoys from another world. These Poles were much less fluent in English than were most of the Lübeckers, but, with a mixture of French and Dutch and German, they were able to converse to fair effect, and were the wiser therefore. They discovered that Poland was very large, extending far south to the Black Sea, Russia to the east, Slovakia to the south and Germany to the west. Its kings had their capital at Warsaw, in the centre, and had a dynastic especial relationship with Bohemia and Hungary. These lands were little more than names to the Scots, as indeed had been Poland itself. But now they saw major possibilities of trade here. It seemed that copper, along with iron and coal, was extensively mined, the former something that Scotland saw little of. Lead also was produced, this seemingly present in several minerals, and produced by roasting the ores in furnaces, the lead content thus extracted. It made the most malleable of metals and did not corrode. They knew of lead in Scotland, of course, but little of it was available. Here apparently were great supplies. Silver also. This Poland seemed to be a great source of minerals, however little known at home. Opportunity for them?

They made detailed enquiries from the Lübeck Poles, and learned that their own merchandise, especially salted and smoked fish, meats, whisky and beer and barley products, would be welcomed. Sailcloth, rope and cordage for shipping, such as that made and woven from the rough-coated blackface sheep, would sell well. Altogether there was scope for much trade here.

The Scots sailed for home well pleased with their enterprise.

3

There was no problem in finding other vessels heading north and west, as convoy partners, with all that sea-going traffic, most sailing for the Netherlands, France and London. The easterly breeze took them up past Denmark and into the Kattegat and Skagerrak in fine style; but thereafter the Norse Sea's south-westerly winds changed that, and they made much less speedy progress.

Presently, of course, they lost the Low Countries ships, and later the French. But when next day the London-bound craft left them, and they were on their own in the *Merlin*, Gavin Muir became distinctly anxious. They must hope to link up with some other north-going vessels fairly soon. Single ships were all too often the prey for those English pirates.

A heedful watch was maintained. They saw various craft heading southwards but none northwards. That is, until, level with the Tees estuary, they did see a vessel sailing in their direction. But when this turned towards them, it was to perceive the red and white St George's cross banner hoisted at its mainmast – the symbol of English government approval and sanction of privateers.

Muir and his crew cursed, as well they might.

There followed a hasty collection of weaponry, swords, daggers, axes, boat-hooks, anything with which to protect themselves. Andrew, casting about, could find nothing better than a length of chain. Doubled into a sort of swinging club, this would have to serve. At least there appeared to be none of the new cannon being aimed at them. Lindsay had a hatchet.

Muir sought to make avoiding tactics, of course, but the English were as expert shipmen as themselves. He endeavoured, by twisting and turning, difficult to manage with sails in a tossing sea, to prevent the other craft from drawing alongside, this to shouts and fist-shakings on both vessels.

But grapnels, attached to ropes and chains, were soon being thrown, these wretches well trained in the like; and although some were cast back at them, others held fast, and enabled the enemy to pull their craft close enough for the timbers to grind together.

The two ships were much of a size, but undoubtedly the foe had the greater number of crewmen, and these trained fighters. They came clambering and leaping over on to the *Merlin*, armed to the teeth and with the padded leather coats that could serve as armour, yelling their hate.

Andrew jumped away from Lindsay's side to give his friend greater freedom and to swing his chain round and round above his own head in dire and general threat, it reaching beyond any sword-thrust or dirk-stab. He had the prompt satisfaction of striking almost the first blow of that affray, to effect, as he leaped at a boarder vaulting over the bulwark, who raised a sword-arm to protect himself, and had the chain wrap itself round him and knock him off his feet, the sword clattering to the deck. Dragging loose the entangled chain, Andrew dropped it, and stooped to pick up that sword. Grasping it halfway down the blade, he drove it into the throat of the sprawling man with all his force. The pirate spouted blood, arms thrashing on the boarding, but did not rise.

Swiftly deciding that his chain was a more effective weapon than the man's sword, he discarded the latter and grabbed up the former again. Lindsay was seeking to beat down the English sword with his hatchet close by, and whirling his chain in the air Andrew smashed it against the back of the man's neck, to send him reeling and down on to his knees. He left his friend to finish off the injured man.

He now came to the conclusion that this chain-swinging was the best contribution he could make to the defence, and sought another victim. Everywhere Scots and English crewmen were fighting each other, and he was able to bring down his third victim as he was stabbing at a defender armed only with a boat-hook, the heavy chain toppling the man.

Panting with the effort of it all and the weight of the chain, he gazed round at all the battling, to decide who to assail next. Then a thought occurred to him, wits in a turmoil as they were. It was the fact that he nearly tripped over one of those grapnels tossed aboard that triggered it off. The surge of the waves was causing this to drag along the planking. If this, and those other anchoring links were cast overboard, the two vessels would tend to drift apart. And with undoubtedly most of the pirates now on board the *Merlin*, this would surely much distract and concern them.

Hurriedly he ran, to pick up and throw overboard the nearest grapnel and, all but falling over a prostrate victim, he reached and jettisoned another. There appeared to be two more.

Then another notion struck him. If he was actually *aboard* this other ship he possibly could do more for their cause. How many men would they have left there in this attack? Few indeed, probably. He could see only the helmsman up on the poop at the wheel.

Leaving the remaining grapnels in place meantime, he vaulted over the bulwark and on to the other vessel. Would that steersman recognise him as a foe? Probably not, their garb none so different.

Still carrying that chain, he slipped across the lower midships section of the privateer, out of sight of the poop. There were no signs of crewmen. At the far side, he climbed the ladder up to the poop-deck, and peered over. The man at the wheel still stood there, gazing down at the struggle going on in the *Merlin*. It seemed a sin to slay the unsuspecting Englishman, but he was a pirate after all, and his fellow-scoundrels assailing the Scots.

Moving over quietly – although the din and clash going on in the other craft would drown any noise he made – and careful not to let the links of the chain clink, he raised his odd weapon high and brought it down slantwise on the man's neck and shoulder, this with major effect. A groaning gasp, and the helmsman fell. Not waiting to examine the new victim's state, he dragged the body over to the stern rail, and heaved it over the side with an effort.

Drawing deep breaths, Andrew stood there for moments. He had become a killer, and a multiple and determined one. But what was the choice? To kill or to be killed.

Now, how many, if any, were left aboard this ship? He had seen no others. And undoubtedly the enemy's greatest strength would have gone to board the *Merlin*. No one was to be seen on the forecastle.

Would any come back to seek to deal with himself? Would indeed any of the fighting men realise that he was not the helmsman, if they saw him at all? Were all too busy? Questions, questions.

If there *were* no others left aboard this vessel then, glory be, it was now his. His alone!

What next, then? Separate the two ships? Only a couple of grapnels held them together now. If they were seen to be apart, what would be the effect on the fighting Englishmen? Upset and worry them, or make them the more determined to capture the *Merlin*? It was impossible for him to tell how the struggle was going, in the chaos of smiting, thrusting, yelling men. But at least his fellow-Scots were nowise subdued.

He made up his mind. He ran down the poop-steps, to go to the side where the two craft nudged each other, and without pause vaulted again over into his own ship, as though to rejoin the struggle. But, no – his targets were those two grapnels that held the vessels together. Stooping, he grabbed one and flung it over on to the ship he had just left. Then the other, stepping over a jerking body on the way.

Since he had to get back on board the privateer before the surge of the tide drifted the craft apart, he had to act quickly. He only just managed it, the gap widening. Nobody seemed to be aware or interested in what he was doing, all too busy battling.

Once over, it was back up the poop-ladder again, to reach that wheel. He had to control the craft if he could, single-handed. Unless there were other crew still aboard?

By the time he got to the wheel he saw that fully six or eight feet separated the ships. None would leap that. The tide was strong. There was still no sign of anyone else on the English vessel.

He sought to steer his capture further away, as far as he was able. The only sail still hoisted was the triangular foresail stretching out to the bowsprit. The south-westerly wind was tending to push the craft astern gradually. Better if the canvas was down. Andrew hurried off across and up the forecastle steps, to reach and pull on the rope to lower that sail. Would the result be to increase the drifting apart? He hoped so.

Whether his efforts were the cause or not, the distance between the craft *was* increasing. Fifteen feet, now? Twenty? As he hastened back to the wheel, Andrew Wood was telling himself that he had captured an enemy vessel by his own efforts!

Was there any way in which he could assist his friends, other than this "stealing" of the enemy ship? There were two brass cannon on board this craft, but he knew not how to use these, load and fire them. Anyway, to what end? He was not going to bombard their own *Merlin*.

But suppose he could somehow manoeuvre this vessel so that it again touched the other, not broadside-on but at some narrow point? Would some of the English then be apt to seek to jump back aboard to reclaim it? This a distraction and lessening, at least temporarily, their fighting

strength? If he wielded his chain at the point of contact –
the bows it would have to be – might that not be of some
effect?

Could he somehow work this vessel so as to approach the
other's stern? There was sufficient wind to draw the
necessary movement, if he could master the sails, or some
of them, and at the same time steer with any accuracy.

He had had no experience of working the sails on a full-
rigged ship. But he could see that there was the canvas and
tackle for no fewer than four sails between foremast and
bowsprit. If he could hoist all these it would almost
certainly give him the power to propel the vessel in some
fashion. He could try, at least.

Leaving the wheel to steer itself meantime, he went
forward to discover which coiled ropes were the means of
raising which triangular sails. Selecting the outermost one,
he began to pull. The canvas was heavy, much more so
than he had anticipated, and it took all his strength to hoist
it. Far from setting it up in its proper position, he nevertheless managed to get it heaved sufficiently aloft to catch
the wind, and tied the rope. The second one, less far out,
was somewhat easier. The third likewise. Would that
serve? All three were filling, and he perceived that the
vessel was swinging round.

So far, so good. Now to steer it to effect.

He could enforce no very accurate control of his prize,
but did achieve a semicircular movement, wider than
intended, indeed possibly a couple of hundred yards from
the *Merlin*. He must aim for the other's stern.

With such modest sail-power, advance was only slow,
and distinctly erratic. And his target itself was drifting
uncertainly in the wind, no one aboard it presently concerned with direction. The same wind, of course, affected
both ships, so that Andrew's approach could be mastered
none so indirectly.

He had all but automatically assumed that this stern
contact was what was called for. Now he had to consider it

more factually. One of those grapnels, or two, hurled from this bow on to the other poop, and the ships ought to remain linked. And if he stood there, at point of contact, with his chain, he would be in a position to attack any of the pirates who might seek to reboard their craft. Would they, in this fighting?

Nearing the *Merlin*, he tried to assess how the battling went, less than easy as this was. The impression was that the Scots were having the best of it. Almost all the struggle was going on up on the poop, near and around the wheel. He could distinguish Lindsay and Muir there, so his compatriots still had their leadership. Had the enemy?

Only his grip on the wheel saved Andrew from being jerked off his feet by the impact as his ship bumped against the other, its bowsprit thrusting spear-like into the fighting men, adding to the confusion. So he was not the only one unsteady on his feet as he lurched forward with his chain.

And he had been right in his guess that some of the Englishmen would seek to regain possession of their vessel. Two promptly did so, one wielding a sword, the other a bloody dagger. The first took the chain across face and throat, and fell sideways as he was mounting the bulwark and collapsed on to it, and thence over to the water. The dagger-man hesitated at the sight of this, and his hesitation was fatal, for it gave time for the chain to be swung back and round again, with fair accuracy, and to strike him in turn. He did not fall overboard but, staggering, went down among the stamping, stumbling feet.

Two more accounted for. That chain was a godsend. Thankfully, no spears were apt to be used in ship warfare.

As it happened, the privateer's bowsprit, the movement of the surging tide causing it to sweep one way and the other like some mighty lance among the combatants, friend and foe alike, had major effect, the more notably on the aggressors, who inevitably were more scattered and who could not be other than distracted and fretted by their losses and their ship being used against them. The tide, other than that of the sea, was turned against them.

Quickly the Scots were aware of it, and heartened in their smiting. Andrew was able to bring down another escaping Englishman. Then enemy arms began to be raised high and weapons flung down in surrender, as the enemy recognised their hopeless position and defeat.

The day was won and lost.

And there were no doubts as to where the Scots should look to account for their victory. Young Andrew Wood was the hero. Great was the acclaim and praise. Embarrassed, he disclaimed overmuch credit. He had merely used the opportunity that had presented itself, and in less than expert fashion. He was, however, much gratified. He had somehow won himself a vessel of his own, none could deny that. And a quite large one, possibly of near three hundred tons. He had become a shipowner in that hour or two. And he could now be a trader – although he would have to find and pay a crew. That would be a problem: money. Harry Lindsay might help. A loan, meantime? That was until he had time and opportunity to examine the contents of the privateer's holds, and discovered that they were part-full of what were undoubtedly ill-gotten goods, stolen property. Whose? Lindsay, Muir and others declared that could never be found out, and that he could lawfully claim it all as his own now. The spoils of war. These pirates were wholly indiscriminate as to whom they attacked. This haul was not to be identified as belonging to any specific victims. Now it was all Andrew's. And it would fetch good prices at markets in Leith and Edinburgh, Lindsay would see to that. Andrew would have moneys to hire a crew, and now had a ship to trade with. His next voyage to foreign parts would be as an independent merchant-trader.

He went home to Largo all but in a daze at the thought of it. What would his mother say? And their neighbours?

He left his captured ship at Leith. He was going to rename it *Kestrel*, to complement Lindsay's *Merlin*. Largo's haven was too small for the like, however pleasant to have shown it off. So it had to be the ferry for him.

4

It was not long before Andrew was back at Leith, to deal with the situation that he had managed to create and its consequences. These were quite major. He found himself to have become renowed, the young pirate-slayer. Not only that but being looked upon as now wealthy, good prices having been forthcoming for the captured stolen goods thanks to Lindsay and his colleagues. No doubt they had gained their own commission thereon, being practised merchants, but that left ample for himself.

At the port he set about, with Gavin Muir's help, finding the crew for his *Kestrel*. This was not difficult, Leith being full of seafarers, and not a few pleased to be taken on by this successful young man. Muir found him a competent, indeed quite well-known shipmaster, James Barton, brother of the adventurous Andrew Barton and son of the murdered John; the family was involved in sea warfare with the Portuguese, the monarch, James Stewart, third of that name, having granted them letters of fire and sword against that nation. This James Barton, youngest brother, was presently without a ship, and ought to make a useful associate.

So now there had to be a trial sail for *Kestrel* and its new skipper and crew, with Andrew himself requiring to learn much about competent navigation and ship management.

Out into the estuary they went, Andrew choosing to head seawards in order to take the vessel to the Isle of May, he wondering how often it might have hidden there in the past to assail Firth of Forth shipping. They moored in its secret corner, Barton proving his skill as shipmaster in the process, reaching the narrow twisting anchorage. The new crew were told something of the story of the isle and how grateful all mariners should be to the monks who kept the age-old beacon burning on its topmost height to guide shipping in the dangerous waters, and how, there being no trees to provide fuel there, wood had to be ferried out from the Fife shore regularly by the brothers from the Priory of Pittenweem, in barges, an ongoing and noble task of charity towards their fellow-men. Their king, James the Third, a pious monarch if no warrior, had made a pilgrimage here.

Well satisfied with James Barton as shipmaster, and the crew recruited, Andrew informed them that, while he anticipated that much of his merchant ventures hereafter would be with the Baltic area and the Hanseatic League, he knew that the Netherlands had long been considered the most profitable trading centre of northern Europe, the Dutch rich, prosperous and of great initiative. He judged that there could be much to be gained by visiting there and prospecting what they had and what they would be pleased to import. So the first voyage of his new *Kestrel* would be thither. He knew that most of the Lammermuir Hills' wool, this the greatest sheep-rearing area of all Scotland, was exported to the Netherlands port of Veere, for onward transportation to the cloth-weaving cities elsewhere in the Low Countries. So – a voyage to Veere to prospect the possibilities. They would sail in a week's time.

Their voyage to the Netherlands was pirate-free: this because Andrew had found various flags and banners in his captured ship, among these the St George's cross of England and others bearing a fox's mask and a death's-head, privateers' and pirates' symbols. These he now hoisted instead of his saltire. They passed two other ships flying similar flags, and were actually hailed by one of them in salutation. And they were heedfully avoided by a convoy of merchantmen.

Barton knew the Netherlands coastline, and approaching the Walcheren peninsula they lowered these false flags and ran up the St Andrew's cross of Scotland. They were then able to join a group of wool-bearing vessels from Dunbar, Eyemouth and Berwick.

Veere lay near the tip of the great isle of Walcheren, this between the twin mouths of the Eastern and Western Schelde, a quite large town of tall pantiled buildings with a cathedral and impressive town hall. Andrew was interested to see other saltire banners flying above houses, and learned that there were numerous Scots residents, even the burgomaster being a fellow-countryman, the wool traffic being its principal industry and Scotland the source of most of its imports. Indeed the annual price of raw wool was fixed here, by the council, and was accepted elsewhere, and known as the Staple at Veere.

This town, however, was not their chosen destination, but Bergen-op-Zoom, a score of miles up the Eastern Schelde, and then Antwerp, the centres of general trade, and where the wool was spun and woven into cloth.

At Bergen-op-Zoom, to distinguish it from the similarly named port of Norway, Andrew learned much as to what would sell here from Scotland, but also from the Baltic. He could initiate a triangular trade of it. He decided that, meantime, he need not go on another twenty miles to Antwerp. The merchants here taught him all he needed to know, which goods would be welcome from the Baltic and Scandinavian countries, and which from Scotland.

He filled the *Kestrel* with bricks, pantiles, glass, iron-ware and woven cloth, all of which would sell well at Leith and Edinburgh. Lace was another manufacture here which might be welcome at home. And he heard of something hitherto but a name to him: the demand for ivory. It seemed here to be accounted as more valuable than gold. It was gained from the tusks of the walrus, and used for a great variety of objects, especially by the churchmen, such as devotional decoration, sculptures, altars, book covers, caskets and crucifixes. It could be set with gems. So here was a notable source of wealth. Walruses inhabited the cold northern seas in great herds or shoals, and were to be found at the Orkney and Shetland isles, and certainly on the Norwegian coasts. Here, surely, was one more commodity that might be exploited to advantage. Andrew imagined that it would do well at Lübeck of the Hansas. There were unlikely to be walruses in the Baltic Sea. To be a successful trader meant ever seeking new merchandise. So much to learn for a young man from Largo.

His ship well filled, they sailed down the Schelde and into the Norse Sea for Leith, some five hundred miles. Obviously he was going to have to get used to calculating miles by the many hundred, and a life spent mainly at sea. But that was none so ill. It all seemed somehow to challenge Andrew Wood.

Once again they flew pirate flags to avoid opposition, and were successful in this; that is until, off the Northumberland coast, they saw two ships fairly close inshore and side by side, one considerably larger than the other. Even at a distance they appeared to be stationary. Andrew decided to investigate.

Soon it was apparent. It was a privateer in assault on a smaller craft. Here was more challenge. He ordered his men to readiness.

Nearing the pair, and themselves seeming to be another pirate, no alarm was evident. The victim, on this occasion, was of an unusual construction, the forecastle very high and the poop lower and shorter. Also it had an extra very short mast, to add to the other three, rising right in the bows. It had a foreign flag at the masthead.

Andrew gave his orders. Board the attackers, on the far side from the attacked. Detach the grapnels. Draw away after dealing with such crew as might remain aboard. Then, after the enemy ship had drifted off, replace it and aid the foreigners.

Alongside the privateer and leading the way aboard, he wondered whether these pirates, English as they all seemed to be, at least in these waters, ever assailed each other? Took over other's prey? Or was there a sort of shameful partnership among them, of mutual support when this might be called for? At any rate, no opposition met him and his as they leaped on to the assailant.

On this occasion they found a number of men still aboard, possibly because the vessel being harried was not large. But these, although looking surprised at the new arrivals joining them, clearly did not envisage attack, their pirate flags seemingly sufficient warranty. So their shocked overthrow was not difficult.

This was the most simple and undemanding attack ever. Those aboard the foreign ship, if they saw another pirate coming to the affray may have wondered, but did not interrupt their own activities.

Getting rid of the helmsman, Andrew appointed another in his place, and led the way on to the attacked vessel, chain swinging. This of sea assault was becoming all but second nature to the young man from Largo.

On the Portuguese ship, the *Caetano* from Mértola, he found its skipper, one Pedro Peres, wounded but not seriously, and still able to command. He announced that he was on his way to Berwick-upon-Tweed with a cargo of goods from Africa and India, the Portuguese being great colonisers and explorers, there to pick up wool, its strong fibres in much demand as against the lighter, finer fleeces of his homeland's sheep. His crew had suffered many casualties. Andrew offered to escort them to Berwick, explaining, as best he could with language difficulties, that *he* was no pirate. This was gratefully accepted.

From this Peres he learned that King Alfonso of Portugal, nephew of the famous Henry the Navigator, had consolidated much of his uncle's conquests in Africa, India and central America into what was now being called the Portuguese Empire, and himself emperor. He, Pedro Peres, did not think that he would again venture into this Norse Sea, with its danger from the devilish pirates. The greater oceans were under Portuguese domination, and safe to sail in.

Andrew learned something that might well be of value to him. That was of caravello- or carvel-built vessels favoured by the Portuguese, as against the northern clinker construction, where the planking overlapped. The carvel boarding was flush, streamlined, nailed to basic framing, this improving speed and steering. He took note.

Leaving the *Caetano* at Berwick, with good wishes, he sailed back to Leith with his new prize.

At Leith and Edinburgh he was becoming known as the pirate-slayer, which he took as a compliment although he would have preferred to rank as a successful merchant-trader.

This of pirate-assailing had an unexpected consequence. A summons came to him at Leith, and from, of all things, the king. James the Third, a peace-loving and religiously inclined monarch, was tending to dwell at his capital's Abbey of the Holy Rood rather than at the royal castles of Stirling or Edinburgh, the abbot's house being put at the royal disposal. Andrew Wood was called to the royal presence.

Hiring a horse, and dressed in his by no means magnificent best, he rode the couple of miles to the foot of the capital's soaring Arthur's Seat. There he found his liege-lord, along with the abbot and two of his monks, with pen and paper, translating Latin scriptural texts. A courtier presented him, somewhat superciliously.

"Ha, the pirate-master!" the king greeted him. "A young man much to be blessed! I hear tell of your exploits. Come, sit you here."

Andrew bowed. "Your Grace, you do me too much honour."

"I but repeat what others declare. This of the English pirates is a grievous burden for many in my realm. I have sent for you, seeking your aid. It is my wish to make a second pilgrimage to the Isle of May, a most holy place. I did this some years back, and would do so again. I am told that, sadly, it is a favoured haunt of these wicked pirates, who hide in its lee, to issue out and prey on passing shipping. I would have you to take me to the island for another visit."

"Sire, that would be a great privilege. I am at your royal service. When would you wish to visit?"

"So soon as you find convenient. And the weather is favourable."

"Any day, then, Sire."

"The morrow? I have the Papal Nuncio coming the next day, and he may stay awhile. If that is suitable to you and your ship?"

"Entirely, Your Grace. I am honoured. Tomorrow. My *Kestrel* is docked at the St Bernard's Quay. And at your service."

"I shall come there in the forenoon. Perhaps my lord Abbot will come with me?"

"That would be my pleasure, Sire," Abbot Henry said.

Early October as it was, the wind was light next day and the seas not rough. King James came down to Leith with more than the abbot, with quite a party indeed, including an indication of the monarch's rather strange partialities, one of his closer friends, Leonard, a shoemaker. Also his small son by Margaret of Denmark, five-year-old James, Duke of Rothesay, a lively child. The king declared that he hoped that there would be no pirates lurking at the isle, to be assured that Andrew had had a small vessel go out at dawn, and the anchorage was reported as empty.

They set sail without delay, Barton and his crew much concerned by having the monarch and his heir aboard. Not that James Stewart presented an impressive figure, clad as though for a long voyage in stormy conditions. The illustrious passengers were interested in the hoisting and management of the sails. And once out of the port and into open waters, the child-prince actually asked to be allowed to take a turn at the wheel, which was taller than himself. Andrew stood by, heedfully.

It was only some sixteen miles out to the May, exclamations uttered as they passed the mighty cliffs of the Craig of Bass under the whirling clouds of screaming seafowl. Andrew told the story of the sixth-century King Loth's daughter Thanea and her drift out here in her paddle-less coracle at the mercy of the sea god, Manannan, which the present monarch knew not of.

The May did not fail to impress and excite those of the visitors who had not been there previously, including the young heir to the throne, who declared that he had seen a whale; actually it was a grey seal, balancing on a skerry. He was for searching for more, but before his father allowed him to be taken to do so, prayers had to be said at the tiny monastery. This was not now used as such, save as a base for the two monks always on duty, from Pittenweem, to tend the beacon-fire. These, distinctly overawed, all but hid themselves until told to look after the little prince. The king, who was much interested in astrology, declared that he had been told that there had been a Pictish standing stone somewhere up on the ridge, and he wanted to see it and discover if it was lined up for the sun's positions at the solstices. Andrew could not help in this, nor could the monks, who admitted that they had never seen anything such, although among all the rocks and stones such might be there.

So the visitors started to explore, the energetic and agile child leading. The king's previous pilgrimage had been merely to the ruined chapel-shrine dedicated to St Ethernan, a Celtic missionary, which the saintly Queen Margaret had renamed St Adrian's after the then pope; and to the monastery founded by her son, David the First. The monarch demonstrated his erudition by telling them all that the island got its name from the Norse *Má-ey*, meaning sea-mews isle, *maew* being the Norse for gull.

Up on the higher ground they found a small loch, where

ducks swam, until young Jamie threw stones at them and they flew. One of the monks said that a predecessor had told him that there was a spot called the Altarstones nearer the north end of the isle, but he had never found anything there of significance. Probably it had been the site of the Pictish shrine. The king had to go on to inspect this.

Unfortunately none of them could discover any indication of the works of man thereabouts; but then the storms and constant high winds of this so-exposed rocky island would tend to demolish all but the basic stone. So King James had to give up his search, and they all returned to the *Kestrel*.

It had made an interesting excursion, even though their liege-lord was disappointed in his searching.

5

Andrew made a cruise up to the northern isles of Orkney and Shetland, much more extensive then he had realised, and populous, this to be able to purchase, and at no great expense, a large number of walrus tusks, the islanders there not valuing the ivory as much more than useful material for the making of tools and arrowheads. He urged that they collect more, much more, and he would come for them on another occasion – this without actually indicating to them the destinations he had for it, nor stressing the value put upon it by the Baltic traders and others.

Thereafter, with this and other supplies, which he had discovered would be welcomed by the Hansa merchants, he made another visit to Lübeck, this to his profit.

He was amassing quite a substantial fund in gold and silver at Leith. And this with a definite purpose. He intended to *build* a ship for himself, not content just to capture such. And this to be on the Portuguese model, with his own ideas and preferences. It was to be carvel-built, not clinker, the planking sides flush, not overlapping; costly no doubt, but hopefully worth the outlay.

He arrived back at Leith to learn that, only two days previously, an urgent plea had come from King James. He was needed with his ship, or better, ships, in the Clyde, where an English squadron, not pirates this time it seemed, had come to harry the towns of that estuary, in especial Glasgow, and were presently besieging the royal castle of Dumbarton.

Andrew could not ignore this request, even though it was not put in the form of a royal command. So with his captured craft to accompany the *Kestrel*, it was northwards again, up to the Pentland Firth, near to Orkney, and through it to the Sea of the Hebrides, and down by all the straits and sounds among the isles to round the Mull of Kintyre and enter the Clyde. Up past mountainous Arran he reached the narrowing at the great bend eastwards, where rose the twin-peaked rock crowned by the royal stronghold, the Dun of the Britons, Dumbarton Castle, the town nearby.

Despite the inevitable delay in responding to the royal request and the quite lengthy voyage entailed, the castle had clearly not fallen; and four ships lay at anchor below, the besiegers. Summing up the situation, Andrew judged that this would not be one of his most difficult confrontations, moored vessels, and many of the crews most probably ashore in the town, sampling its attractions while the castle held out until starvation forced a yielding.

Indeed, it did prove to be all very simple. Sailing his two ships up to the four, he led boarding. At first it seemed that there was no one left on this vessel, but then they discovered three men, who promptly surrendered in the face of many boarders. No doubt the next crews left on their vessel were warned now, but that did not help them against their numerous attackers. They yielded likewise, without a struggle.

The third craft's people, seeing what was happening to their fellows, at least did not wait to be assailed, but were lowering a small boat to escape to the shore. Andrew was unable to put a stop to this, but one more ship was his.

The fourth crewmen had had time to see the danger, and had also got a boat down and the five men into it, also to pull for the town's quaysides. So the English ashore would be told of the situation. But had four enemy ships ever before been so easily taken? Presumably the leadership had not visualised any relieving squadron coming to the aid of Dumbarton. The Scots had no navy of warships.

What now? The English in the town could sail out in

their small boats to try to retake their vessels; but they were unlikely to succeed, in the circumstances. Andrew ordered half of his crewmen in his two ships to man, in the best manner possible, the four enemy craft, raise the anchors and enough sail to get them well out into the estuary waters, so that small boats would have difficulty reaching them, he with his now reduced crews doing likewise.

Presently he did see many small boats putting out from the town, but did not think these capable of regaining their vessels. Soon, apparently, the Englishmen perceived the same, and the boats turned back.

Now he had six ships instead of two, but inevitably all much under-manned. What best to do with them? He could not, with any hope of success, assail the town. The English would outnumber them greatly. He could not aid the castle other than by preventing any attack on it. If the townsfolk were to rise against the invaders, that would be different. But were ordinary citizens likely so to do against armed fighting-men? Probably not.

But what of King James? This was a royal castle. And although he had no suitable vessels to attack, he could surely raise large numbers of men, armed. Was he doing so? Where was he? Glasgow could produce many, likewise Paisley, Greenock, Renfrew and other nearby towns. Could the monarch march a host here? He must be doing something, not just leaving it all to his pirate-slayer.

Andrew decided to land on the castle rock and climb up, under the Scottish saltire flag, to consult with the keeper thereof, whoever that was.

He lowered one of the *Kestrel*'s small boats, and was rowed to the rock-foot, with a banner, there to land and climb up the hundreds of steps cut in the steep ascent. Nearing the summit there were three gatehouses barring the way. Challenged from the first, he shouted that he was Andrew Wood, in command of the Scots ships that had captured the English ones, as would have been seen. He would speak with the keeper of this royal hold, in King James's name.

The guards would not know who Andrew Wood was, almost certainly; but this of naming the monarch, and with the St Andrew's cross flag, ought to serve.

It did. After a brief wait, he was admitted through the gateway, and the chief guard told him that the keeper of Dumbarton Castle was the Lord Darnley. He was present above. Men were provided to escort Andrew up past the other two gates to the fortress itself.

He found Sir John Stewart of Darnley, a far-out kinsman of the monarch, who was assuming the style and title of Earl of Lennox, a youngish man of confidently assured manner, who however welcomed the visitor, declaring that he had watched what went on below and realised that the English besiegers were not having things their own way. He had indeed heard of the pirate-slayer, and saluted him and his efforts, if in a somewhat superior way.

As to King James, he understood that he was assembling men at Glasgow to counter this English threat. But the need for ships had been vital, and so Wood had been sent for. There were many merchanters at Glasgow of course, but their crews not trained for warfare. These might well be used to carry men, but would not be able to assail the English squadron. Now, with the invaders deprived of their ships, the king's men would be well placed to challenge the foe. The enemy might be able to take over sundry craft at Dumbarton harbour, of course; but these would be small, and not to be measured against Wood's vessels and his captures.

So Darnley urged Andrew to wait meantime until the royal force came up, and then to assist in the conquest of the foe.

How long would it take for them to reach Dumbarton? Up the north side of Clyde, by Yoker and Dalmuir and Kilpatrick, was some sixteen miles. And such a force, afoot, would not march fast. It depended on various factors: the assembling of a sufficiency of men, leadership arrangements, and of course when a start had been made. The king would not be aware of the new situation, that the enemy's ships had been captured. So he might take his time, awaiting more men from Paisley, Elderslie, Kilbarchan and the like.

Andrew declared that the sooner the royal force arrived and was able to clear the English out of Dumbarton town the better. For it could be that this group of the four enemy vessels was only the forerunner of a larger fleet. These had not been pirate craft, so their arrival might well indicate a more serious assault on Scotland. The two nations were in a state of permanent if undeclared war, and this of Dumbarton only the commencement, a first preparation.

Darnley admitted it. What could be done to improve the Scots position?

Andrew thought that the king and his host should be informed speedily as to the situation – that the English were now without their ships and stranded in the town. If the royal force attacked, the citizenry would probably rise against the invaders, and it ought to be complete defeat for the foe. How many of them would there be? It could well be that they had brought many more men than just the ordinary crew members. At most say one hundred per ship? Four hundred men? The king would have many more than that. The English could seek to escape in small Dumbarton craft – but *he* would attend to that.

Best, then, that he sailed up Clyde to find the king's people, inform them, and arrange a joint assault on the town.

So it was back to the *Kestrel*, and instructions left with the five other ships, scanty as to crews as they were, to remain cordoning off the town's waterside, while he went in search of the monarch.

Actually it took no more than twenty minutes' sailing to meet the scattered array – it could scarcely be called an army. Four miles east of Dumbarton the estuary narrowed quite abruptly into a river, at Erskine, and here, on the north bank, came the straggling hundreds, variously armed, the monarch with a company of knights and lairds leading, but in the main ordinary town and country folk, gathered in haste and at random.

The *Kestrel*, drawing in, was recognised by King James, who halted all, to greet his friend the pirate-slayer when he landed, indeed embracing him warmly, thankful to see him.

The situation explained to him, he was much encouraged; a joint attack on Dumbarton town then. When? They were still some four or five miles from there, and this not very disciplined or battle-trained force would have to be marshalled and given clear instructions. Two hours? Three?

Andrew said that he would land a few men, to create a distraction more than anything else, for he really had only two crews and these were manning six ships now, and some must be left aboard to maintain the barrier to prevent an enemy escape by boat. It would be evening by then, and the English might well not be looking for any attack.

James Stewart was no warrior-prince but he had the advice of some lords and knights, who were fairly confident that they could take the town if those hundreds of the enemy were sufficiently distracted. So that was up to Andrew. He must do more than merely bar their escape. A landing at the waterside quays. Some demonstration. How many could he put ashore, and yet leave the ships manned in some fashion?

Head ashake, Andrew said no more than thirty. They might set alight one or two of the harbour sheds, this to draw attention to the landing, that distraction.

This was accepted. In about three hours, then.

The *Kestrel* tacked its way back westwards, to rejoin the waiting five.

And still they had to wait, Andrew sending his instructions out to the other crews.

At least they could see the eventual approach of the king's force. Dumbarton lay at the mouth of the River Leven, flowing down from Loch Lomond and the Highland hills, none so far off. The town lay on both sides, with two bridges over the river. But the main part, like the castle, was on the east bank, and the lesser suburb could probably be ignored.

When time had been given for the royal manpower to mass around the eastern outskirts, Andrew gave the signal. Boats were lowered from the ships to carry the landing-party ashore, with whale oil to help start the desired blaze.

Landed, Andrew found, among the various sheds and warehouses near the shore, two old wooden cabins in which were stored old fishing-nets. These would burn readily, doused with oil.

They did, and soon the huts were ablaze, with clouds of smoke, reddened by flames, blown over into the town's streets. That ought to serve their purpose.

The fires certainly had their effect, but not without confusion for the attackers as well as the foe. For the narrow lanes and alleys became filled with alarmed folk, and in the smoke and gloom it was difficult to distinguish friend from enemy. Andrew shouted to his people to look out for *armed* men, for such would be the English.

They did not see many such, no doubt the king's large attacking force preoccupying most. Such as they did encounter they dealt with readily enough, save where these took refuge among the thronging townsfolk, as they were apt to do; and these latter, uncertain who was friend or enemy, were no help. Attack and defence can be like that, frequently chaotic.

In the event, Andrew's party did little fighting, the Englishmen being much more fully taken up with the king's major onset. Dumbarton became a series of minor battles in its various market-places, streets and alleys as the evening merged into nightfall, and no one knew what went on elsewhere, Andrew's group probably the most coherent and organised of all the contenders.

At what stage it could be recognised that the town was delivered from its invaders would be hard to say; but before long it was only fellow-Scots whom Andrew's people encountered.

Dumbarton was freed. And Andrew Wood had won four more vessels.

6

Those new ships: what was Andrew to do with them? He had no desire, or need, to build up some sort of fleet of his own; two vessels were adequate for his trading. Moreover he was constructing a fine new one to his own design. So he might sell these captured ones, if he could find buyers.

It occurred to him that, instead of having them sailed all the way round Scotland to Leith, he might well find a market in Glasgow, which was probably the largest port in the land. Sail them up Clyde then, the sixteen miles, and see what he could do among the Glasgow merchants.

Before leaving Dumbarton he had to take leave of King James, a grateful monarch. And in telling him of this of selling the ships, his liege-lord said that it would be to his realm's advantage to have its own ships, as these captured vessels were England's, whether King Richard's own or belonging to his government or parliament. As it happened, Bishop John Laing of Glasgow was Lord Chancellor of the Scots parliament, and Abbot Crawford of Holyrood High Treasurer, these churchmen ever the most able administrators. He, the king, would sail up to Glasgow with his friend, and introduce him to the bishop, and see what could be done with these ships, and payment therefore.

This was, needless to say, much to Andrew's satisfaction. So instead of riding back to the city with his troops, the monarch embarked on *Kestrel* and the six ships sailed upriver for the great port.

The cathedral of St Kentigern, or Mungo, was not hard to find, none so far from the river, its spires soaring above all, and Bishop Laing's palace nearby. James had actually slept there two nights before, and was on excellent terms with the Chancellor. The prelate had of course heard of Andrew Wood's exploits, and greeted him in amiable fashion. And hearing his, and the monarch's suggestions as to building up a number of ships to form the nucleus of a national fleet, showed much interest. This would be a matter for a parliament; but if recommended by the king and himself, the probability was that it would be agreed. Would Andrew be prepared to hand over his captures to the nation, at some suitable payment? Andrew certainly would.

Just how much would be paid was a matter for the High Treasurer, Abbot Crawford. He was at Holyrood, in Edinburgh. But since the captured vessels would be more usefully left here at Glasgow, he, the bishop, could make some token payment meantime, and the treasurer settle the details later, this to the king's commendation.

Andrew found himself given a quite substantial amount of silver coin in return for leaving the four craft with the Chancellor. It seemed that James was remaining at Glasgow for the time being before returning to Edinburgh; so there was a leave-taking. Considerably the richer, Andrew and his two ships set off down the Clyde again for the quite lengthy sail to Leith.

What to do with all this extra money? He did not actually require it for his trading, which was doing sufficiently well on its own. He judged that it would be best invested in land. And if this was in the Largo area, it could be of benefit to his mother and young brother. Purchase some property at or near Largo, and become something of a laird? Largostone was well enough as a house; but lands to go with it would be advantageous. He would consult Harry Lindsay, and his father Sir John, at Pitcruvie, on this.

His return to Largo, and now being so evidently successful and all but famous, he was welcomed by more than family and kinsfolk. As to buying land, at Pitcruvie he met an interesting young woman, Elizabeth Lundie, the niece of Lady Lindsay, herself a Lundie, this a presentable and lively female, dark of hair and bright of eye, who was full of questions for the pirate-slayer: how he managed to board other vessels at sea, what he did with the ships he captured, did he find them full of booty, and what of the evil men whom he took prisoner? Did he hang them?

Andrew answered these questions as best he could. He was not used to coping with well-bred young women, never having had much association with the like, his experience with the other sex being little more than some huddles and cuddles with cottage girls of a summer evening. This one was otherwise, pleasingly frank and friendly, but with an innate assurance as well as good-looking; and being the only young people there, and much of an age, they tended to get together.

Beth, as she said she was called, came of a notable Fife family, the Lundies of Balgony. They had originally been Lundins of that Ilk, Lundin being next to Largo westwards on the great Largo Bay. But the name of the family had become Lundy or Lundie centuries before, and now they held the lairdships of Condland and Benholm as well as Balgony.

Andrew did have a word with Sir John regarding this of the purchase of land, and was advised that he would be best to invest in property that might yield a profit rather than mere acreage. Mills, for instance, to grind the farmers' grain, then sell the flour, a sure source of revenue. Land should be seen as a responsibility and a productive holding, not, as so many lairds viewed it, as a name to enhance their status, or mere sporting ground. Also there were fulling mills, where the grease was pounded out of sheep's fleeces to make it fit for weaving. These could be profitable. He added that the miller at Coitlands had just died, leaving only a widow and two daughters, and they were looking for a buyer. There was a possibility for investment and he could find some miller's young son to run it for him.

Andrew said that he would take a look at this Coitlands Mill. When he bade goodbye, he told this Beth Lundie, since she had sounded interested in his pirate campaign, that, if she would like to visit and inspect his ship, the *Kestrel*, she would be very welcome. It lay presently at Methil, where there was good docking, Largo's haven itself being suitable only for small fishing-boats. He could bring horses to collect her. She said that she would much like to see his famous vessel and have his activities described to her; but pointed out that her home, Balgony Castle, east of Markinch on the River Leven, was only five miles from Methil. So she could meet him there and save him the longer ride.

Andrew would have none of that. He would come for her, take her to the ship and escort her home again. She did not say him nay.

They agreed to do this two days hence when she would be back at Balgony from this Pitcruvie, for he would be off to Leith the day following.

He went to inspect Coitlands Mill, five miles away on the Lahill Burn, approved of it – but learned that it did not belong to the widow, but was only rented from Arnot of that Ilk, chief of that name. He went to Arnot, and had no difficulty in buying the mill, which was to be the first of many.

Balgony Castle, where he duly picked up Beth Lundie, was a fine place, built early in that century by a Sir John Sibbald, whose daughter and heiress married Sir Robert Lundie and was now Beth's mother. It was a tall square keep of five storeys, with parapet and wall-walk within a curtain-walled courtyard, all built of good squared stone, ashlar as it was called, not the random rubble of so many tower-houses, and so requiring no outer harling to prevent damp seeping in through the mortar. The doorway was at first-floor level, reached from a detached stairway and little

platform, the gap to which could be spanned by a remo-
vable gangway or bridge, a notable safety device which
Andrew commented upon when he reached the welcoming
Beth. She observed, laughing, that although *he* might be
well guarded, in his ships, she was likewise not to be taken
easily! He promised to remember it.

She was the youngest of the family. Her eldest brother
was actually the Sheriff of Fife, her father elderly and in
failing health, uncle to the present Lundie of Lundie.
Andrew was well aware that he did not come of such
background, and was received in friendly fashion because
of his exploits, fame, and known closeness to the monarch.
He had little doubt that, but for this, he would not have
been allowed to conduct the daughter off alone to visit his
ship.

They rode down the Leven for three miles to the
Cameron bridge, where they struck off for Methil, Beth
obviously a competent horsewoman. Without being deliberately so she made a challenging companion for a man,
sparkling-eyed, of attractive bearing and figure, all woman, Andrew far from unaware of it.

Reaching the quayside and the *Kestrel*, the tide being
low, they had to mount the gangway in a steep climb, and
getting over the rail called for a high-stepping clamber in
which long female legs became very evident and were duly
admired, Beth accepting that along with his helping hand.
He retained a grasp of her arm thereafter, for her guidance,
there being much to show her. It occurred to him that this
was the first time that a woman had been on *Kestrel*, at
least since it became his ship.

He took her up to the forecastle first, proudly to show
her the bronze cannon which he had acquired on his last
visit to the Netherlands, the first such which he had
installed on one of his ships, thus copying the Portuguese.
He admitted that he had not yet used it, save to try out one
or two practice shots against rafts as targets, cannonballs
being too precious to waste. He explained the use of the

various sails, so important for manoeuvring one vessel against another, as was so often his task. He took her to see his cabin quarters below, with its bunks, and she remarked that the basic facilities were somewhat elementary, especially for women, he confessing that such had not as yet demanded his attention.

The aftercastle was inspected, the wheel's and the helmsman's vital importance emphasised, especially when attacking another craft.

Beth showed considerable interest in it all, and declared that she would like to sail in such a vessel one day. She had been on small fishing-boats with her brothers, and enjoyed that; but never on a large ship. Andrew did not fail to propose a short trip once he got back from his next voyage, which was in two days' time. This, he admitted, would be something of an adventure, taking him into unknown waters and to territories hitherto only names to him. He explained about the great value put upon ivory by the Hansa merchants, and how this was to be won from the tusks of walruses; and that while these were to be found among the Orkney and Shetland isles, great numbers of the creatures were said to inhabit other islands further north still, these called the Faroes or Bird Isles, and better still at Iceland, a great and little-known territory thought to be their breeding-ground. He intended to prospect its possibilities.

She declared that she admired his questing and venturesome spirit, but hoped that he would not take undue risks in these strange lands – although she supposed that they would probably be no more dangerous than his pirate-attacking. Must he ever be such a risk-taker?

"I appreciate your concern for my safety," he told her. "But a man must meet challenges if he is to retain any opinion of himself. And this of the ivory is no small opportunity. You yourself strike me as an adventurous young woman. I would have thought that this project would have commended itself to you?"

"There are ventures and ventures," she pointed out. "And what made you think me adventuresome?"

That he found difficult to answer. "Something about the way your eyes dart and gleam," was the best that he could do.

She turned those dark eyes on him, and possibly without so intending, confirmed his assessment.

When it came to disembarking, Andrew demonstrated his own initiative by stepping over the vessel's rail first, and then, on the top of the gangway, turning to bend and lift her bodily over, and hold her there heedfully on the steep descent. Beth nowise shook him off although, smiling, she shook her head over him.

Back at the horses, her mounting provided him with further opportunity for contact and limb and limber approval. And, when they returned to Balgony and he aided her down again, he was bold enough to plant a kiss on her cheek in the process. She looked at him, dark head to one side judiciously, and then, leaning over, did the same for *his* cheek.

"Let it not be said that I do not give as good as I get!" she declared, and started to lead her horse into the courtyard.

He promised a short sail for her in the *Kestrel* when he got back from the far north; and rode homewards thoughtful.

7

Andrew judged that this would probably be one of the longest voyages that he had ever undertaken, further than to the Baltic by far. Reckoning as best he could, it would be four hundred and fifty miles to the northern tip of Shetland, one hundred and twenty more to the Faroe Isles and another two hundred and fifty to Iceland, over eight hundred altogether. With the prevailing south-westerly winds it would take four or five days and nights sailing, although he could not rely on the wind direction, especially the further north he got, where the Arctic was said to produce its own winds, and often gales. Warm clothing was going to be called for. It was to be hoped that it would all prove worth while, and the walruses were to be found in their hundreds, even thousands. Hopefully he took the two ships, in case *Kestrel* was unable to hold all the ivory gained; was that expecting too much? He was calling the other vessel the *Goshawk*. A pity that his new-building especial craft, carvel-planked, which he was going to name the *Yellow Caravel*, on account of the pale colouring of the timbering which he had brought from the Baltic, was not yet finished. It would have been a notable launching voyage for it.

After cautious negotiation of the roosts off the Orkneys, they proceeded on to pass the Shetlands, making good time of it. Then came waters hitherto unsailed by him, to the Faroes. He understood that they could risk sailing by night, reportedly no islets nor skerries to endanger navigation.

It was not rocks or obstacles that delayed them thereafter

but a gradual change of wind into the east and then north-east, this involving much tacking and sail adjustment. Andrew rather feared that the further they went, the more northerly the winds would get. And the air was already colder.

Beating this way and that, they reached the Faroes, a long string of islands extending to over seventy miles, with steep cliffs and deep fjords, colonised by the Danes. They did not halt here, for although there were said to be walrus here, they were alleged to be in nothing like the numbers to be found at Iceland. So, another two hundred miles at least, and in uncharted waters.

The wind in their faces now at least was producing no gales; and the seas were consistently great rollers, causing the ships to dip and rise seemingly endlessly. And it was cold, cold. Their progress, in these circumstances, was not speedy.

Oddly enough, although the sky was actually cloudless, it was cloud that eventually heralded their approach to Iceland, smoke clouds. Not the dark smoke of fires but many tall columns of grey-pink towering into the air ahead. Presumably these were from the many volcanoes Andrew had been told about, hundreds of them allegedly. This Iceland was a country of strange contrasts, heat and cold, boiling springs and icy glaciers, soaring mountains higher than anything in Scotland, and great bare moorlands. Although they were apt to think of it, if thought of at all, as a great island, it was much more than that, as large as Ireland and said to resemble it in shape.

Gradually pale-blue mountains began to rise above the horizon under the smoke, although as they drew closer these turned from bluish to gleaming white.

Approaching their destination, Andrew had to consider carefully. He had been told at Leith that these Icelanders, of Norse extraction, were not numerous, and settled necessarily round the coasts, inland being all those high mountains, glaciers and lofty barren tableland. Although a few sheep and cattle were bred, the folk were mainly fishers. So this of his quest for walrus tusks demanded caution. The folk here did not seem to realise the value of the ivory in far southern lands, using it only occasionally for making carved utensils and decorations. But they did greatly value walrus hides and blubber, oil and meat. They called the creatures *morse*, or seahorses, and would not approve of strangers coming to slaughter them. So some arrangement would have to be made with them. Could it be agreed that they had the carcases if the Scots could have the tusks? Some sort of bargain struck, without revealing what ivory would fetch at Lübeck?

Suppose that he declared that he had a market for the tusks, not referring to them as ivory, in a far land where elephant tusks were highly esteemed but very scarce, and these would serve as substitutes. And he had no wish to retain the bodies with their skins, blubber and meat and would transport such to the nearest communities for the folk to use as they wished. Would that arouse suspicions? He could, he supposed, offer to pay for the tusks. Presumably these people would have use for silver? He must wait and see what the situation demanded. One thought did keep recurring to him: he was not looking forward to the actual slaying of large numbers of walrus.

They saw, as they neared the land, that it was none so different from most other sea coasts, however unusual was the scene inland, a succession of long sandy beaches, rocky strands, bays, cliffs and inlets, some of these last narrow enough to be called fjords. At first no communities were evident; then he perceived a small cluster of low thatched-roofed cottages just within the shelter of an inlet. This did not look a good place to moor his ships, although there were small boats drawn up on the beach. He steered further along the coast westwards.

Crossing the mouth of a wide bay, just behind a small headland at the far side, they came on a much larger scatter of houses, not what could be called a village, more of a crofting township. He saw nothing like a dock or harbour for larger vessels. These Icelanders must have sea-going craft for their voyaging – but not here apparently.

He drew the *Kestrel* in, to anchor just behind the headland, the *Goshawk* following. Lowering one of his two small boats, he was rowed to the shore. He now saw quite a number of folk waiting and watching there.

Talk with them would almost certainly be difficult. He had only a smattering of Danish, picked up at Copenhagen and the Baltic ports. And it seemed highly doubtful that these Icelanders could speak English. James Barton did know Dutch and German. They would just have to make themselves and their wishes known as best they could.

They found themselves eyed with not unfriendly interest by the watching men, women and children, waiting behind a row of boats drawn up on the sand, coracles in fact, made out of grey skins on sapling frames. Timber would be scarce in this strange land; they saw no woodlands, only small scattered and stunted birch.

Grounding, Andrew leaped ashore, hand upraised high in greeting, Barton close behind.

"Friends!" he called. "Scots friends. From Scotland. Good friends. Scotland." He added Shetland and Orkney, even the Faroes. They might know these names better. "Come to trade." Would they make anything of that?

It did not look as though they did, by the enquiring expressions. But these were not hostile, at least.

Andrew tried a few words of his scanty Danish. This did produce some effect, a chatter of speech that was unintelligible to him. One man took a step forward, elderly, presumably an elder or headman. He too held up a hand in salutation.

No antagonism, at any rate.

Andrew uttered such words, in Danish, as he could think of, then adding Scots, Schottishe, Celts, Albannach. This produced noddings of heads.

Then he remembered the Icelandic word for walrus, *morse*. He announced it, twice.

That did have its effect. More nods and chatter, even pointings, these eastwards along the wide bay.

Andrew repeated the word enquiringly.

More nods and pointings.

He looked back at his friends. They too nodded.

So he waved in that direction, and took a step or two. Some of the Iceland men turned, obviously to lead him on. It seemed as though he were to be escorted along the beach, not to the coracles, just along the shore. Did this mean that there were walruses somewhere nearby?

He walked beside the older man, exchanging glances and nods. This was an unexpected reaction, being taken, apparently, not just directed.

Not far along that beach there was a reef of black rocks to form a slight projection into the tide, covered in seaweed. Picking their way over this, the old man pointed. The shoreline, at this half-tide, curved away for at least a mile. And some way along it there was a stretch encumbered by something, objects, shapes, a considerable area, greyish against the sand. Could it be . . . ? So soon?

He pointed. "*Morse?*" he asked. "*Morse*, there?"

The Icelander nodded, and repeated the word, smiling.

They had perhaps a quarter-mile to walk before, even to the Scots' eyes, it was evident that there was movement among the mass ahead. Andrew for one had hardly expected to be seeing walrus as early on as this.

As they drew near he was able to see individual creatures. They were huge, perhaps a dozen feet long, heavily built, grey-skinned with reddish hair at the wide shoulders, these reared up, producing thick forelegs ending in flippers. There were small heads and bulging eyes, quill-like whiskers, and, to be sure, great white tusks thrusting and curving downwards to sharp points, what they had come so far to see. The Icelanders, laughing, pointed at them all, chanting, "*Morse! Morse!*"

At their approach, most of the great beasts began to waddle and flop their way down to the water, and soon it became a general move. Without actually seeking to count, Andrew guessed that there could be over one hundred heading for the sea. But it was not this exodus that riveted his attention, but what they left behind. Hitherto hidden by the great clumsy bodies, the upper beach was seen to be littered with stationary objects, flat, not rearing up, bones, skeletons by the score, the hundred. And gleaming among them all, white tusks.

He all but ran forward to the carcases, or skeletons, to stoop and grasp at one of the tusks projecting from a quite small skull, all out of proportion. It was firmly attached.

He turned to look back at his friends and such crewmen as had accompanied them, shaking his head in wonderment. So easy, so simple, and yet so extraordinary. The ivory there in vast quantities, just waiting to be collected. Axes and hammers to break it off the skulls, that was all. There were hundreds of these skulls, all with their tusks. The carcases had obviously been skinned, flayed by the locals, the blubber and meat taken and the debris left, including the unwanted tusks, and this presumably over a quite long period, to account for the great numbers in this walrus graveyard.

Andrew could hardly hold himself back from shouting his astonished elation. The ivory harvest lay waiting for him, presumably to take as he wanted. This was beyond all belief. Could it all be his? Did the Icelanders seek payment?

Those who had brought him here revealed no such attitude. They kicked contemptuously at the bones and skulls, and pointed seawards, laughing still. The inner waters of the bay were so closely dotted with seal-like heads, all gazing shorewards, as almost to show more grey skin than water. This is what *they* were interested in, proud of: the numbers of live walrus there for their catching.

Andrew searched for and picked up a skull which had got detached from the rest of the bones, this with tusks still in place, and heavy as it was, weighing he guessed not far off a dozen pounds, and over three feet in length, hoisted it on to his shoulders, this obviously amusing the locals. James Barton and other Scots kicked other skulls apart, and followed suit. They would carry these back to their boats, in a sort of triumph.

At the vessels, they ordered the full crews to come ashore, with their implements, to hack off tusks from skulls and load them on to the boats, a lengthy and laborious process, the resultant haul weighty indeed, so that it demanded a great many boat-loads to get it all back to the ships, and there to have the ivory hoisted aboard. This last was the slowest part of it all, for only one at a time could be lifted up on ropes; that is, until Andrew organised sailcloth hampers which would take half a dozen. Some of the local men watched this proceeding, heads ashake.

It occurred to Andrew to ask, by signs as well as repeating the word *morse*, whether there were other bays and parts of the shoreline where these carcases might be found? He learned that there were, pointings in both directions. So there was further harvesting for the Scots. But this must suffice for that day. On the morrow, then . . .

The holds of the two vessels could take a lot of ivory. But two days later they were full, the tusks stacked as closely as possible considering their shapes.

Payment now? Some gesture must be made to the Icelanders, however little *they* seemed to esteem the cargo. There was no measure by which Andrew could assess what might be a suitable recognition of appreciation – and he wanted it to be adequate, for he certainly intended to come back one day for more. He counted out what he deemed to be a reasonable amount of silver, and took this to that elderly individual of the little community, which seemed to be named Dyrhulaey, or something such. This was received with astonishment, and indications that it was certainly not necessary. But after a little awkward urging, he accepted about half of it, with head-shakings.

So, the enterprise was completed, and most satisfactorily, this part of it at least. Now to see to the selling. The Lübeck merchants would almost certainly never have had such a haul of ivory delivered to them before. Would the sheer weight of it all bring down the price? Or would it be wise to split it up, offer it to various markets, not just the Hansa one; the Netherlands, for instance? They would have to see what the reaction was.

Andrew decided that there was no point in heading back to Leith. Much better to sail directly south-by-east for the Baltic, passing between the Shetland and Norwegian coasts. From this Dyrhulaey or whatever it was called, at the southern tip of Iceland, to the Skagerrak could be, he assessed, not far off one thousand miles, lengthy voyage as it was, but better than making for Scotland first, by-passing the Faroes, open sea all the way. And with these northerly winds giving way presently to the prevailing south-westerlies, they ought to have reasonable sailing conditions and no need for night-time heaving-to. Four or five days, then?

It was Lübeck for them.

They made the Baltic in four days of steady and uneventful cruising by which time all aboard were getting tired of feeding on walrus meat. And at Lübeck, however surprised the Hansa traders were at being presented with two whole shiploads of ivory, there was no lack of buyers and no fall in prices, the market apparently assured, far and wide.

So Andrew found himself well rewarded indeed. He passed on a fair proportion of the proceeds to his friends and crews. He was able to fill his two ships with goods that he could sell at a profit at Leith and Edinburgh, and still retain a very large sum in gold and silver for his own coffers. He decided that he would use this to build a second ship in the caravel design, convinced that these would be of great advantage in sea-worthiness, speed and manoeuvrability, to rival the Portuguese craft, if not better them.

It was home for Leith, then.

8

Andrew had not failed to bring home a present for Beth
Lundie, a jewelled brooch. Also a little ivory ornament
from Iceland, in the shape of a whale, which might appeal.
So he had to hire a horse to take him to Balgony.

He was well received at the castle and, arriving in the
early evening, was invited to stay for the night, although he
said that he could easily ride back to his bunk on the
Kestrel, at Methil.

Beth declared that the brooch was far too valuable a gift
for the likes of herself, and made her wonder whether the
giver was seeking especial favours in return?

When he denied anything such, she said, "A woman has
to be careful, see you, friend Andrew. Especially in accepting such as this from a man used to making conquests!"

"My conquests, lass, have all been at sea thus far. I am
an innocent where women are concerned. Compared with
the many more practised admirers who must seek your . . .
attentions."

"So you present me with a diamond and rubies set in
gold, to win the said attentions?"

"They come with no such intentions, Elizabeth Lundie!"

"I thought that it was to be Beth?"

"Beth, then. Say that it is to persuade you to risk a small
voyage in my ship. Instead of the only brief inspection you
made that day."

"I do not require jewels to coax me for that! I have been
waiting for it. I judge that I should be safe with you
aboard, with all your crew present to restrain you, if
necessary?"

He wagged his head over this so challenging young woman. Was she like this with all the other sex? Surprising that she had not been captured well before this by eager suitors. Or was she well able to defend herself? She had said, that time, that she could give as good as she got.

"My *Kestrel* is at your disposal, woman. Whenever you wish."

"Tomorrow, then?"

"Why not. If the weather is not unkind."

Andrew was glad to accept the invitation to stay the night at Balgony. Over the excellent meal he entertained the company with tales of strange lands, the Baltic, Iceland and the walruses. There was music and ballad-singing thereafter, Beth contributing tunefully.

At bed-going, she escorted Andrew up to his chamber. She inspected all, to see that it was in order, hot water for washing, a warming-pan in the bed, and wine and oatcakes for possible night-time appetite – although as the young woman checked on all this, the man's appetite tended to be otherwise than for his stomach.

When she made for the door, to wish him peaceful sleep, he mentioned, "A goodnight kiss might be helpful in that!"

"Is that a hostess's duty, sir? Then I must not fail you. I would not wish you to feel deprived!"

Clasping her to him, she offered him her lips, this time, not just her cheek, he demonstrating his appreciation by reluctance to release her.

"It is only slumber that you are here for, Andrew Wood, not . . . dalliance!" she observed. "Do you wish *me* to have a wakeful night?"

"I, I could not truthfully deny that!" he told her, as she slipped away, and closed the door behind her.

He was in no hurry to close his eyes that night.

The morning proving breezy but sunny, the promised sail in *Kestrel* was readily offered, and accepted – although Beth's youngest brother Michael's request to accompany them was acceded to less than enthusiastically by Andrew. The trio rode off down to Methil. Offered the choice of the Isle of May, or up-Forth to the further off islands of Inchkeith, Inchcolm, even Inchgarvie and Inchmickery, Beth said that she had sailed round the May in her brothers' fishing-boats. But she would like to visit Inchcolm, called after St Columba, of whom she was a great admirer. Had he ever actually visited that isle, or was it just named in his honour? And was it possible to sail round the Craig of Bass on the way? She had often gazed over at it from the Fife shores, but never been close. Andrew declared that no problem.

Hoisting Beth aboard *Kestrel* was less productive of appreciation with brother Michael present, even for the crew.

Sailing well west of the May, they headed across the score of miles to the Bass, not far off the Lothian shore, to round it, Beth duly exclaiming over the enormous cliffs, white with bird droppings, the clouds of wheeling seafowl above, including the great solan geese or gannets which made this their nesting-place, these diving into the sea vertically, with much splashing, in search of their prey, and usually coming up again with flapping fish in their large beaks. They inspected the peculiar cavern-like tunnel, through a spur at the south-east, not far off two hundred yards long, which small boats could sail through although not the *Kestrel*. This looked almost man-made, although almost certainly was natural. Andrew recounted how the eighth century missionary, St Baldred, had had his hermitage here, from which he was said to commune with the seals, as well as with his Maker.

From the Bass they beat their way westwards, almost another score of miles, to the quite large island of Inchkeith, lying in mid-Forth between Leith in Lothian and Kinghorn in Fife, cliff-girt but not soaring high, not unlike the May, half a mile of it, where allegedly there were prehistoric remains referred to by the second-century astronomer Ptolemy, who presumably must have visited it in his famous travels.

There was no call to land here. But none so far off was a very different isle, Inchcolm, the one Beth wanted to see. Andrew, who was well versed in islands, needless to say, told how King Alexander the First, in 1123, had been marooned hereon for three days while the land was searched for him. He had been crossing the Forth to Aberdour from Leith in stormy weather when a gust capsized the boat, drowning the oarsmen, but the king, a strong swimmer, managed to reach this island. He found it inhabited by a hermit monk, who apparently lived on shellfish and the milk of a single cow, and this had to be the royal diet until, on the third day, their smoke signals managed to attract the attention of Kinghorn fishermen, and Alexander was rescued. In gratitude he founded an Augustinian abbey on the island, dedicated to St Columba the sea apostle. The famous chronicler Walter Bower had been abbot here for a time.

They did land now, and at the abbey were eyed apprehensively by the monks, who, reassured, explained that twice they had been raided by English pirates and their precious relics, even their food, stolen. Andrew assured them that this would not happen again if *he* could help it; and they were hospitably entertained. They were taken and shown the graves of Danes, with carvings on the stones, these the followers of the King Sven defeated by the Scots, and still tended by the monks, even though the Vikings were not Christians.

The remaining islands of Inchgarvie and Inchmickery were small and barren, little more than rocks for seals. But near the last they passed a group, to be carefully avoided, more skerries than islets, known as the Cow and Calves, with the isolated rock of the Oxcar nearby, this traditionally said to be the sire of the calves.

They turned back here, having covered a fair mileage, and with the westerly breeze made a speedy return to

Methil, Beth expressing her approval of it all, and her gratitude.

Andrew was to spend another night at Balgony. They found the eldest brother, Robert Lundie, who was Sheriff of Fife, present. He lived on the subsidiary estate of Pitlour. He was interested to meet the pirate-slayer, declaring that he doubted whether all the tales told of Andrew Wood could be true, but recognised him as a remarkable man and a credit to Fife. He had heard that he had bought a couple of mills. But had he ever thought of purchasing an estate and becoming a laird? Would that not be suitable?

Suitable for what? Andrew wondered. This from Beth's brother. He admitted that he had considered the matter. His home territory was Largo. And there were the mills that he had bought. If the barony itself came up for sale, he might well make a bid for it. Meanwhile he was sufficiently concerned, money-wise, in his shipbuilding which, with his notions of what was advisable and worthy, was expensive. The *Yellow Caravel* was almost completed and the second one, to be called the *Flower*, all but half so.

Lundie, who as sheriff was very knowledgeable about affairs in the county, mentioned that he had asked this because he had heard that the laird of the barony, Arnot of Largo, was dying. And he was leaving no son, only one daughter. The probability was that, on his death, widow and daughter would move out to the dower-house of Strathairly, and Largo estate might well come on the market. Just a thought . . .

Andrew pondered over all this, and the fact that Lundie was speaking of it to him. Did it indicate that the sheriff, aware of his friendship with Beth, was anticipating their marriage? And if so, would wish his sister to marry into the lairdly caste, not just to a merchant-trader, however successful? It was a thought. *Would* Beth marry him? This was not the first time that he had wondered that, of course. But this conversation rather brought it to the fore. He had the money now, for marriage and land-buying. James Barton was off to Iceland again in the *Goshawk* to collect more ivory to add to his wealth. He *could* become Andrew Wood of Largo, in more than just having been born and residing in the parish. And not only was it a parish, but actually a barony, Lundie had said. And that gave a seat in parliament, for holders of baronies. Did he want that? No disadvantage, at any rate.

Another notion had been simmering at the back of his mind. This of the *Yellow Caravel*, and the king's friendship. Suppose he was to ask James to launch it, and he then to present it to the monarch, in token at least, as ever available to take the monarch and his queen to the Isle of May, which he so esteemed as a place of pilgrimage? Might not that be an appropriate gesture? An expression of his loyal support, as well as marking their so kindly association.

So, at Leith, ascertaining that the king was at Holyrood, he rode thither and sought audience. He found James in a state of much anxiety and distress. Queen Margaret was sick, very sick, and her physician, the famous William Sheves, was not expecting her to recover. There was even talk of her, at court, well known as a most pious woman, being proposed to the Vatican for canonisation. In these circumstances, Andrew felt unable to propose his plan for the *Yellow Caravel*. After commiserating with the monarch and the three young princes, he returned to Leith.

There, a few days later, he learned of two deaths, that of Queen Margaret, and that of Arnot of Largo.

So now he was in a position to seek the purchase of the barony in which he had been born. And because it *was* a barony, it required royal permission under the Great Seal of the Realm to change hands. Attending the funeral of the queen, he had James telling him that were it not the custom to inter Scotland's queens at Cambuskenneth Abbey, close to Stirling, he would have buried Margaret on the Isle of May which she loved. Now, to be near her resting-place, at least, he was going to occupy the royal quarters at Stirling Castle, instead of this Holyrood.

Before the king left finally for Stirling, Andrew saw him again, and obtained the warranty under the Great Seal to hold the barony of Largo, which the Arnot widow had been glad to sell. So now he was a feudal barón, with a seat in parliament. Dare he hope for such position to enable him to put to the test his longing that Beth Lundie would be prepared to marry him?

9

With the *Yellow Caravel* in the water at Leith docks, Andrew proceeded with his plan to have the king officially launch it. He sailed *Kestrel* up Forth as far as Airth, eight miles from Stirling, the nearest point he could get a large ship to that town, to request his liege-lord to come to Leith to perform the ceremony. This James declared himself prepared to do, especially when he was told that nominally the great new ship would be his royal property, a vessel at his disposal when he so required. In two weeks' time his engagements would allow him to come to Leith for this especial occasion.

So Andrew made his arrangements, and rather notable ones. He would invite Beth and her mother and brothers to attend the ceremony, with Harry Lindsay and many other merchant-traders, and seek to make a memorable event of it indeed − and for more reasons than one. With this objective he sailed over to Methil and rode to Balgony. He was going to take Beth to see his new acquisition, Largo Castle, no longer an Arnot house.

She was interested to see it, and they rode the five miles eastwards. The castle stood on highish ground midway between the Lower and Upper communities, just west of the Kirkton, its land verging on that of Pitcruvie, along the valley of the Boghall Burn. It was no large fortalice, a typical square tower within a small courtyard, less impressive than Balgony but of about the same age, and with better views up Largo Law to the north and over the Firth of Forth to the south. It had a little group of cottages to the east to form a modest castleton. And there was an orchard to the west.

He took her within, to view the vaulted basement kitchen and cellarage, and up the winding narrow stair to the hall on the first floor with its wide fireplace and ingleneuks, its recessed buffet, its garderobe in the thickness of the walling, and the small withdrawing-room off, then upstairs further to see the two bedrooms on each of the second and third floors, and the attics above giving access to the parapeted wall-walk with its open rounds at the angles, from which they admired the vistas.

"What think you of it all, my dear Beth?" he asked then, holding her arm.

"I like it," she said simply.

"How much? It is no great mansion. But . . ."

"But what, Andrew? It is adequate, convenient – and I can see my favoured Craig of Bass from it."

"Adequate for what, lass?"

She eyed him assessingly. "For living in, no?"

He took a moment to consider that, drawing breath. "Could *you* live in it?"

"Ah!" There on the parapet-walk, she likewise paused for a space. "I see no great . . . drawbacks!" she said.

"I, I am glad of that. For, for . . . that is why I bought it!"

This time she looked away and away. "You bought this house hoping that *I* might be prepared to live in it?" she asked carefully.

"I did! I did! Oh, woman dear, can you wonder at it?" Still he had hold of her arm, but now he pulled her round to face him, not the Bass Rock.

"I want you! Need you! I ache for you, all of you, all of *me*! Have you not seen it? Known it? I love you, Beth – *love* you!"

Those dark eyes turned on his were warm but almost amused. "It has taken you a long time to announce it," she declared.

"But, but . . . you *knew*?"

"Do you take me for a ninny? Why have you been

visiting Balgony, taking me in your ship, telling me of your ventures, bringing me gifts? Were you not courting me?''

"Many men are courting you, I think.''

"Some do, yes. But they are not Andrew Wood!''

"And he, *I*, mean more than these?''

"What think you, foolish one? Do you find me gone off with these, sailing, riding, visiting their castles and houses?'' It was her turn to do the grasping, all but shaking. "Do I behave so with all? Give my kisses?''

"You mean . . . ?''

"I mean that you are not the only one who can love! That is what I mean.''

"Oh, my heart! My heart's darling! My Beth! My own Beth!'' He flung his arms round her almost to lift her off her feet. Dispensing with words, he used his lips to better effect, kissing her brow, her hair, her cheeks and her lips – and they opening to receive his.

There they stood, holding each other on that walkway, for how long they did not know nor care, man and woman, admitting, showing, proclaiming unity, and with still greater unity envisaged.

"You will marry me?'' he got out presently, amidst less coherent murmurings and endearments.

"Think you that I . . . would be here . . . and in your arms . . . giving myself to you, if I would not?''

"You *give*?''

"And take! I told you – I give as good as I get. In this as in all else. I am that sort of woman.''

"The woman that I would have.''

"And have got! Let us go elsewhere than this. Down within.''

"Aye. Would that we were on my ship. My cabin at hand . . . !''

"Cabins are for . . . later!''

Arms around each other, they descended the narrow turnpike stairway, which certainly demanded closeness. The castle was empty of furnishings, but in the hall there were stone seats lining the ingoings of the windows. On one of these they sat, and hard as it might be, Beth made no complaints – but then, of course, she was plumper for the sitting than Andrew was.

More than his lips were busy quickly, his hands, fondling, caressing, exploring her warm, lovely, rounded person, she contenting herself with stroking his cheek. The division between her breasts especially appealed to him.

"When will we wed?" he asked. "I want you – all!"

"You must be patient, my eager man," she said. "Women have to consider such . . . timings. And there will be much to think of, and arrange. After all, it will be the start of a new life for us both. But I will not delay overlong, I promise you."

"The king is coming to Leith, to the launch of my *Yellow Caravel*. Would it not be pleasing to have him there, at the wedding? So, immediately after, and James to be present to witness it? He calls himself my friend, as well as my liege-lord. How say you?"

"When is this?"

He said in two weeks' time or thereabous. That was three days ago."

"Two weeks? Yes, that would suit, I judge. But, to have the king at our wedding! Would he do it?"

"I would think so, if affairs of state allow it."

A considerable time elapsed before they moved from that window seat, however hard the accommodation, Beth having to rearrange her bodice.

They both had much to see to during those two weeks, once Andrew had confirmed that the monarch would participate in the launching of the ship. Beth and her family had assumed that the wedding would take place in Balgony parish kirk; but, as it happened, it was James Stewart himself who suggested otherwise. Why not hold the ceremony in the little chapel on the Isle of May? The bride loved that place, the groom had known and esteemed it all his days, and he, the king, made pilgrimages there. It was only early September, so the seas would not be such as to trouble those attending. This proposal was gladly agreed by both of the happy couple – in fact, Beth scolded herself for not having thought of it.

Then there was Largo Castle to be prepared for their occupation. It need not be fully furnished and staffed for their initial entry, but quarters must be made comfortable and welcoming. Fortunately money was amply available.

The *Yellow Caravel* itself had to be fully crewed and readied, with James Barton its skipper, and all Leith tidied up for the royal presence and celebrations. And of course there was the cleric arranged to perform the marriage ceremony on the May. The parish priest at Balgony, who had known Beth all her life, and had indeed christened her, must be present, but King James felt that he was old and insufficiently prominent for the occasion. And it so happened that the monarch had made his own secretary, Andrew Forman, the Prior of Pittenweem, under which sway the monastery and chapel came; so he could suitably officiate. He was due to become Bishop of Moray; but this would be a worthy ending to his priorship. The couple had no reason to object.

Robert Lundie, the sheriff, would deputise for his father in presenting the bride to the groom; and after the nuptials all present would sail over to Pittenweem Priory for a banquet, this more accessible than Balgony. Andrew wanted his crews to be present.

The great day approached. They would have it on St Ninian's Day, the 16th of the month, he who had brought Christianity to Scotland for the first time, a century before Columba, and who had established his little cell on another island in a firth, the Solway, at Whithorn, Candida Casa.

With so much to attend to, Andrew did not see much of his beloved in those two weeks; and when he did she had to restrain his impatience for closer intimacies, declaring that it would be a shame to anticipate the delights of their wedding night.

Since it was customary for a bride and groom not to meet before the ceremony on the day of bliss, Andrew sent the *Kestrel* over to Methil to collect Beth and her family, and to pick up Prior Forman on the way, while he himself awaited the king's arrival at Leith, the timing to be carefully planned and adhered to.

James Stewart, boarding the *Yellow Caravel*, duly inspected it all, and declared it quite the most splendid ship he had ever seen. He was conducted even to a royal cabin.

"It is yours, Sire, the vessel at your royal service whenever you so require," he was told. "See it as such."

"And you my admiral, Andrew – as well as my friend."

"Admiral, Sire? That is too grand a style for me. Pirate-slayer I accept. But admiral!"

"We will better even that. Hereafter."

Concerned over the hour, Andrew ordered moorings to be cast off and sail to be hoisted, and the *Yellow Caravel* moved out into open waters for the first time, its designer eager, even anxious, to test how it behaved, gained speed, answered the helm and took the cross-seas. Well pleased, he could find no faults.

They had gone perhaps two-thirds of the way to the May when he saw *Kestrel* heading out from the Fife shore, mutual timing accurate.

The two vessels drew in to the hidden haven of the island almost side by side, *Kestrel* looking all but insignificant beside the *Caravel*, so tall and lengthy, with its royal banners and saltires flying from the mastheads.

Despite this of bride and groom not meeting prior to the ceremony, the king on this occasion commanded otherwise. *Caravel* moored first. Landing, the monarch said that they should wait for the Lundies to come ashore. Surprised as he was by this, as obviously was Beth when she disembarked, they were still more so when James beckoned the young woman forward. As she curtsied doubtfully, he bent to kiss her cheek.

"Stand there, Elizabeth Lundie soon to become Elizabeth Wood," he told her. He turned. "And you, Andrew, do not stand so, kneel rather."

Astonished, the man, eyeing Beth, did as he was told, while the king turned to his Captain of the Guard, the only man who could go armed in the royal presence, Sir David Guthrie of that Ilk.

"Your sword, Sir David," he commanded.

And there, on the rocky shore of the May, he took the weapon, to tap it on each shoulder of his kneeling admiral.

"Thus and thus, I hereby dub thee knight, Andrew Wood, Baron of Largo, and my admiral. Be thou good knight until thy life's end. Arise, Sir Andrew Wood!"

Shaking head in wonderment, the new knight got to his feet, amidst cheers and congratulations from all present, including Beth, who clapped her hands.

The monarch turned to her. "This also in salutation to yourself. In that you will presently be the *Lady* Wood!" he said.

She curtsied again, more confidently this time.

"Come, then – let us no longer delay the happy event," he ordered.

So Andrew and his brother Jamie, who was to act groomsman, on one side and their liege-lord on the other, were led first into the little chapel. Most present could not enter, so small was it, and must remain outside, standing to face the door, which was to remain open, so that something of the occasion might be glimpsed. Perhaps there were certain disadvantages about holding a wedding on the Isle of May.

There were no chancel steps in this tiny shrine, so the groom and his attendants had to wait up quite close to the altar. There being no vestry either, Prior Forman had to come up behind them, pass them, with a brief bow to the monarch, and so turn to face them at the altar itself.

No choir nor singing was possible here either, only the cheers from those outside heralding Beth's and the sheriff's approach.

She came, to stand beside Andrew, and their fingers entwined.

The prior, in the circumstances, made the nuptials as brief as might be, without omitting any vital part, this with no complaint from the couple, nor anyone else. The prayers, the address, the ring-fitting, the kneeling, the declaring of them as man and wife, and the benediction went smoothly. It was the monarch's hearty congratulations that really made them realise, scarcely believingly, that they were indeed now joined together for all time, despite the brevity of it all. Almost in a daze, the newlyweds turned, eyeing each other, and after a pause, went hand in hand towards the waiting crowd and the greetings of all. The nuptial mass would be held later, at Pittenweem.

Preliminary felicitations and salutations given and received, it was back to the ships, to sail the eight miles to the priory for the mass, and then the celebratory feasting being provided by the monks, who, with Andrew Forman being the royal secretary, were quite used to large-scale entertaining.

Excellent as the hospitality was, needless to say the pair, while being duly appreciative, and saying so, were in fact anxious to get away and be alone. The proceedings could go on for some considerable time. So, after making a short but grateful speech of thanks to all concerned, and declaring how blessed he was, Andrew fairly soon sought the royal permission to retire, Beth looking suitably bashful, unusual as this was for that young woman. He announced that they were off to Largo Castle, at least for the meantime; but told the monarch that the *Yellow Caravel* was his to take him back to Leith, and would remain there, at his royal disposal. For such sea travel as might be required, the *Kestrel* would serve himself and his wife.

So, to much benevolent well-wishing and even some experienced advice, this modified in view of the royal and monkish presence, the couple made their escape while the evening was yet young.

It was a ten-mile ride westwards to Largo, by Kilconquhar and its loch, and the Muircambus moorland, and they went joyfully, even though on one occasion, as they paused to ford the Cocklemill Burn, Beth did announce that she was wondering about what was to come, and the night's proceedings, and how she would perform. It was all very well for Andrew, he, like all men, she supposed, being not inexperienced in such matters. But she was a virgin still, however much he had sought to initiate her previously, and she was a little concerned as to his masculine demands. She said this with a shake of the head and a gleam of eye, which scarcely indicated dread.

"I imagine, my dear, that you are less innocent than you sound!" he observed, smiling. "I do not mean that you are less virginal than you say, only that, being the woman you are, you should have some fair notion of what is ahead of you."

"Save us, is that how you esteem me, Sir Andrew!"

"I esteem you in all ways, lass. But judge you . . . knowledgeable! And, for myself, while I admit to some slight association with young females in the past, it was, shall we say, fleeting, trifling."

"But giving you the advantage – as you have sought to demonstrate to me ere this!"

"We shall see!" he said. "But, mind this. I *love* you, and shall seek to prove it, and kindly."

She reached out to pat his arm, as their horses splashed through the water side by side.

At the castle they made no delay about going upstairs to the principal bedchamber, the keeper's wife having prepared all for them knowledgeably. Thanking her, they closed the door and eyed each other.

Throwing her arms around Andrew, and kissing him,

Beth laughed, and promptly began to cast off her clothing, clearly not going to play the blushing bride.

The man watched her appraisingly, and as she discarded her last covering and stood before him naked, even swinging round, arms out in frankest display, she trilled another laugh.

"Shall I serve, husband mine?" she asked challengingly. "Or . . . do I disappoint? You have seen the upper half of me, now the rest. How say you?"

He found words hard to come by, for she was loveliness personified, all of her, long of neck, wide of shoulders, full of breast, slender of waist but not of belly, dark of groin and well rounded of buttocks, with lengthy and shapely legs.

He all but groaned in his reaction, but not in any distress, save perhaps at his inability to express his delight in what he saw, in words at least. In action it was otherwise. He strode forwards to grasp her and pick her up bodily in his arms, carrying her, face buried in her heaving bosom. Back and forward he bore her, mumbling against her warm flesh, while she chuckled and bit at his ear and declared that his doublet buttons scratched her, silver as they were. And that he should get *his* clothing off before behaving thus.

At that he set her down and hastily began to disrobe, she seeking to aid him however ineffectually, her fumblings actually getting in the way.

At length he was as unclad as she was, and together thus they waltzed round the room, in spirits as high as was his masculinity, this until he could delay no longer, and picked her up again to carry her over to the bed. There, laying her down and throwing himself upon her, he had to remind himself that he had promised to be as gentle as he could be, however taxing this was for him, the more so in that she was equally eager, however slightly apprehensive of the initial pangs while welcoming him into her.

Thereafter, presently, she uttered a little cry, part pain,

part satisfaction and fulfilment, as they became one indeed, as the prior had pronounced them.

He, perhaps, was less gentle then than he was telling himself to be, but apart from one more little cry she made no complaint, gripping his shoulders almost fiercely, and jerking her head from side to side.

With a different groan this time, Andrew reached his climax, and more or less collapsed on top of her, to Beth's whispers of love and caring and assurances that *she* would do better hereafter, he beyond words.

So they lay together, man and wife indeed.

Presently the man's breathing deepened and became regular, and he slept. But she did not.

Somnolence was not part of Andrew Wood's attitude to life however, now or at any time; and quite soon he was awake and eager for more of her, and competent to fulfil his desire. And this time, she was more able to take active part, even though she still suffered discomfort as well as more of satisfaction. At least he was now able to be gentler, however possessive. Sleep followed, more prolonged sleep, and for them both.

As wedding nights went, it was probably a success.

10

Husband had a proposal to make to new wife, less usual than such were apt to be. He had one of his voyages to make, this not to be put off longer. The king had made him admiral, and indicated that he wished to have a number of vessels, not perhaps a fleet at this stage, but at least a flotilla, scarcely to rival Henry of England's, but to be ready to face a challenge. There was word that a London shipowner, he could hardly be called an admiral, had a number of vessels, and was asserting to King Henry that he could purge the seas of this man Wood who was proving such a menace to the English privateers, he by the name of Stephen Bull. And he was said to arm his ships with cannon of bronze and brass, and carry armed pikemen and archers, the artillery not the sort that had slain the monarch's father, James the Second, at the siege of Roxburgh by exploding in his face, this of iron bars welded together with metal rings to form a great tube, and breech-loaded. The newer cannon were constructed of other metals, moulded, and so not likely to burst apart when the powder was ignited. Also muzzle-loaded, to make the detonation safely confined within the barrel, not bursting from the breech. Andrew had gained the name of the expert in founding such cannon, in the Netherlands, one Hans Poppenruyter. He was going to visit this gun-founder, and seek to purchase such cannon. This ought not to be any dangerous mission. He wondered whether Beth would like to accompany him in the *Caravel*? Make a longer voyage and see new lands?

She was delighted so to do, and not to be parted from her beloved for these lengthy periods.

The five-hundred-mile voyage was uneventful, and although they did see the odd privateer, these kept their distance from such as the *Yellow Caravel*, obviously not a vessel to be assailed. The Low Countries coastline, needless to say, interested Beth, with its many river-mouths and the largely level islands that separated them, making even England seem hilly by comparison. They entered one of these, a channel of the great River Schelde, to proceed some fifty miles up, past seemingly endless stretches of absolutely flat land, seamed by long lines of wide drainage ditches, for the land was scarcely above sea level, these stretches, largely cattle-dotted, apparently called polders. On these, far and wide, the only outstanding features were church spires and tall windmills, with occasional clusters of villages, reachable not by roads but by canals, these, Andrew explained, tending to be composed of groups of farmhouses and their cottages, clustered together however wide their watery lands stretching to seeming infinity. It all made a novel landscape for Beth, unlike anything she had ever visualised.

The ground level became somewhat higher, although far from lofty, as they neared Antwerp. They passed large numbers of ships and innumerable barges, these last sometimes towed by horses pacing the riverbanks, the Schelde being a highly busy waterway, Antwerp claiming itself the commercial capital of the world, whether accurately or otherwise, making even London look modest. Because of the level nature of the land, they saw the city ahead of them for perhaps nearly a score of miles, its towers and spires and tall buildings, all under a pall of smoke, outstanding.

In due course they entered into actual miles of riverside docklands. It was difficult to judge just where to seek to moor, but Andrew assessed that the nearer they got to the soaring steeples of the great cathedral was probably the likeliest place to seek the whereabouts of this Hans Poppenruyter, the cannon-maker.

They had a problem finding a space to dock the *Caravel*,

so crowded was the scene. When they did, Andrew's mixture of Dutch, German and French in due course gained him the information he required, the Antwerpers being well versed in languages. It seemed that they were none so far from the great foundry where the cannon-maker moulded his pieces, the smoke rising from his furnaces pointed out.

Beth found it all as intriguing as it was unusual, the narrow crooked streets crowded with chattering folk, the market-places, the tall warehouses with their hoists from the brick-paved lanes, stone being scarce here, the innumerable churches and oratories, the monuments and statues, wells, and the stalls of street-traders – all this and the gabble of strange tongues by the noisy passers-by.

The foundry, their goal, proved to be enormous, and the din emanating therefrom deafening, the hammering and clashing and beating, the grinding of metal wheels and chains, and the shoutings of the workers. Andrew himself had much shouting to do to learn the whereabouts of its master founder, Beth well aware of the undisguised inspection of the workmen, women no doubt being but seldom seen on these premises.

Poppenruyter, when found, proved to be a huge man of jovial manner, who made a great, all but bellowing display of greeting Beth, with shouts of laughter and a sort of ponderous gallantry to which she responded with spirited appreciation. Andrew had to put up with this before he could get down to the reason for the visit. He wanted to know the advantages of different makes of cannon, and which were advisable for use on ships, the ranges of shot, the kinds of powder advised, and the supply of cannon-balls.

Fortunately this larger-than-life character spoke quite good English, however loudly, as well no doubt as other languages, his trade being with many nations; and Andrew learned much, in between bouts of banter between the giant and Beth, who got on with him in great style. Her husband was able to learn which cannon were best to order for his purposes, and they were taken to see a large selection of pieces and informed of the various prices. None was cheap, by any standards, but he was in a position to afford them, and did not attempt to bargain, which in the circumstances was unlikely to have been effective. He actually bought four pieces there and then, and arranged for these to be delivered down at the dock; and he ordered eight more, for the *Flower*, the *Kestrel* and the *Goshawk*. Poppenruyter beamed and hooted laughter. Payment he was told would be made at the ship, in silver. The bronze cannon were less expensive that the brass, but the latter had the longer range.

This over, they went to visit the famous cathedral of the Holy Virgin on the east bank of Schelde, erected some century and a half before, and worthy of its renown. It was as large and spectacular as seemingly all else in Antwerp, no less than five hundred feet long, with no fewer than one hundred and twenty-five decorative pillars to support the lofty groined roof; and all adorned with carvings, paintings, banners and magnificent stained-glass windows, at clerestoreys and side chapels. The wealth of Antwerp was amply demonstrated here.

After some further inspection of the city and its prominent features, it was back aboard ship to head for home, Beth much pleased with her visit, and indeed the voyaging also. She said that Andrew must frequently take her on his travels.

Back at Leith with the cannon, they found a summons awaiting Andrew from the king, not from Stirling but from Holyrood. He saw no harm in taking Beth with him up to Edinburgh.

There they found James, with his three sons and two daughters. Father and his heir, James, Duke of Rothesay, were very different, the prince dashing, ardent, impatient and romantic, all that his sire was not. They were seldom in each other's company these days, scarcely getting on well together.

In fact this difference in temperament was demonstrated on this occasion, for the monarch was seeking Andrew's help to make a gesture towards some of his nobles who were demanding action against the Lord of the Isles and other Highland chiefs who were making invasions into the Ross area of the north, and claiming the western parts of that great territory as belonging to the Isles lordship by ancient tradition. The Lowland magnates were declaring that the insolent Islesman should be shown in no gentle fashion who ruled in mainland Scotland, and taught a lesson. The unwarlike monarch was against any such demonstration of force; but his son, Rothesay, was all for it. These nobles, under the Lords Fleming and Seton, were assembling a force at Stirling, and calling on James to join them. He now wanted Andrew to take him up-Forth to the Stirling vicinity and make it clear to these that civil war within his realm was not to be considered, his son vehemently of the other persuasion.

This was no sort of mission for Beth to be involved in. Andrew agreed to take the monarch to Stirling, but they would land his wife at Largo beforehand. Young Rothesay announced that he was coming with them.

So it was down to the *Caravel*, and *Flower* following, across to Fife to deposit Beth, then on up Forth to where the estuary became a river.

The shallows prevented the ships from getting close to the town and castle, but it so happened that the lords were assembling their men on the levels where the great Battle of Bannockburn had been fought, well away from the town and its distractions for their forces. Andrew dared not risk running *Caravel* and *Flower* aground, which meant that they had to moor some way off from the encamped host. How to make their presence effectively recognised, and the royal authority emphasised? It occurred to Andrew that here was a use for his new cannon, not to fire ball but to make a loud and challenging impact by firing blank shot, detonating gunpowder. Both crews were ordered so to do, the first use, other than practice, for the artillery.

The *Caravel*'s pieces crashed out first, in thunderous noise, even impressing Andrew himself, especially as it echoed back from the Ochil Hills to the north; and when this was added to by *Flower*'s three guns the din was almost alarming.

They kept it up for some minutes. Then Andrew had a boat lowered, and with young Rothesay he was rowed upstream the necessary distance, to land near the large encampment. Their arrival attracted considerable attention. They demanded to be taken to the leaders of the assembly.

Led to tented pavilions, they found a group of lords in discussion over wine, no doubt concerned over that cannonade. Announcing the Duke of Rothesay and his own identity, Andrew declared that they had come to order the commanders of this large force to attend His Grace on the ship, a royal command. This was not to be ignored; and the Lords Seton, Fleming and Montgomery, who appeared to be in charge, distinctly haughtily agreed to accompany Andrew back to the ship, demanding what all the cannon-firing had been about.

Andrew said briefly that it was by way of being a token of the royal authority.

Rowed back to the *Caravel* they climbed aboard, and James received them. He demanded the reason for this great muster of armed men. He was told that it was to restrain the arrogant Lord of the Isles from further invading Ross, which was mainland not Isles territory.

The king declared that if anything such was required, *he* would order it. But such matters should be settled by discussion and negotiation, not civil war, and that he would see to it. This force must be disbanded forthwith.

The three lords made no answer to that.

"You hear His Grace!" Andrew said. "Obey."

The trio eyed each other, but still none spoke.

"Agree. Or bear the consequences!"

"The Islesman needs to be taught a lesson," James of Rothesay intervened.

"Not by force of arms, James," the king told his son.

"He, Father, speaks loud with his galleys and longships, not gentle words."

"Nevertheless, he is my subject, as are these lords. If necessary, I will go and speak with him. Up to those parts of my realm."

"Then we shall accompany Your Grace, with our men," Fleming asserted. "To ensure that your royal will is obeyed."

"Not so. I will have no such demonstration in arms. I will go myself."

"This is folly, Sire!" Seton declared. "That one, with his clansmen and galloglasses, will not heed you. Indeed he might well take Your Grace prisoner! He looks upon himself as an independent prince, as did his forebear, Somerled. Our strength with you, and he will think better."

"No. I go alone. Or with Sir Andrew here. And forthwith. Disband your men."

The lords looked stubborn, and did not reply.

"You have heard His Grace's royal command," Andrew said.

"Keep your insolent tongue in check, shipman!" Montgomery said.

"Sir Andrew speaks with my authority," the king asserted. "See to it. The dispersal."

The trio inclined their heads, scarcely bowing, and turned for the boat.

Andrew looked at James. "Sire, I would advise that you detain two of these lords here in my ship until you see that this force is indeed being disbanded at your command. One will be enough to order it. Two held here will serve as indication of your royal will. Hold my lords Fleming and Seton, I counsel."

"Very well. You, my lord of Montgomery, go and have that army broken up and sent off. Your friends will remain with me here, meantime."

The three, frowning and looking rebellious, continued on their way to the ship's side and the rope-ladder to take them down to the small boat.

"Halt you, my lords," Andrew exclaimed. "I have sufficient crewmen to keep you aboard!"

"Montgomery may go, the others remain," James said.

Young Rothesay hooted laughter, apparently seeing it all as an amusing charade.

Rowed back to the shore, Montgomery glanced back at his colleagues, and shrugged.

On board, all waited.

It was some time before they saw any real movement in the camp. The bringing down of those pavilions was the first sign. Then gradually the marshalling of troops and companies became evident, and some of these began to ride and march off in various directions.

"How know we that they will not reassemble elsewhere?" James asked.

"We shall gain these two lords' word on it before we release them," he was told.

Presently, as the movement continued, Andrew turned to Fleming and Seton. "You heard His Grace? You may go free if we have your promise that this force disperses, and the move against the Highlanders and Islesmen ceases, my lords. Otherwise, you remain captive."

The pair nodded, unspeaking.

"Your *word*, I said!"

"You have it, shipman!"

"It is agreed, Wood."

"Very well. You permit it, Sire?"

The monarch agreed also. So the two nobles were allowed to depart.

"What now?" Rothesay asked. "How keep the Northerners in order?"

Andrew answered him. "I agree that His Grace should go and visit them. We could sail up yonder. Learn at Inverness, if we can, where the Islesmen are. They will not be far from their longships, I judge. Speak with them."

"Is there not danger in that? They could hold my father."

"I think not. His Grace could remain on my ship. I would bring John of the Isles to him. And my cannon would speak sufficiently loud if he proved . . . awkward. How say you, Sire?"

"It is a long way to the Isles from this Stirling, my friend Andrew."

"We may hear of him at Inverness."

So it was accepted. Back to Largo and Leith. Then, after the king had made his arrangements with Colin, Earl of Argyll, the Chancellor, to act deputy during the royal absence, and sundry directions issued and papers signed, head north.

Nothing would do but that Beth came with them. Why not? If King James was assured that there was no danger in it for him, there would be none for her either. And she would greatly like to see the Sea of the Hebrides and its islands, of which she had heard so much, the wild beauty of it all. None thought to deny her.

In due course they sailed out of the Forth, past the Tay estuary, and on up the Angus, Aberdeenshire and Moray coasts to Inverness, Beth and the youthful prince getting on notably well, both eager, adventurous.

At the Highland capital they learned that John of the Isles, who was also Earl of Ross although he seldom used that style, had been there only a week previously, or at least at nearby Dingwall, the main seat of the Ross earldom, seeing to affairs in what was known as the Black Isle of Cromarty, even though it was a great peninsula not an island. He had sailed off northwards, presumably for his own Isles.

So that was the route for them also.

Up along the rugged coasts of Sutherland and Caithness they went, under the sway of the Islesman's son-in-law, the Earl of Sutherland, they rounded the great headlands of Duncansby and Dunnet to enter the Pentland Firth. Passing the Orkneys, Andrew told his royal passengers about far Iceland, the glaciers and volcanoes, the walruses and the ivory. Rothesay asked if they could not go on there and see it all? He was told that it was hundreds of miles, and his father pointed out that he could not leave the rule of his realm for overlong, however able was Colin Campbell of Argyll. This of the Islesman would take up a sufficiency of time, probably, as it was.

They rounded Cape Wrath, and Beth asked how that mighty headland got its name. Was it because of the Atlantic storms striking it, the most northerly as well as westerly point of all mainland Scotland? Andrew said that no, he had heard that it was but a corruption of the ancient Norse word *hvarf*, meaning a turning-point.

Southwards now, they proceeded down a very different coastline and scene, all mountains and islands, great inlets and long sea lochs, even the water seeming to be of a different colour. This was caused by the underlying white cockleshell sand reflecting, and the different shades of seaweeds on rocks and gravel, as a result of the warmer currents and shallower seas of the Hebrides. Not only Beth was enchanted, the royal passengers almost equally so. Andrew was thankful that the weather was kindly, for these isles could be very different, with storms, driving rain, fierce tide-races and overfalls, also down-draughts from the hills.

Where would they find the Lord John? He could be anywhere among literally hundreds of islands and islets in both the Inner and Outer Hebrides, for there were the two main groups, separated by what were called the Minches, North and Little, Norse again, for the Vikings had had a great and enduring influence here. But Andrew had heard that the Isles lordship had its principal seat well to the south, on the large and fairly level island of Islay. So unless they learned otherwise as they went, they would try to seek him there first.

Down the North Minch they sailed, with most careful navigation, for the seas were littered with reefs and skerries many of these covered at high water, making them dangerous indeed to sail over. Fifty or so miles of this and, with darkness descending, they moored for the night in the shelter of the Summer Isles, so called for sheep being summered there. Enquiring ashore they learned that the lord's longship fleet had passed nearby those days before, without halting.

Next day they entered the Little Minch, between the Outer Isles of Lewis and Harris and the northern tip of Skye. All aboard were greatly impressed by that famous and huge island, said to be fifty miles long, and dominated by the mighty range of dramatic peaks known as the Cuillin Mountains, so named after the legendary hound of Cuilann of Ossian fame. Andrew was taxed indeed to expand on it all to his distinguished fellow-voyagers.

They called in at Dunvegan, the seat of the MacLeod chief, seeking word of Lord John, and were fortunate to learn that MacLeod had been with him on his Easter Ross excursion and that the former had headed on for Islay, his normal base, where lived his wife, the Countess of Ross, she unlike her husband preferring that style to that of Lady of the Isles. She was a daughter of the southern Lord Livingstone, and had brought John the castle of Greenan and the lands of Kineddar in Ayrshire, which gave him a foothold on the Lowland mainland. Her father had been Great Chamberlain of Scotland.

So it was on down southwards, past the spectacular islands of Rhum and Eigg and Muick, to round the huge mainland cape of Ardnamurchan and sail between Mull of the Macleans, even larger than Skye, and the fertile level islands of Coll and Tiree, the latter known as the Garden of the Isles, so low-lying that the white crests of the great Atlantic breakers could be seen across the waist of the island from the mainland side.

Ahead now soared the twin shapely peaks known as the Paps of Jura, and just beyond, Islay.

The narrows of the Sound of Islay at least allowed them to find where, in that large isle, they should look for the Lord John; for halfway down, at the haven and anchorage of Askaig, were moored the fleet of longships, low-set, narrow, many-oared vessels with single masts and great square sails, known as the "greyhounds of the seas" so fast could they move.

The arrival of *Caravel* and *Flower* among these brought prompt demands from fierce-looking armed warriors with horned helmets as to who they were and how they dared to sail the Isles seas without the permission of the lord thereof? To which Andrew replied that they were His Grace James, King of Scots, his heir the Duke of Rothesay and the admiral, Wood of Largo. When this failed to produce any notably respectful reaction, he gave orders for his cannon to make their own announcement, with blank shot. That certainly had its effect, as the thunderous din was re-echoed from the peaks of Jura and more distant mountains, the like undoubtedly never before having been heard in these parts.

Suitably impressed now, helmeted leaders declared that they would conduct the visitors to the Lord John.

A landing was made, and king, prince, Andrew and Beth were escorted up a quite steep track to the community of Askaig, and thereafter some way to the edge of an inland loch, no very notable feature save that it had two islets in it on which rose a castle and what looked like a large church or chapel, with a spire. A few houses were grouped at the shore, and boats drawn up on the beach.

Their escorts halted them here, king or none, while men rowed off in one of the boats to see if the Lord of the Isles would receive them, an unusual experience for the monarch.

They could only wait, Andrew frowning, Beth laughing at it all.

Eventually the boat came back, and it was announced that the Lord John would admit them into his house.

They climbed aboard and were rowed out to the first of the islets.

The castle was no great strength, the Isles lords no doubt relying on the might of their manpower to protect them.

It was the countess who received them, duly deferential to the king, as became a daughter of a Lowland lord, and declared that her husband was presently over at the chapel islet, which in fact was the caput, or seat of judgement, of the entire lordship, conferring with some of his chieftains. But she expected him to return shortly.

They were given refreshments while they waited, the countess apologising for the delay but clearly unwilling to send for her spouse.

The reason for her reluctance was demonstrated when John of the Isles did arrive. He was a huge man, of commanding appearance and bearing and, unlike his wife, not at all perturbed by the presence of the monarch who, in fact, made a considerably less impressive figure than himself. Indeed the big man looked more heedfully at Andrew, of whose exploits he no doubt had heard, ignoring the prince and Beth.

"I judged that it must be Andrew Wood who was visiting me here by the unseemly din made at my haven of Askaig," he declared, still not bowing to the king. "None other would have such cannon aboard. What was the reason for that flourish and mummery, may I ask?"

"I was announcing the presence of His Grace, James, King of Scots," he was informed. "Come in person to the Isles."

"For what purpose?"

"I came because of stirrings among my subjects in the south," James told him. "They were concerned that you, my lord, appeared to be making your influence felt over-strongly in the Inverness area and thereabouts, and seeming to—"

"I am the Earl of Ross as well as Lord of the Isles," he was interrupted. "And Ross extends thereto."

"Inverness is in Moray. No part of your lordship. They were assembling men, many men, to assert this, to march north and challenge you. I, with Sir Andrew Wood's aid, had them to disperse, declaring that all matters in my realm should be settled by discussion and peaceful means, not by armed force. And *I* would deal with disputes between my subjects."

"I am no subject of yours, James Stewart!" the other declared.

The king drew breath. "These Isles are in Scotland, are they not? And I am King of Scots. And you are one of my earls."

"The Lordship of the Isles is mine, and mine only."

"As are the holdings of other lords. But under the superiority of the crown."

"I recognise no such superiority here. In Ross, perhaps, the earldom. But not in the Isles."

"You cannot be part of Scotland and not acknowledge the superiority of its monarch, sir. That is impossible."

"Then the Isles are not part of Scotland."

There was silence.

Andrew intervened. "My lord, you cannot change the facts of the land. Your islands are but extensions of the mainland. Ardnamurchan is part of the mainland, yet you claim it as Isles territory. Skye is an island only in name, separated only by a narrow channel that could be bridged. Kintyre is but a great peninsula, attached to the main-land, yet you claim it as in your Isles. So, this is all part of the realm of Scotland. And you are a subject of King James."

"I am not, sirrah!"

"The earls of Scotland are, by tradition, the lesser kings, yes? The *ri*," the monarch pointed out. "But I am the Ard Righ, the High King. You cannot deny that, my lord."

"Then I shall renounce such name of earl. I am, and will remain, independent. If you do not admit it, the King of England does! He calls me his dear cousin!"

"That merely because he seeks your aid against me in any warfare. Your fleet of longships."

Andrew again spoke up. "These southern lords were preparing to assail you, my lord. His Grace had them to desist. To return to their lands. Saying to all that differences should rightly be negotiated, not by war. And you thereby greatly benefited."

"They could do nothing against my Isles, nothing!"

"They could against Ross, Easter *and* Wester."

"My birlinns and longships can sail round to the firths of Dornoch and Cromarty, Inverness and Moray."

"But not with a sufficiency of men thereafter to challenge a Lowland host."

"At any rate," James said, "I convinced them that this was not the way to serve my realm. That all should be debated, and differences settled round a table. That is my way of ruling."

Young Rothesay, listening, sniffed and shook his head.

"So what is there to discuss?" the big man demanded.

"This of Inverness and the lands to the west. Down the Great Glen, Loch Ness-side, Badenoch. The Mackintosh country. The Cameron's, MacIan's and other clan chiefs'. They see you, my lord, as menacing them. This should cease. Confine your actions to your Isles, my lord, and we shall have peace."

"You would have me to relinquish my hold of my Ross earldom? Even though I do not use the empty style? Never!"

"No. But do not threaten these parts with your armed

strength. Act the lawful earl, even though you do not use the title. Have the folk esteem, not fear you. As should I."

"And to what advantage?"

"No more threats from the southern lords. No animosity from the Highland chiefs. And, see you, I could have your sway here bettered, enhanced. And lawfully. You could even be sheriff here, Sheriff of Inverness. That would give you greater authority, lawful authority. To your advantage in much. How say you? Administer the law, but fairly. And yourself within the law, the law of my realm."

The other stared, calculatingly.

"Consider it, my lord John. Consider well. You could serve me and my kingdom as well as yourself."

"Why? Why offer me this?"

"I would have the Lord of the Isles my friend. Even with Edward of England's 'dear cousin'."

"But . . . the Isles lordship remains independent."

"If so you wish to name it. But the earldom of Ross cannot be named so. I would have you to resume that title. And to take an earl's part in the rule of the land. And in parliament. That would be to your advantage, no? At present, your goodson, the Earl of Sutherland, has to be your informant on such matters. Better to see to it yourself. And make a mark on all Scotland, not just your Isles. You could well do so."

The other looked at them all, then took a pace or two back and forth, clearly debating with himself the obvious advantages but the price to pay. If John of the Isles was debating, so was Andrew Wood. Now he spoke.

"Sire, if my lord John was to be made Justiciar of the North, as was his father for a time, as I recollect, as well as Sheriff of Inverness, this would make his contribution to the peace and well-being of your realm still the greater, acting as your representative. And so keeping in touch with Your Grace."

"Ah! Yes, Andrew, that is a notable thought. How say

you, my lord? Would that appointment appeal to you? Justiciar North of the Forth? The Earl of Arran is that, but is now old and frail, using a deputy. Justiciar, and so my trusted commissioner. In frequent collaboration with myself and my council."

Slowly nodding, the Islesman said, "I do not know why Your Grace is offering me this!" It was the first time that he had accorded the king the style of monarch.

"I do so because I see our association to be of value for Scotland," James said. "That is ever my concern."

"Very well — so be it," the Lord John declared. "I will accept your charge. And your royal authority." That, from the independent Lord of the Isles, was a major concession indeed.

"Let us shake hands on it, then."

As they all adjourned to the hall of the castle, where the countess announced that a repast awaited them, Beth pressed Andrew's arm. She whispered.

"You achieved that cunningly, husband! Gained the Lord of the Isles to be the king's ally. A feat indeed! Am I wed to a wily schemer? I shall have to watch my steps, in that case!"

"I but sought the weal of James and his realm," he told her. "Is there ill in that?"

"We shall see. But I am warned!" She shook her head. "A pirate-slayer is one thing. But a foxy intriguer is another!"

With the Lord John's chieftains all there in the islet's buildings, and the castle itself not very large, there was no room for the king's party to stay overnight, even had they wished to do so. It was back to Askaig haven and the ships, the leave-taking being at least somewhat more friendly than had been their reception. The cabins in the two vessels were probably more comfortable than would have been the accommodation in the crowded castle.

In the morning, then, it was back north-about for Cape

Wrath and the Pentland Firth, and then all the way south, to deposit the king and his son at Leith, for Holyrood. It would be good for Andrew and Beth to get back to Largo and their domestic bliss.

11

The Woods' bliss was distinctly disturbed soon thereafter by the news emanating from Edinburgh and Stirling concerning the king and his activities. His interest in matters of fair and worthy government and the weal of his people had long been suspect by his nobility, the lords asserting that this was not kingly, royal, unsuitable for the monarch. In especial his fondness for, and association with, common folk, in particular his influence in getting the Vatican to elevate William Scheves, astrologer and alchemist, one of the monarch's friends, to be Archbishop of St Andrews. Also another favourite, the mason and master builder Robert Cochrane to a prominent position at court, where, at Stirling Castle, he was erecting a new hall for meetings of parliament, and rebuilding St Michael's Chapel as a music school, at the king's instigation; he was enabled so to do by the king's giving him, Cochrane, the temporalities of the rich Abbey of Coldinghame in the Merse, to the fury of the great borders family of Home, who had long sought the same. Now the news was that James had actually conferred on Robert Cochrane the royal earldom of Mar, left suddenly vacant by the death of his younger brother John. To make a mason and builder, however competent, into an earl was an extra-ordinary gesture, and bound to raise anger among the established earls, and lords who might covet that status. Andrew had not actually met this Robert Cochrane, but had of course heard of him. Now this royal favour had produced an eruption of fury from the realm's magnates, who demanded the withdrawal of the earldom from this wretched upstart and an end to his influence over the monarch. If they were not heeded, they were threatening to take matters into their own hands. And James of Rothesay was said to be siding with and encouraging them, he seeing Cochrane as something of a menace.

Andrew and Beth agreed that the king was being unwise in this matter. His concern for freeing his ordinary subjects from the powers of the nobility was worthy perhaps; but this of presenting a builder and craftsman with a royal earldom was surely folly. Beth urged her husband to go and tell the king so, his influence with James possibly effective.

Andrew was by no means eager to attempt this, but recognised that the monarch might be well served by such advice. It occurred to him that *he* himself could possibly be looked upon by the lords as an upjumped nobody, with overmuch sway with the king who had created him admiral.

He would go and see James at Stirling. Should Beth come with him? She should, it seemed. The king, lacking a wife, and over-fond of men such as Scheves and Cochrane – and perhaps Andrew Wood?—might do with some female guidance.

So it was up-Forth from Methil in the *Kestrel*, scarcely an occasion for the *Yellow Caravel*.

At Airth they left ship, as did so many visiting Stirling, and hired horses for the eight-mile ride.

Unfortunately, James was closeted with Cochrane, poring over plans and drawings for the new parliament hall, so this presented hardly an occasion for advising him. The new Earl of Mar was a bulky, square-jawed individual of early middle years, with great powerful hands. He was very definite about what should be done over the proposed building, even dismissing James's suggestions. Beth took an instant dislike to him.

This subject, however, was not one on which the visitors were competent to speak; and Cochrane was in no hurry to yield up the king's attention to them. James was evidently in some measure under the sway of this man. They could not interrupt. It was Beth who eventually managed to get the monarch detached, by declaring that she and Andrew had come on a private matter concerning the Largo barony and its Strathairly appendage. This was effective. James rose, and conducted them into an anteroom.

There Andrew began by declaring that he was sending his ship, the *Flower*, to the Low Countries, to Antwerp, to purchase more cannon to install on the *Kestrel* and the *Goshawk*, probably going himself. He wondered whether the king would have the like brought back for the royal use, for his castles of Stirling, Edinburgh and Dumbarton? He would present such, as a gift, if so desired. James said that he was glad to avail himself of this offer.

Then to the delicate matter of Robert Cochrane, next door. Andrew felt it his duty to inform the monarch of the feelings aroused among the nobility and prominent folk over this of creating the master mason, effective and useful as he might be, to the status of earl. There was much concern over this, an unheard-of situation hitherto, the appointment doing the crown's reputation no good. There was talk of the lords taking the matter into their own hands, in just what fashion was not disclosed, but it was not likely to be pleasing. Admittedly the king, and only the king, could create earls; but this of someone not of noble or even lairdly caste promoted directly to that rank, and without consultation with the other earls, was creating much upset. There would be questions in parliament about it, indubitably. Would it not be possible to rescind the nomination, and bestow on Cochrane some other appointment or office?

James looked unhappy at this, coming from his friend Andrew, shaking his head.

"It would be a grave embarrassment if questions were raised in parliament from the earls' benches," Andrew went on. "You could assert the royal prerogative. But that

95

would not serve the crown well. Could you not make him some sort of minor officer of state? Create a new style? Master of the Royal Palaces? Master Builder to the King? Designer Royal? Something of that sort. And so prevent any outcry."

"Having made him earl, could I unmake him?"

"I do not see why not. Your royal prerogative again. None could contest it."

"Could you not appoint him keeper of the Chapel Royal, Sire?" Beth suggested. "He is restoring St Michael's Chapel here. Call it the Chapel Royal, and make him its keeper? None could deny that. And it sounds well. Some dignity to it."

"I must think on this," James said. "I mislike changing it. Keeper of a chapel is scarcely a fair exchange for an earldom!" The monarch glanced towards the door, obviously indicating an end to the discussion.

They bowed. They could do no more.

"I will purchase Your Grace cannon," Andrew said, as James left them.

Andrew decided that, in the circumstances, it would be wise if he personally went to Antwerp to see Hans Poppenruyter, and inspect and buy the cannon. There could well be refinements, improvements, newer types which he had not yet discovered. He wanted the best. And there might be other foundries in other cities. Beth would accompany him. He would also take his brother Jamie, who was becoming more and more involved in the trading matters, if not in the admiralty ones; indeed he was now in charge of the ivory enterprise at Iceland.

This Low Countries visit was successful in that from Poppenruyter they learned that he was co-operating with a brass-founder in Brussels in the making of much lighter cannon, of smaller calibre and shorter range admittedly, but which could be much more easily handled and were quicker firing. These were being called demi-cannon.

Andrew ordered four of them, visiting the Brussels works to test them out.

When they arrived back at Largo it was to learn dramatic and very significant news. Cochrane was dead, along with others of the king's so-called "low-born" associates: Rogers, a musician involved in the chapel music school; Torphichen, a dancing master; Preston, an Edinburgh merchant; Stobo, a clerk; and Leonard, a leather-dresser and maker of boots and shoes for the monarch. All were now hanging, by horses' halters, from the bridge over the River Leader at Lauder in the Borderland.

Apparently it had all been something of a rebellion against the monarch's odd preferences, led by John Stewart, Earl of Atholl, James's uncle. Involved had been Archibald Douglas, Earl of Angus and other powerful Douglases, with the Lords Home, Gray, Hailes, Hamilton, even Avondale the Chancellor, these supported by the Duke of Rothesay, this last perhaps the most telling of all. The heir to the throne was now making his presence felt in the nation's affairs, and often in opposition to his father's preferences.

The king's younger brother, Alexander, Duke of Albany, long all but exiled in France because of his ambition to replace the gentle James, had persuaded Edward of England to support him with armed force, and to march north to gain him the crown, dangerous a device as this was. This had greatly upset his nephew Rothesay, who on his own initiative but with major Douglas and other borders lords' aid, had ordered a great force to assemble at Lauder to repel anything such. The king, learning of it, had hastened thither to seek a peaceful settlement, with some of his strange friends, including Cochrane – all this while Andrew was in the Low Countries. The inevitable had followed. While James and his especial young page, John Ramsay, had gone to examine some Pictish remains in the neighbourhood, the lords had taken and hanged the other favourites, as lesson to the monarch as to who should be his associates. James Stewart had returned to Holyrood, a man devastated.

Andrew did not know just where his duty lay. The unhappy king was his liege-lord and friend. Yet he recognised the folly of alienating the nobility by this of ever preferring the company he did, and especially in making Cochrane an earl and having the man Scheves promoted to archbishop. Even his son Rothesay was siding with the lords.

Beth said why not go and bring their sorrowing sovereign over to Largo? He trusted Andrew, and they might be able both to advise and cheer him somewhat. Get him away from all his sorrows and problems for a space, in their comfortable home.

This was agreed. Andrew would cross over to Leith and seek to persuade James to it.

He was sending *Caravel* to the Low Countries for the demi-cannon, which ought to be ready and awaiting him by now. He would go in it, collect James if he would come, bring him to Largo, and then send the ship on to Flanders. He suggested that Beth came with him. It was her notion; and the depressed king might well be more amenable towards a woman's sympathetic guidance.

They found the monarch all but in hiding, alone in a chamber of the abbot's house. They had difficulty in gaining the royal presence, even the officers of state having the same problem with their papers to have signed and the like. James clearly needed to be taken out of himself, as Beth put it.

Told that it was his admiral who sought audience, with his wife, they did gain access, to the displeasure of sundry lords who were being refused it. And there it was Beth, with her arts, who was able to persuade James that a spell at Largo would be to his benefit and a change from his brooding seclusion – for he was even refusing to see his son, blaming Rothesay for siding with the lords.

Inducement, mainly Beth's, did eventually get their

liege-lord down to the docks and aboard the *Caravel*, no trappings of royalty involved, James tending ever to dismiss such. There Andrew told the harbour-master to have *Flower* in a state of readiness for any sudden call, for the *Caravel* was off to Flanders for the cannon, that man and his assistants impressed by the monarch's presence, however gloomy of aspect he seemed, despite all Beth's efforts.

They sailed; and it was only later that they heard that the story going round Leith was that the king himself was off to the Low Countries in his admiral's ship, despairing over his Scotland.

At Largo, James did regain something of his self-possession and concern for his realm's affairs. They heard some good news, at least: that the English army, confronted by the Scots nobles' force, had turned back for their own land. However, this borders army was now all but in rebellion, claiming that the king was failing his nation in his reluctance to use armed strength, and he should be replaced on the throne by his son, Rothesay, who would make an infinitely better monarch, such as Scotland needed. They would urge his abdication, and his son's accession.

James, needless to say, was much distressed and worried by this. He had no intention of abdicating, judging that his son was much too impetuous, as yet, to make a good monarch. No doubt he would learn, in time. But meanwhile, *he* must continue to reign. These lords must have this made clear to them.

Andrew agreed with this. But how to convince Rothesay's supporters was the problem. Armed force, whatever James thought, was the only way to show them.

Some demonstration, then? And one that would impress armed men would serve. How to convince the peace-loving James?

Andrew did his best. He declared that some military gesture was absolutely necessary. His ships and cannon could be used to help make an impact; but men, armed and landed, was the only flourish that would really teach them. His own crews, disembarked, would make a nucleus of a force; but many more than that would be needed, although his estates and their villages could produce a fair number. If he could call, in the king's name, for a rally from the men of this East Fife territory – Methil, Leven, Buckhaven, Wemyss, Kirkcaldy and inland, to the west, and Elie, St Monans, Pittenweem and Anstruther to the east, armed as best they were able – such could make the required demonstration, and warn the rebellious nobles that the king could use force when necessary.

James took a deal of convincing, but eventually he gave his consent. Andrew sent his emissaries east and west, for an assembly, at the royal command. No real battling was envisaged, only a gesture with men, many men, armed.

The response from the Fifers was, if not exactly enthusiastic, at least adequate, pride in their admiral helping. Andrew reckoned that he could field between seven hundred and eight hundred men. That should serve.

How, then, to display this force? Some sort of challenge? Rothesay was said to be based at Stirling Castle, the traditional royal stronghold. So presumably his supporting lords would be thereabouts. Andrew felt no hostility towards young James himself, but only to those who were using him against his father. A sally, then, with his ships, up as near to Stirling as they could get. A cannonade of blank shot to announce their presence and to emphasise threat. Then a landing of the Fife force somewhere to constitute the necessary warranty. Not at Stirling itself; that would be too dangerous. There was the dowery palace of Linlithgow considerably nearer, the port for which was Boroughstoneness. A landing there. That would imply action, and could bring the rebel army to cope with it. Then cannon-fire, not blankshot. This of the artillery was the great advantage. Only he, the admiral, and in the name of the monarch, had that, so far as he knew.

The plan, then? Go to near Stirling, and make a challenging din. Then back to Methil and collect the Fife men, and take them to land at this Boroughstoneness. If, as was to be hoped, the rebels came, take the loyal men aboard again before any fighting could commence, then deposit groups of them along various stretches of that shoreline to confuse the enemy. Cannon-fire, ball and blank, as intimation of the royal authority and strength. It was probably the best that Andrew could do, at this stage.

Sailing his ships up-Forth, beyond Airth to opposite the town of Alloa, brought them as close to Stirling as was possible without the risk of running aground in the narrowing and shallowing estuary. There they used up much gunpowder in a lengthy cannonade, which could not fail to make the rebels fully aware of the kingly authority. Then, leaving Barton on the *Kestrel* lying off Boroughstoneness, Andrew took his other vessels back to Methil to embark the Fife contingent.

This occupied a full day. Heading back westwards, they were met by *Kestrel* and Barton announced that the challenge had indeed been met, and a large force from Stirling had arrived in the Linlithgow and Boroughstoneness area.

So far so good.

Now for the tactics Andrew had devised. Eastwards between where the enemy had arrived and Queen Margaret's ferry port, a distance of some eight miles, was an empty stretch of rocky coast with, midway along it, a small thrusting promontory of no great height called Blackness, this on account of the colour of the rocks, on which rose a ruined castle. This had twice been burned earlier in that century, in the reign of James the Second, the present monarch's father, once by the competing Livingstone and Crichton lords in their efforts to rule in the young king's name, and once by the invading English. Using this as a centrepoint, Andrew dropped off groups of his Fife men, one hundred or so at a time, along three or four of these miles on either side of the headland, this to cause the rebel force to split up and hopefully make its central leadership lose control. Then they would see what the ships' cannon could do. Meantime the vessels hid behind the out-thrusting headland.

They had to wait and wait, and Andrew grew agitated. Had he calculated amiss? Were the rebel lords not going to contest his manoeuvres? They must realise that they were vastly superior in numbers to anything that the ships could bring against them, and surely would not remain idle at Boroughstoneness.

Calculations were proved to be accurate. The enemy's scouts no doubt informed the lords of the situation, of the groupings along the coast, and that this must be for some tactical purpose. In consequence they divided up their own strength to go and deal with this.

Well pleased, Andrew led his ships out from behind Blackness, and, their skippers warned of the danger of running aground, they moved in as close to the shore as they dared, *Caravel*, *Flower*, *Kestrel* and *Goshawk*.

So, along that shoreline the strange battle commenced, the various Fife groups well aware of their role, to bring the enemy within range of shot, if possible, yet to keep clear of the danger themselves, no simple matter. But, warned and guided, they played their part. Soon the miles of coast resounded to the continuous thunder of gunfire – Andrew only concerned that his supplies of powder and ball would not run out.

It was not possible to estimate enemy casualties in the confusion and the clouds of smoke generated. But at least it became obvious that the enemy, scattered and unable to strike back, were at a grievous disadvantage. It was not long before, through the mirk and reek, it was fairly evident that the foe, or most of them, saw their position as hopeless, and withdrawal their only option. Dispersed and inevitably confused as they were, this recognition was far from simultaneous; but gradually the retiral became general, this the signal for the Fifers to change from defence to aggression, thus hastening the process.

The Battle of Blackness, if such it could be called, was won and lost. King James could claim victory, or his admiral could.

Andrew's satisfaction was tempered by the realisation that he would fairly promptly have to send ships to the Low Countries for supplies of gunpowder and shot. He could possibly send men to try to retrieve quite a number of the cannonballs by search parties, precious ironware.

What now? The royal cause was in the ascendant. But Andrew often wondered what actually constituted the royal cause? The rebel lords were the opposition, and using young Rothesay's name as their authority. But what of the rest of the nobility and lairds and chiefs? Indeed of the nation at large? What of Holy Church? The vast majority, undoubtedly, were not opposed to their peace-loving monarch. Yet all seemed to be quiescent. Why? Was it because of James's fondness for low-born companions, for music and astrology and book-learning and the like, which did not appeal to most of his subjects of whatever rank? The Scots looked to their monarchs to lead, in affairs of state, as well as in warfare, not leave it to ministers and officers. Most, probably, saw Rothesay as a much more effective king-to-be, not only these actual rebels. Was that why the admiral seemed to be left to champion the royal cause?

What indeed was King James doing with his time at the moment? In all probability he would be closeted with some artist or alchemist discussing heaven knew what. Andrew could well see why most folk did not enthusiastically rise in support. He himself was fond of James Stewart, as well as loyal to his liege-lord. And possibly he was somewhat suspect, for that very reason? But the friendship was there, and duty was duty.

12

The news rang through Scotland only a month after these happenings. The rebel lords had, as it were, officially renounced their allegiance to James the Third, and proclaimed Rothesay monarch as James the Fourth. That young man's reaction was uncertain; but undoubtedly much of the nation was sympathetic towards that development.

Nevertheless, since all the lords and chiefs had sworn to support the monarch with all their might at his coronation, some still held to their vows. Such included the Earl Marischal, Keith; Lindsay, Earl of Crawford; Cunninghame, Earl of Glencairn; Gordon, Earl of Huntly; and Sinclair, Earl of Caithness. These, and sundry lesser lords, recognised that it was time for action, however disinclined for warfare was their liege-lord, and without waiting for any royal commands called all loyal men to arms, and this at Perth at the soonest. The fact was that the king's main support came from above Forth and Clyde, so to some extent it was a contest between north and south.

Andrew viewed the developing situation apprehensively and sadly – it being turned into a struggle nominally between father and son. There could be no doubt as to his own support. He was the king's admiral and friend.

He summoned his Fifers, although not all were eager to become involved, and found himself with only some five hundred to take north to the Tay and Perth. There he consulted with the Marischal, traditional leader of the royal armed forces, and the Gordon Earl of Huntly who was providing the greatest contingent of men. What was the best service *he* could contribute to what looked like developing into a major battle?

It all depended, of course, on where such conflict was to take place. The rebels were based on Stirling, with its all but impregnable citadel – not that they would be likely to hide themselves there, with their thousands. But they almost certainly would not seek to march north to assail their opposition at Perth. So, if fight there must be, it would be apt to take place somewhere near the first possible crossing of Forth – as had been Stirling Bridge with Wallace, Bannockburn with Bruce – the Tor Wood, Plean, or Falkirk, that area. Unfortunately, but inevitably, this had to be where the estuary became a river, and as such became too shallow for Andrew's vessels with their cannon. It was unlikely that he could influence events, save by providing a fairly near presence, and demonstrating it by a cannonade, showing a measure of support.

It was St Barnabas Day, the eleventh day of June 1488.

He sailed his four ships as far as he dared take them, to what was called the Pows, or pools, of Forth, opposite the little community of Polmaise, and there dropped anchor. Had the Perth force crossed yet? That would have to be further west, of course. There was no means of telling. It was as near to any likely battleground as he could get, if he was needed.

They settled to wait.

It was late afternoon before any indication of events reached them, this in the form of groups of men arriving in haste at the riverside from the area just south of Stirling, folk obviously in flight, seeking to find a way across, defeated troops undoubtedly, but rebel or loyal? Some few did plunge into the water to seek to swim across, but most turned up- or downstream. Andrew sent his brother Jamie in a boat to ferry some of these across and question them, finding if possible someone who could tell of events with some authority.

Jamie was soon back, with three tartan-clad Gordons,

which in itself was significant. One of these, wounded in the shoulder, and promised that he would be rowed across to the north side, told a more coherent tale than most of the others.

It was disaster. The king was dead. He had failed them all, and paid the price. Battle had joined at Sauchieburn, back there, and, the fighting going less than well for the royal side, the king himself, a curse on him, had fled the field, deserting his supporters, fled alone. But reaching where the Sauchie Burn joined the larger Bannock, at a mill, his horse had apparently reared in fright and thrown him, to his injury. The miller and his wife had carried him to their stable. And there, following him, had come the Lord Gray, one of the rebels, and being led to the stable, recognised him, and stabbed him to death.

The flight of the king, needless to say, further lowered the morale of the loyalist fighters, and it had become retreat and escape. The Duke of Rothesay, who was with the victorious rebels, had been taken to see his father's body, he now King of Scots, James the Fourth. The sorry reign was finished, and rebels were no longer that but the new king's men. Those, like themselves, who had fought for the father, were now for home if they could get there, battling over, Scotland entering a new order.

Andrew heard all this, confirmed by other fleeing men who sought to cross the river, and recognised the new realities. He had loyally supported the unfortunate and foolish monarch. Now, there could be no doubt where his duty lay. He was Admiral of Scotland, and whatever his attitude to Rothesay in the past, now *he* was his monarch and liege-lord. Duty bound, he must make prompt recognition of this. He must go and declare his due allegiance.

So, while streams of defeated men were seeking to cross Forth for the north, Andrew, with James Barton and a company of his seamen, left his brother in command of the ships and, landing, set off on foot against the tide of flight to seek the victor of the battle, in a strange reversal of role.

It was fully two miles to the battle-site; but they did not have to go that far, for they came to a quite large party of the former rebel lords, some of whom Andrew recognised, such as the Earl of Angus and the Lord Home, this at a mill, presumably that at which the monarch had died, or been murdered. And there he learned that Rothesay, or rather James the Fourth, was himself in the mill-house, with the corpse of his father, in a state of some upset and confusion of feelings, as well he might be. Declaring that he was the admiral, come to pay his respects to the new monarch, Andrew gained admittance.

He found the young man sitting alone beside his father's body, this on a bunk bed beyond the kitchen, where the miller, wife and a child huddled in obvious anxiety and distress.

It proved to be a moving sight, the new monarch with, of all things, an iron chain around his waist and loins, sitting gazing at the corpse, lips moving wordlessly. He did not look up as the newcomer entered.

"Sire," Andrew said, bowing. "You know me, Andrew Wood, your royal father's admiral. And now yours. I come to assure you of my loyal duty. As you are aware, I was in a fashion close to your father. I would wish you to learn that I well understand your feelings in this pass, and to assure you that I will serve you as I did him." He gestured towards the corpse.

The son looked up and shook his head.

"The past is past, Sire. You are now my liege-lord. I will seek to prove it, as required. The days of struggle and faction are over. My ships and men are at your royal disposal. For the realm's weal is all-important. I would have you to know of my support."

James was fingering that chain. "I will wear this," he declared thickly. "For all my days. Before Almighty God, I will! To remind me that I slew my own father!"

"Not that, Sire – not that! *You* did not. He who did must bear the blame. The Lord Gray, I am told."

"He did it for *me*! For my cause. I cannot escape the curse of it. I will wear this chain next to my skin. So that I shall never forget."

"As you wish, Your Grace. But you now have a realm to rule. If the chain aids you in this, so be it. But let the like not cost you, and your nation, too dear."

"It hung in the stable where he was slain. I took it down."

"Use it to hang the Lord Gray, then – who did the slaying."

"Was ever a son so accursed! Gray thought that he was serving me, making me the king by doing it. I cannot escape the blame."

"He misjudged, direly. But you cannot blame yourself."

"I do, I do! I led an army against my father."

"With fair intent, no doubt. But you were used by others, including this Gray. Now, rule your people the better, Sire. To make up for it all. Your father, there, would so wish it."

"You knew him well, Sir Andrew. Probably better than I did. We were never close. As son and father should be. And now – it is too late! Leave me, to my shame and sorrow . . ."

Bowing, Andrew turned and left them there, father and son, himself much moved. What more was there to say?

13

He had not been long back at Largo when there was an unexpected development. The former rebel lords, now in effect masters of Scotland and holding the new king in their grip, sent for Andrew to appear before them, claiming this as a demand from the Privy Council. He sent word back that he was quite prepared to do so, provided that he received pledges for his safe return. They must send a couple of their lords to his keeping, as security.

Whatever they thought of this, apparently they were sufficiently eager for Andrew's presence, for in due course the Lords Fleming and Seton arrived at Largo. They were well received as guests in the care of Beth and brother Jamie, but left in no doubt that they were as good as prisoners until the admiral came home in good order.

He sailed for Leith in the *Caravel*.

Landing, with James Barton, he presented himself at the Tolbooth as requested, where he was surprised to find King James present, the new monarch casting a quick and significant glance and a brief nod of the head, where he sat, then turning away. The lords were being led, as so often, by the Douglas, Archibald Earl of Angus, as spokesman, who was haughtily demanding.

The first point raised was quite astonishing, in the circumstances. Did he, Wood, hold the body of the late and unworthy King James the Third?

Another quick look at James the Fourth, who again looked away, left Andrew wondering indeed. When last he had seen the latter he had been sitting beside his dead father. And various of the lords had been nearby, in the other room of that mill-house.

He wagged his head, and declared that he did not. Why should he? They had had the late king slain, murdered, after Sauchieburn. The corpse was in *their* bloody hands. Why ask him this?

"The royal body is amissing," Angus declared. "And *you* were in a position to take it, to your ships nearby. Some are declaring that he, the former king, is still alive. And possibly in your keeping."

Another darting glance at James, who continued to stare away, had Andrew hurriedly calculating. That young man well knew that he, Andrew, did not have his father's body. Yet these, his former supporters, thought that he might have it. So what had happened to their support, and to his father's body? Had the new king somehow spirited it away for private burial? Some sort of remorseful gesture for the sense of guilt over all the opposition? The young monarch's silence, and very obvious distancing himself from this enquiry, could possibly indicate that.

"You, my lords, had the late king slain. And held his body," Andrew declared. "Why ask where it is? *I* know not."

"There is this talk that the former monarch is not dead, only held somewhere," Angus went on. "Possibly escaped in one of your ships. To Flanders or elsewhere."

"*You* know that is not so."

"It would be best for His Grace, here, if his sire's body was displayed. And then duly interred, probably in Dunfermline Abbey, along with other kings."

"Possibly so. But I know naught of this. The whereabouts of the, the remains."

King James remained silent.

"Somebody knows," Home said. "And we are told that you saw the body after the battle."

"As did others. *Your* friends!"

There were head-shakings and signs of frustration. But they had to accept Andrew's disclaimer.

He bowed to the seated monarch. "Have I Your Grace's permission to retire?" he asked.

James half rose and then thought better of it, raised his eyebrows at Andrew in a telling fashion, and turned head to stare down through the nearby window, and nod.

Andrew interpreted this as some sort of signal, concerned with outside. Bowing again, but certainly not towards the lords, he left the chamber.

Down in Tolbooth Wynd, he wondered. What was James intending by that last indication? Out and down? Was it a sign to wait for him? A private meeting hereafter? He told Barton to return to the *Caravel*. He would join him presently.

Downstairs, he went over to the entry to a tenement of houses, from which he could see the Tolbooth doorway. There he waited, part hidden.

It was not long before his guessing was proved accurate. The young king appeared, with a single companion, and, glancing along and over, clearly saw Andrew waiting. He pointed in the other direction to the young man with him, and sent him off. Then he came across to the doorway, to move with Andrew inside, and so out of sight of the Tolbooth windows.

"I have to tell you, Sir Andrew," he said. "You should know that *I* took my father's body. It is now in his music place, the Chapel Royal at Stirling. They, Angus and the others, were going to have it interred at Dunfermline. I would have it placed beside my mother, his wife, at Cambuskenneth Abbey. This the least that I can do. Can you sail your ship up to that abbey, near to Stirling, beside the Forth?"

"Cambuskenneth, Sire? It is further up than I usually take my ships. But, yes, I think that *Kestrel* could win that far. It is fairly shallow of draught. Why, may I ask?"

"So that I may have my way. They want my father beside the Bruce's body, for some reason. I say beside my mother's. They heed me not. So, I thought of you. And your ship. I can have the body taken there. Your cannon fired as token. You were his friend. Here is something that you can do for him. Help to have him laid beside his queen. Then cannon-fire. And those cannon would make it clear that man and wife were not to be disturbed by any disinterment. You have it? Buried at Cambuskenneth to loud gunfire. My last salute to my mother and father. And proof that, even in such as this, *I* mean to rule Scotland hereafter — not Angus and Home and Hailes and the rest. You were my father's friend, Andrew Wood. Be now mine!"

"I am that already, Sire. But, yes, I will do it. But how to get the body to Cambuskenneth in my ship?"

"No need. I will get it from the Chapel Royal by night. I have friends. William Dunbar, and the Frenchman, Damian, and Andrew Miller, whom I trust. We will carry it by pack-horse. Your crewmen could help at the abbey. Here is something that I can do. And show that I am king, not just these lords' puppet."

If it seemed an odd way to demonstrate kingship, at least it showed spirit, determination and enterprise, and a son's regard for his parents, if belated. Andrew promised co-operation. How soon?

The sooner the better. Or the corpse might be beginning to stink. How quickly could he get his vessel up to Cambuskenneth?

By noon next day, probably.

That was it, then. The body to be taken there by night. Hidden. The *Kestrel* to come. Cannon-fire. The late monarch to be laid to rest beside his wife. And the ship to remain nearby, just in case the lords sought to interfere, to disinter even, and have their way. Those cannon were ever an unchallengeable threat.

So the strange compact was made. Andrew wondered whether ever before a royal burial had been so contrived? James the Third had been a strange monarch. James the Fourth, romantic and venturesome, looked like being as strange, but stronger. The Stewart line was certainly not dull and humdrum, whatever else.

In the morning *Kestrel* sailed westwards the nearly thirty miles, Beth insisting on attending this peculiar funeral. They duly found James and his assistants awaiting them, with Abbot Henry. Cambuskenneth was a fine abbey, dating from 1147, one of the many founded by the pious David the First, with mainly English moneys gained by his marrying the richest heiress in all England, but dedicated to the Virgin Mary. The name meant the creek of Cainneach, one of St Columba's disciples. Here, highly suitably Bruce had received the surrender of the English nobles after the victory of Bannockburn.

The abbey consisted of a large cruciform church and chapter-house, with monastic buildings nearby in the quite tight crook of the winding river. It had a great square parapeted tower seventy feet high, and dominated all those watery levels.

Rowed ashore, the newcomers found all in readiness. The dead monarch was in a simple oak coffin, this lying in a cavity in the stone flooring before the high altar, beside the grave of Queen Margaret, a great plain slab ready to place over it. There was no delay now. Abbot Henry conducted a brief and simple burial ceremony, prayers were said for the soul of the departed, holy water was sprinkled on coffin and cavity, and the body lowered into its resting-place. All stood in silence, heads bowed, for an interval, and then the heavy slab was levered into position, hiding all, no indication left that there was any partner for the queen's tomb. In due course a suitable carving would be made on the slab, but meantime there was to be nothing to draw attention to the new grave.

Abbot Henry gave his blessing to the new monarch and his friends, and it was farewell. The pack-horse and James's helpers went off whence they had come, and the king accompanied Andrew and Beth and their crewmen back to the *Kestrel*. He would be taken to Leith, and thence to Holyrood and thereafter Edinburgh Castle.

Not to draw attention to the abbey itself, the ship was turned about, quite a difficult manoeuvre in these shallows, and then sailed off round no fewer than six of the extraordinary windings of the Pows of Forth, to opposite the Haugh of West Grange, one of the many granges of farmland belonging to and worked by the abbey's monks. There the *Kestrel*'s demi-cannon fired off their salute to the dead king, no doubt to the wonderment, question and possibly alarm of all who heard it, which would be many, for the thunder of it was re-echoed from all the range of the Ochil hillsides.

Duty done and James satisfied, it was back down Forth, for the estuary and Leith.

From now on, Scotland was to learn what it was to have a vigorous, determined and enthusiastically imaginative monarch.

14

Andrew and his wife had an especial royal invitation to attend James's coronation, to be held, as was traditional, at Scone, on the Tay, where the estuary became a river and fresh water triumphed over salt, this revered from earliest times as a symbol of the nation's fertility.

It was a great occasion, the new king determined to make it even more so than usual, as a means of uniting his quarrelsome lords and chieftains. To help achieve this, after the initial religious ceremony in Scone Abbey, the focus of all was transferred up to the top of the nearby Moot Hill mound, where the oaths of allegiance were sworn before the new monarch. He initiated a new clause in the oath-giving whereby the lords, kneeling before him on his throne, with handfuls of earth brought from their various properties, had to swear not only fullest support and leal duty to the monarch, but association and co-operation with all other subjects of their liege-lord, whatever their previous alignments, factions and feudings, so help them God. However many eyebrows were raised at this, it was a royal command, and the declaration had to be repeated.

Andrew, as Admiral of the Realm, watched all from behind the throne with the other officers of state.

Duly crowned, and after the subsequent feasting in the abbey's refectory, James sent for Andrew to attend him in a side chamber. There he declared that he intended to establish something new for Scotland, a proper royal navy. France, Portugal and Spain had national navies. Scotland should have the same. England did not, Henry the Seventh merely giving shipmen royal authority to call themselves privateers and be available for the king's service when called upon. Better than anything such was required, a fleet of the realm, under the admiral. How said Sir Andrew?

That man wondered. The notion was certainly good. But had His Grace considered the cost to his treasury? Shipbuilding was expensive. A fleet of large warships would demand vast moneys.

James declared that the cost would just have to be found. Extra dues and taxation. He would have Archbishop Scheves and other churchmen to deal with that, Holy Church's riches enormous. Meanwhile he, with Andrew's help, would draw up plans. He had a vision of the sort of great ship he wanted for his own; larger, much larger, than even the *Yellow Caravel*. Capable of carrying many men beyond just its crew, armed men, pikemen, bowmen and even knights. And many cannon, to be sure. Andrew would have to see to this last. He, James, was determined on this. He would cow all those English privateers into submission as far as Scots shipping was concerned.

Andrew held his peace as the monarch elaborated on his ideas for this naval flourish. He would have the vessel built at Leith. He already had a name for it. He would call it the *Michael*, or better, the *Great Michael* – that being his favourite saint, Michael the Archangel, God's vice-regent, warrior leader of the heavenly hosts and principal adversary of Satan.

Listening, his admiral looked doubtful. Enthusiasm was all very well – and this James was a born enthusiast. But what was practical had to be considered. Silver. Money. The cost of even this one great craft would be daunting. *He* knew, from his experience with *Caravel* and *Flower*. But the monarch was not to be dissuaded.

This was early in 1489. And not long thereafter there was what James declared was proof of the need for his intentions. From Stirling the king sent word to his admiral that five large English ships had entered the Clyde, although a period of truce had been agreed with King Henry, and these were ravaging and laying waste the towns and communities flanking that estuary in shameful fashion. Appeals for help were resounding. Sir Andrew must see to it.

Kestrel and *Goshawk* were away to the Low Countries for the cannon for the king, so Andrew had only *Caravel* and *Flower* to tackle this royal call. And in windy March weather it would be a blustery voyage round Scotland to the west, through the Pentland Firth's fierce tides and the troublesome waters of the Sea of the Hebrides.

It proved to be so – and a strange time, really, for the English privateers to have come up to the Clyde; but whatever else, these would be seasoned seafarers. Would they be as effective fighters? And five of them reported.

Rounding eventually the Mull of Kintyre and entering the Firth of Clyde, Andrew sailed his two ships cautiously up the Ayrshire coast. They saw signs of devastation as they went, fire-blackened ruins, roofless sheds, wrecked fishing-boats. Where were the invaders likely to be at the present? How to catch them unawares?

It was across on the Isle of Arran shore that presently they saw smoke, three different clouds, somewhat south of Lamlash Bay and the offshore islet called Holy, where there was a monastery and sacred well. Some distance apart, these columns of smoke looked significant. So it might well be possible to deal with the kindlers of these fires, assuming them to be the enemy, separately. His ships would be seen heading inshore, so surprise would be difficult. But if the raiders were burning some way inland, they might take time to get back to their vessels. Probably only skeleton crews would be apt to be left aboard.

They saw the first ship at the mouth of a wooded glen, in a small bay a couple of miles perhaps below that Holy Isle. Make a start here.

It was almost too easy. Moving in, they drew up their

two vessels on either side of this craft, and grapnels were thrown to pull them in close enough for boarding. Clearly there were not many foemen left to man it, these eyeing the large and impressive newcomers in evident alarm. Assailed from both sides, the eight or nine Englishmen saw that they had no chance of defending themselves. They surrendered without a blow struck.

What to do with them? Andrew had them disarmed, and taken aboard *Caravel*. Then he ordered a few of his men to sail the captured ship out into the firth, there to await developments.

Four more, reportedly, to seek.

Guided by those inland smoke clouds they moved southwards, and found two moored vessels in another bay. Andrew did not know Arran intimately, but he did recognise Dippen Head, not far from the southern tip of the island, and this bay was just a little north of that headland. They saw that the thatched roofs of a group of cottages had been burned, and no sign of the former occupiers, the smoke rising further inland. *Caravel* and *Flower* had to tackle these two craft separately, for they were perhaps a hundred yards apart. But the taking of them was no major task, again only a few crewmen left on each. This was proving to be the simplest of operations. Three of the enemy ships taken. The problem was now sparing men to hold them.

Where were the two remaining ships? There was no more smoke to be seen, a quite lofty hill rising just to the south. Round Dippen Head for them, then.

There they came to a much larger bay, And coming across it, towards them, were two vessels close together, almost certainly the foe they were looking for, craft of that size seldom to be seen in these waters.

The three captured ships were following on, in rather laboured and unsteady fashion, with the scanty men crewing them. Andrew was now faced with various problems, this shortage of men in particular. The English prisoners, even disarmed as they were, might just rise in revolt, outnumbering their captors.

At least there was no question as to what to do about the two approaching craft, the likelihood of them being equipped with cannon remote.

He ordered a salvo of blank shot to be fired. What the oncoming crews thought of it all was not to be known, their own three ships tailing behind the two great war vessels. But this cannonade would make the immediate situation clear to them, at least: they were being summoned, threatened.

And reaction quickly became apparent. Sails were lowered, and the ships waited.

Andrew was now racking his wits to decide on effective action. Men! Numbers of men! Enemy men much more numerous than his own, and these last now distinctly dispersed. His cannon gave him ample superiority as to strength, but did not guide him as to what to do with the captives, ships and men.

He sailed up close to the waiting English vessels, and from his forecastle shouted.

"Heed me, shipmasters – heed! I am the Admiral of Scotland! You, and these others now in my grasp, are invading and ravishing this realm. And in time of truce. It is outrage! You burn and slay. I should hang you all. Blast your ships with my cannon!"

There was no response from the others.

"Answer me. How say you? Surrender, or be sunk?"

The reply to that was the hauling down of the three red and white St George's cross banners of England from the mastheads of one of the ships, quickly followed by those of the other.

What now, then? Decision. They were less than one hundred miles from the Cumbrian coast of the Solway Firth, England. It was unlikely that more enemy privateers would appear, but not impossible, these five merely showing the way. And burdened with his captures of ships and men, he wanted no contest further. Back then, all the way round Scotland, with all his prisoners, a prolonged process. Could his crews face that, dispersed as they were?

He ordered the captains of the captured vessels to be brought to him on the *Caravel*, as hostages, and had the English crews told that these would be hanged, and not only them, if there was not strict obedience to his orders. Let it be understood, he would stand for no least indiscipline, and would not hesitate to sink any ship, with its crew, his own men rescued. Obey, and behave wisely, and he promised that he would appeal to the King of Scots, in due course, to let them return, unharmed, to their native land. That ought to ensure their co-operation.

It did. The seven vessels, however odd the manning, set off in a column led by *Caravel*, south by west, to win out of the Clyde, rounded the Mull of Kintyre, and started on the lengthy voyage up the Hebridean Sea.

They had to sail at the speed of the slowest, so it made a lengthy-seeming voyage indeed. Andrew feared that there might well be revolts among some of the captive crews, but thankfully there was none, the promise of a petition to the monarch for freedom to return home unmolested having its effect.

At last Leith was reached, and King James's presence sought. Being the man he was, he took little persuasion to agree to give the Englishmen their freedom, and even told their captains to give his respects to King Henry, declaring that *he* at least was prepared to maintain the truce, whatever these had done.

Andrew proposed that he should take the enemy crews to Newcastle-on-Tyne, the nearest large English port, there send them ashore in small boats, and return with the captured ships. This was enthusiastically agreed, James even offering to come with them to demonstrate a royal presence off the English coast; but Andrew advised against this, in the interests of the alleged truce.

So the further voyage was made, another hundred miles,

to the mouth of the English Tyne, where, to salvoes of cannon-fire as salutation, the enemy crews were sent ashore, this without any hostile reaction from the local shipping.

Well satisfied, Andrew turned his vessels for home. He would have much to recount to Beth.

15

The word reaching Scotland was that King Henry of England was furious indeed at the defeat and capture of his privateers, and even more so at the insult of sending his captured seamen home unharmed as of no least concern to the Scots. He was reported to be offering a pension of one thousand pounds per year to any warrior shipmaster who would go up to Scottish waters and suitably chastise the arrogant Scots, especially the one who was calling himself an admiral, and end this offence against English shipping.

It was being said that Stephen Bull was for taking up this royal challenge.

Andrew had heard of this Bull, so aptly named, a quite renowned trader and shipowner, who had made his mark against pirates of various nationalities, and had been spoken of by the Hansa merchants, and indeed by Hans Poppenruyter of Antwerp, who had sold him cannon. So here was an adversary to be respected and watched out for. Would he come north?

King James was much impressed with the efficacy of the modern cannon, which did not seem to endanger the gunners thereof by bursting at the breach, as had quite frequently been the case in the past; had not his own grandfather, James the Second, been killed at Roxburgh by one of his own cannon? He now decided that, costly or not, he was going to equip his royal fortresses, Stirling, Edinburgh, Dumbarton, Roxburgh, Perth and the rest, with artillery. And who to see to it but his admiral? Andrew was to go to Flanders and purchase the necessary pieces, whatever the High Treasurer thought of it.

This of cannon-making must be becoming a highly profitable industry in the Low Countries. Andrew wondered whether it would not be possible to forge their own artillery in Scotland? They had the ironstone and the coal, after all.

James was demanding many guns, and they would be weighty to carry, as well as costly. Andrew reckoned that at least four vessels would have to be taken to collect them. He now had a surplus of captured ships, which he was selling at Leith and in Fife to traders. But he preferred to use his own trusted craft and crews. So the *Caravel*, the *Flower*, the *Kestrel* and the *Goshawk* set off for the Low Countries, Beth, as usual, not to be left behind, despite warnings that this Stephen Bull might just possibly seek to make his presence felt.

However, the sail southwards was uneventful, no opposition presenting itself, and they entered the lengthy Wester Schelde, to reach Antwerp in good time.

However, there they met with considerable delay. Poppenruyter, although welcoming them as good customers, declared that the demand for cannon was ever growing, and his ability to meet it stretched indeed. He was actually farming out orders to other foundries in neighbouring cities, this concerning him, for he feared that the quality of their work did not always reach his own standards. But what could he do?

So, it seemed that they were in for a quite lengthy wait. They would have to fill in time. They would visit other cities and towns none so far off, Brussels, Bruges, Ghent, Limburg, Eindhoven and the like. They were assured that there was much to see of interest, Beth especially taken with the prospect of it all, although her husband was concerned for his crewmen, left idling at the Schelde docklands, and possibly getting into mischief as they consumed large quantities of the local schnapps gin. He was also anxious that the quality of the cannon bought might not be as he desired. But Poppenruyter assured him that he would inspect all before handing them over, whatever foundries they came from.

Travel around these Low Countries cities was not difficult, not the usual horse-riding. Since all were more or less at sea level, water lay everywhere, and canals crisscrossed the land in all directions, barge traffic the normal means of wayfaring, some of the barges not only large but comfortably furnished with sleeping quarters and kitchens. It was all a very different way of life from that of the Scots' own hilly land, this in itself interesting, quite apart from all that was to be seen and inspected. Beth was much intrigued by it all.

They had seen much of Antwerp itself previously. It was decided to visit Bruges, since it could be reached readily by ship, lying just south of the mouth of the Wester Schelde by which they had just come. So it was back to the sea and down to Zeebruges, the port, and by barge, on canal, inland to the ancient city. It had been much talked of only two years before, when the citizens had risen in revolt against the excesses of the Archduke Maximilian, and imprisoned him, asserting their independent status. Famous for its lace and linen, its renowned tapestries, its distilling and shipbuilding, it was a place to attract both Beth and her husband.

They duly admired the great market-hall, known as Les Halles, with a famous belfry over three hundred and fifty feet high. Also a town-house larger than any tolbooth in Scotland. And the celebrated Chapel of the Holy Blood. Andrew spent two days at the shipyards, gaining much useful information, while Beth found ample distraction elsewhere.

Then back to Antwerp.

Poppenruyter had their cannon assembled, from makers he trusted, inspected and approved, numbering over fifty, of various sizes and calibres. Also balls to suit, and great quantities of gunpowder. All was loaded on to the four vessels, the cost thereof having Andrew blinking. However, he had the money, as a result of selling those captured ships, and paid up unprotesting. Whether he would ever recoup himself from the royal coffers remained to be seen.

It had been an expensive visit, and personally likewise, for Beth had not been content with admiring all that she saw, and was taking home not a few of what she named her treasures. Why not, when the moneys were there? she asked. What was siller for? Hoarding, or using to obtain objects and gifts to value? Her spouse had to admit the sense of this, especially as he had himself bought a handsome gold and jewelled crucifix, which he was going to present to the monks of the Isle of May, always his favoured shrine. His soul could almost certainly do with some prayers and supplications offered up by those brethren.

They were homeward-bound then, heavily laden. As well that he had the ivory, as well as the ship-selling and other trading ventures to pay for it all.

Andrew's donation of the crucifix to the Isle of May had an odd presentation indeed. They had entered the Forth estuary in their four laden ships, were nearing the island's proximity when out from behind its cliffs emerged three tall warships flying English flags, larger ships than *Caravel* and *Flower*, no mere privateers these. It was Stephen Bull, almost certainly.

Confirmation of this was not long in coming. A puff of smoke and a single bang of cannon-fire heralded a spout of water not far from the Scots vessels as a ball plunged into the sea, its message plain.

Andrew's reaction was not so swift as he would have liked it to be, as he curtly ordered Beth to get below, out of harm's way. His craft were burdened with all the newly purchased cannon, and these were not primed nor loaded. And nearly home, indeed just opposite Largo, he was scarcely looking for battle. But he had to demonstrate whose waters these were, truce or none. Some of the

Caravel's cannon were always primed with powder for blank shot, for signalling, and he ordered one to be fired, in answer, while others were hastily loaded and readied.

Another ball crashed into the sea close to *Flower*.

It was something new for the admiral to be in contest with vessels as well equipped with artillery as were his, and in his own waters, moreover clearly looking for a fight. Even though they were three against his four, they were larger, powerful craft.

His men were well trained, of course, and there was but little delay before their own first shots thundered out.

The two groups were actually beyond effective range as yet, and no ball struck home. Andrew turned off at an angle, not because he sought disengagement, but for time to manoeuvre. He wanted to get to windward of the enemy so that he could bear down on them in full sail and bows-on, presenting the smallest targets. He concentrated his forward cannon on just one of the English vessels, seeking to cripple it, so that he might be able to get his two ships alongside each of the enemy, engaging them on both flanks, and to get grappling-irons out to lash them together for hand-to-hand fighting, which ought to even the odds somewhat.

But although they succeeded in bringing down two of the masts of the target vessel, causing it to be all but incapacitated from the fight meantime, Bull, if he it was, perceived their tactics and swung his ships off, right and left, at the same time firing more ball. One of these struck the *Goshawk*'s foremast, collapsing its sail. Thus far, an even score.

Leaving the two partly disabled craft to cope with each other, Andrew ordered *Flower* to engage one of the remaining foemen, while *Caravel*, with *Kestrel*, bore down on the other, on either side of it, grapnels ready to hurl. One ball struck *Caravel*'s forecastle, carrying away some of the timbering, but not greatly damaging them. Actually the gunfire on both sides was not notably effective, this because the sea was fairly rough, and with the dipping and rearing much ball was wasted. This also affected the grappling process, chains and their anchors having to be thrown, pulled back, and thrown again. Altogether, tactics and strategy were frustrating owing to conditions.

The eventual boarding process was less than successful likewise, for the English ship was manned by strong and competent fighters, and, even though assailed from both sides, put up a strong defence.

This struggle was indecisive, some boarders being repulsed. And when Andrew saw that, despite *Flower*'s engagement, the third enemy craft was coming to place itself alongside *Kestrel*, he had to recognise hard facts. This boarding operation was not going to be a success. He signalled *Flower* and *Kestrel* to back off, while he ordered his own crewmen to come back, unhitching those grapnels and chains, and aiding their wounded to return.

The three ships drew apart.

Thus far, it was no victory for either group.

All this had taken some considerable time, and with an outgoing tide, the struggling vessels had drifted out miles east and north of the May, to opposite Fife Ness, the final point of the land. With daylight failing, and no decision yet reached, Andrew decided to lie off and lick his wounds, as it were. He wondered whether Bull would come to the conclusion that his invasion of Scottish waters was proving unprofitable, and depart southwards overnight? As the late-autumn darkness fell, Andrew ordered no lamps to be lit to give away their positions. No lights showed on the enemy craft either.

Caring for the wounded, repairing such damage as they could, it was a case of waiting overnight to see what daylight would reveal. Andrew and his crews were well aware of their handicap by being laden with all those purchased cannon. Fighter as he was, Scotland's admiral did hope that the foe would choose to depart southwards.

But, no. Dawn revealed that the English were still there

– *there* now being off the mouth of the Firth of Tay, the strong south-west wind having carried them all that far.

Conditions and tossing seas were still not good for any accurate gunfire, ball apt to fly high or down into the water. Andrew came to the conclusion that he should try to make the land itself fight for him, if possible. Unlike the Forth the Tay estuary had a very narrow mouth, between Buddon Point and Craig Head, although it widened out again thereafter opposite Dundee. Could he get Bull's ships driven therein, and so bottled up?

Goshawk's crew had managed to make their craft effective again. So, although no doubt the enemy had also repaired damage as far as was possible, it was again their four against three. The strategy was to form a line seaward of the English, and advance westwards, to force the enemy into that mile-and-a-half-wide mouth.

This device was most fortunately aided, albeit involuntarily, by three merchant ships, sailing in convoy against possible privateer attack, making for the port of Dundee, and, seeing the two battle squadrons and no doubt having heard the cannon-fire, lying well off, out of harm's way. Andrew sent *Kestrel* to order them, under the authority of the admiral, to join his four vessels in approximate line abreast, and so proceed. Thus, with seven ships bearing down on the three, and one of the foe damaged, Bull was more or less forced into the narrow firth entry.

As Tay widened out thereafter considerably, *Kestrel* was sent off ahead at a tangent to pass well clear of the enemy ships, to reach Dundee's dockland and there order all vessels that could be manned at short notice to sail out into the firth, as seeming added threat to the English. No need for any attack, just a presence.

Now with six craft chasing three, Andrew pushed on. Bull was now cooped up in Tay.

Where the estuary widened to a couple of miles across there was room to manoeuvre, and an exchange of cannon-fire followed, the water here fairly calm and more accurate aiming possible. This applied to both sides, of course, and *Caravel* suffered a ball bringing down one of the foremast sails, which complicated effective wind usage, and some consequent delay. But the emergence of no fewer than five more merchant ships from Dundee's port, led by *Kestrel*, however loth might be their crews for any actual action, had its effect. Bull could not fail to recognise that his position was hopeless, greatly outnumbered in hostile waters and unable to win out of these. After one last flourish of all his cannon, as gesture, he bowed to the inevitable and lowered both his sails and his English banners in surrender.

Andrew sailed *Caravel* into within hailing distance of the largest English ship.

"Stephen Bull!" he shouted. "I, Andrew Wood, salute you! You are a notable foeman, but defeated in fair fight. I order you to sail into the harbour of this Dundee-town, where we may discuss terms. Obey me!"

"As you say," came back. "I must submit. But will fight another day!"

"We shall see. Dundee for you."

Preceded by *Caravel*, all the vessels involved turned to sail for the northern shore, with the tall steeples and towers of the city and its hilly background ahead of them.

Docked along Dundee's waterfront, Andrew summoned Stephen Bull aboard *Caravel*. He asked him whether he preferred to give his word to abide by all commands, with his captains, or to be locked up in the city's tollbooth. He chose the former, needless to say. He was then told that he and his men could abide on their ships, until he, the admiral, had royal instructions as to what to do with them. This was allegedly a time of truce, and the King of Scots must decide what was to be done.

James had promised to be at Edinburgh Castle, awaiting delivery of all those cannon Andrew had purchased for him. So James Barton was sent in *Kestrel* to Leith, to urge the monarch to come to Dundee and decide on the fate of

Stephen Bull. Leith was only six hours' sailing, against the wind as it was.

Waiting, Andrew invited Bull and his captains to have a meal with him on the *Caravel*. Beth would enjoy this.

The next evening *Kestrel* arrived back, bringing King James, the monarch much elated over the situation, and loud in his congratulations to his admiral. Ever romantically and chivalrously inclined, he received Stephen Bull with courteous amusement, declared that he had heard much of him, but that he was foolish to have pitted himself against Sir Andrew Wood. Tell Henry Tudor so when he got back to the Thames. Also that that monarch should restrain his privateers, at least as far as Scotland was concerned. He, James, had brought gifts for Henry, and also for Bull himself. Take them, and his ships likewise, free of ransom, and go home. He, and his royal master, would be welcome to visit Scotland hereafter, so long as they came unarmed and in peace.

That was typical James Stewart. Andrew shook his head over his liege-lord, but admired him also.

Now they had all those cannon to deliver at Leith, and then his crucifix to the Isle of May monks. Then it would be home to Largo.

16

Andrew attended his first parliament that autumn. He had been entitled, as holder of a barony, to sit in such; but they were infrequently held and he had always been gone on some voyage or expedition hitherto.

This one was held at Edinburgh, in the great hall of the rock-top citadel. Its main purposes were to renew the so-often violated truce with England, and to further the alliances with France and Portugal, these to help restrain the aggressive tendencies of Henry Tudor. James had specially urged Andrew to be present, since he could act as one of the envoys to these lands, and convey the others thereto. Other business was to consider the problems created by the Lord of the Isles who, like his predecessors, was acting the independent prince and indeed making his own treaties with Henry of England. The admiral's ships might well be required to deal with this also.

Andrew was interested in the procedure. The assembly was known as the King-in-Parliament; and unless the monarch was present it was no parliament, only a convention. James presided, on his throne, but normally did not take any very active part in the debates, the proceedings being conducted by the Chancellor, presently Bishop William Elphinstone of Aberdeen.

On this occasion Andrew was somewhat embarrassed at being singled out for identification and praise, on this his first attendance, James personally introducing the matter of foreign relations and the need for ambassadors to go and establish and confirm these. He promptly declared that Scotland was fortunate in having its renowned admiral, Sir

Andrew Wood, with his ships, to take the envoys to the different countries and to act as one of these himself. The Auld Alliance with France was to be emphasised; and Portugal was seen as a suitable ally, its great fleet able to threaten England if necessary. Who better than Sir Andrew, here present, to visit and so help to arrange with the other envoys? Did parliament agree?

No contrary voice was raised. Andrew stood, in his fairly humble seat among the barons well behind the earls and lords and the bishops and mitred abbots, bowed to the throne, and sat down again, uttering no words – although glancing up at Beth, a spectator in the gallery.

Chancellor Elphinstone took over. He asked for nominations for other envoys to go to the countries specified, suggesting that, in the circumstances, four would be a suitable embassage. Three other names, then?

Robert Keith, the Earl Marischal was proposed and seconded, apt to act with the admiral. Also Patrick Hepburn, Earl of Bothwell. This with a cleric, as necessary because the delegates were also to go to Rome to see the Pope. Robert Blackadder, Bishop of Glasgow was chosen. James was concerned that papal legates were seeking overmuch power in Scotland, and in more than Church affairs; and he wished it to be known that no representative of the Vatican was to come to Scotland unless he was a cardinal or a Scotsman. Also the Church lands were becoming ever greater, and they should not seek especial privileges over tenants. When a bishopric became vacant through death or otherwise, the king was demanding at least eight months before a successor was appointed, this to enable him to make his own preferred nomination; after all bishops, as lords spiritual, had equal power with lords temporal in the Scots parliament, and so could effectively sway decisions made. This might not be so in other realms, but here it was important that prelates did not exercise too much power in the nation's affairs. So the envoys' visit to Rome was of some significance, and to be handled with care and due authority.

Another serious matter before the assembly concerned Archibald Douglas, Earl of Angus, he who was once called Bell-the-Cat, one of the most powerful lords. He was not present, this because he was in fact warded meantime in his own castle of Tantallon, near North Berwick, because of treasonable relations with Henry Tudor. He had been offended against King James who, as a youth, had been in his power, and had since preferred other magnates to favour, including his admiral. Angus was now seeking to build up a faction to regain ascendancy over his liege-lord.

This matter aroused considerable debate in the parliament, for Angus had strong allies, especially among the Douglases of course, but also among other lords, the Hamiltons in particular. The Chancellor had frequently to call for order, beating his gavel. James was restive, he having no love for Angus. Presently he intervened from the throne, and declared that it was his royal will and command that the lordship of Liddesdale, with its mighty stronghold of Hermitage Castle, and Angus's position as one of the wardens of the Marches, was to be transferred to Patrick, Earl of Bothwell, since anyone with links with the King of England was highly unsuitable to be in part charge of the borders area. As further evidence of his enmity to Angus, he pointed out that after the murder of his father, James the Third, much of the royal jewellery and treasures had been placed in the hands of so-called faithful and responsible persons, including Archibald of Angus, and some considerable portion of this had disappeared, and there were questions as to who had purloined it. He left it at that, but the issue had its effect on the gathering.

Parliament had to concern itself with all the usual issues of appointments and offices, tax details, trading privileges and the like, these taking up much time. Andrew sat through it all, his mind tending to be on other matters. But he frequently looked up at the gallery.

When at last it was over, and James rose, all present standing also when the monarch stood, Andrew presently found the Lyon King of Arms coming to tell him that he and his wife were invited down to Holyrood to dine with His Grace.

There they found themselves part of only a very small company consisting of the Master of the Household, Patrick, Earl of Bothwell, and his wife, Mariota, and themselves. Patrick Hepburn had been the Lord Hailes until created earl by James, he who had led the heir to the throne's army at Sauchieburn. Ever close to James, he made good company; and his wife and Beth got on well. A pleasant evening was passed, especially for Andrew when the monarch announced that, in gratitude for all his services, and particularly for all those cannon purchased for the royal fortresses – which he would pay for as funds became available from his treasury – he was bestowing on his admiral the additional lands of North Fawfield, in Fife, and parts of the baronies of Broughton in Edinburgh and Restalrig in the vicinity of Leith, this to provide a worthy house to dwell in when, as so often, he was based there.

They discussed details of the mission to the continental nations and courts, and in especial to Rome, where James announced that he desired Pope Innocent to make Bishop Robert Blackadder of Glasgow an archbishop, this well deserved, but also to help counter the sway of William Scheves, Archbishop of St Andrews, the astrologer and alchemist friend of the late king, who was proving to be something of a problem, and appointing his peculiar associates to offices in Holy Church, to the offence of other senior prelates. Blackadder, a most worthy and reliable cleric, as archbishop, could help the other bishops and mitered abbots to prevent this.

The two ladies present announced that they wished to accompany the four envoys on their progress to foreign lands, although they were not so sure about visiting the Vatican. Their husbands made no objections. They would ask the Earl Marischal if he would care to bring his lady also. James said that he wished that he himself could have gone with them, but this would not do for the monarch; and anyway, he could not be away from his kingdom for any such lengthy period.

It was decided that the two vessels, *Caravel* and *Flower*, were all that was necessary for conveying this embassage, the other ships more usefully engaged in trading ventures. They would set off in some ten days' time, from Leith.

It was quite a large and distinguished company that embarked, in due course, the two earls, with their wives and Beth, and Robert Blackadder. The bishop was a man of middle years, strong-featured but amiable, and with a notable sense of humour, making an excellent travelling companion. Andrew managed to install them all in cabins on *Caravel*. They would visit France first.

The French monarch, Charles the Eighth, would presumably be found at the palace-stronghold of the Louvre in Paris. Unlike the Low Countries, waterways were not so convenient for large vessels in France; but James Barton had been there more than once, and said that the great River Seine would be wide and deep enough to bring them to Paris.

They entered the estuary of the Seine at Le Havre, and found that they had to sail eastwards rather than southwards at first, to pass Harfleur, where it began to narrow to become a river, and a very winding one with great bends, not unlike the Forth in the Bannockburn and Stirling area, but wider and deeper. Nor were there any hills to vary the views of rich farmlands and pastures, with many communities of an obviously large population. Although it was only some seventy miles, as the birds flew, from the sea to Paris, because of all the windings and bends it proved to be fully double that distance. There was quite considerable traffic on the river, but nothing like the numbers of barges to be passed on the Netherlands canals.

They halted for their first night in France at Rouen, where the river did turn south, a large city with great warehouses and ample dock space. They proceeded next day, without delay, for Paris. At that great and splendid metropolis they had no difficulty in finding the Louvre, a huge citadel. There they learned that King Charles the Eighth was presently, of all places, back at Rouen, meeting certain of his dukes and counts. It was not known just when he would return.

The Scots party spent the night in their ships, and filled in the next day visiting and admiring the sights of the capital, all duly impressed. But when, the day following, there was still no sign of the monarch, they decided to sail back to Rouen. If Charles was meantime heading for Paris again, they would surely recognise the royal ship.

They saw nothing resembling such on their return sail. But, docking at Rouen, there was a most handsome vessel, sails painted with the lilies of France, just drawing out of the harbour area and heading south. So there was nothing for it but to turn round and follow it back to Paris, a ridiculous performance indeed.

They reached King Charles eventually back in the Louvre. He proved to be a young man of twenty-four years, interested to meet the Scots, and behaving with all but excessive gallantry towards the ladies, this despite the presence of his queen, Anne of Brittany who, slightly older than himself, seemed to accept it all as normal.

They were allotted rich quarters in the palace, and treated to what amounted to a banquet. But the monarch seemed only mildly concerned with the envoys' mission, declaring that France's alliance with Scotland was ages old and required no confirming by himself. He was off next day, apparently, to the Touraine area, and they were welcome to come with him if so they wished – and it was at the females that he looked invitingly. The husbands and the bishop however made suitably courteous excuses to the effect that they were heading on for Portugal and then Rome, and time was important in their lengthy mission. That night, after much dancing and entertainment, the husbands felt that it might be as well that their wives were kept close.

In the morning farewells were said, kissings among the salutations, and it was back to the ships for more of the Seine navigation to reach the Norse Sea again, and onward, now westwards for the Atlantic. Andrew was quite glad to be spared more of river-sailing, with all the bends and the picking of their way through the small-craft traffic, however much of interest it provided for the passengers.

In due course they rounded the great headland of Ushant, and, among the tossings of the mighty ocean rollers, turned south to cross the vast Bay of Biscay, notorious for its tides and storms, Portugal ahead.

Now, indeed, they were seeing Portuguese warships frequently, some of them coming close, to hail, but none actually challenging these two most evidently powerful and cannon-equipped vessels flying Scottish banners. The Portuguese, great adventurers and explorers, sailing far and wide to Africa and even India, more so than any other nation in Christendom, had no doubt heard of Andrew Wood the pirate-slayer. For his part, Andrew much respected these people.

Reaching the south end of Biscay, at the aptly named Cape Finisterre, they commenced the two-hundred-mile sail down the Portuguese coastline, past Bouro, Oporto and Estramadura, making for Lisbon, the capital, this at the mouth of the Tagus estuary. King Alfonso had died a few years before, and his son John only months later, leaving a cousin, young Manuel, to reign. He was said to be desirous of emulating his great-uncle, Prince Henry the Navigator, whose explorations were famous; but meanwhile he had his aunt, widow of Alfonso and mother of John, to guide him, this with the aid of another explorer, Vasco da Gama.

They found the Tagus estuary crowded with shipping, Andrew interested to note the cannon evident on them all,

Hans Poppenruyter having declared that the Portuguese were his best customers.

Lisbon, although not so large and fine a city as Paris, was more obviously wealthy, signs of this and of artefacts from distant lands everywhere. The envoys, at the palace, were told that the young king was off watching a bull fight on the outskirts, but ought to be back before long; but meanwhile Queen Joan would entertain them. This proved to be an obviously strong-minded woman who, it seemed, was more or less acting as regent for the youthful monarch.

It quickly became clear to the visitors that Queen Joan was the real ruler here, and that such negotiations as might be necessary would have to be conducted with her rather than with Manuel. In her sixties, she made the position very clear.

She was in full agreement that the English, under this Henry Tudor, had to be kept in their place; not that they represented any real threat to Portugal and its overseas territories, but their privateers could be a nuisance, especially where trade with the Low Countries and the Baltic was concerned. As to any sort of alliance with France in this respect, she and da Gama were less sure. King Charles of France was a headstrong young man, and arrogant. And he was laying claim to the kingdom of Naples, near to Rome, to the anxiety of the Vatican, and this could much upset the peace of the entire southern Europe and Mediterranean area. Portugal loyally supported the Pontiff; and there could be a clash with France over this. All the papal states were worried.

The Scots perceived that their Auld Alliance partnership with France could possibly involve them in trouble with the Pope, this much concerning Bishop Blackadder. They would have to go warily, it seemed.

When young Manuel returned from his bull fighting, he proved to be an impulsive and somewhat light-headed character, but clearly under the thumb of his aunt. There seemed no need greatly to concern themselves with him.

Queen Joan's attention to the Scots wives was little short of contemptuous. A dominant and almost masculine female, she practically ignored them. Beth made not a few significant faces at her husband during their visit. Not that they were not well catered for by servants.

The wives urged a speedy move on from Lisbon. The men were not averse.

Their journey thereafter took them almost one hundred and fifty miles southwards, to round Cape St Vincent and then across the great Gulf of Cadiz, with an eastwards trend now, to head for the narrows of the Strait of Gibraltar, representing the entrance to the Middle Sea. It was all new waters for Andrew and his crews, and much intrigued them, especially when presently they could see what must be the northern coast of Africa looming before them – Africa, almost another world.

They had all heard of the Rock of Gibraltar, and were not disappointed at the vast upthrust of it, rising to well over one thousand feet in pointed majesty, making even the Craig of Bass in their own Forth seem modest in comparison. It was said to be penetrated by numerous caves, one being called the Hall of St Michael; and there were reputed to be monkeys, Barbary apes, living on this strange island. The ladies were disappointed at not being able to catch a glimpse of any such, passing below, Andrew much too preoccupied with steering to peer up.

Once into the Mediterranean, they still had a lengthy voyage ahead of them to reach Rome, almost one thousand miles it was calculated, due eastwards. Now they were spared the heavings and tossings of the Atlantic, and the air was noticeably warmer. There were still numbers of Portuguese ships to be seen.

In time they passed the Balearic Isles of Ibiza, Majorca and Minorca, and thereafter sailed out of sight of any land for a full day and night's cautious navigation before they reached the great island of Sardinia, over one hundred miles of it, its own kingdom. Then a further almost two hundred miles across the Tyrrhenian Sea to the Gulf of Gaeta where lay Naples, the kingdom which was the focus of so much controversy and clamour, and which Charles of France was claiming now as his own, this to the alarm of the Vatican. Rome lay to the north, some one hundred and fifty miles.

So now Andrew swung away, destination none so far off.

As they neared Rome, Robert Blackadder, who had made excellent company for them all throughout, became notably silent, his good humour replaced by a sort of heaviness, which Andrew for one found odd. After all, the bishop was on his way to see the Pope, his Master-in-God, and should be looking forward to this, and to his recommended promotion to archbishop. But it seemed as though he had his doubts. Andrew did comment, privately, on his evident reservations, and he admitted that he felt in something of a quandary. It was the reputation of this Pontiff, Borgia, Alexander the Sixth, which worried him. Andrew had heard of this, of course; all Christendom had. He had gained his appointment on the death of Pope Innocent by bribing the cardinals; and his personal life was notorious. He had five illegitimate sons, by different women; and he had cruel tastes. Yet he was head of Holy Church, and as such held a power greater than kings. The bishop did not seek to hide his knowledge of it all; but declared that all popes were not necessarily saints. But then, *all* men were sinners, and the Almighty had to deal with that, and consequently must use sinners to do His will. He, Blackadder, was a sinner. He agreed that God's will would be better done and His people led by saints. But presumably the Creator, although He had made mankind in His own image, had to accept them behaving even so. For himself, as a bishop, he had to endeavour to distinguish between man and office. It was the Pontiff, not Borgia, he was going to see on this mission.

Andrew shook his head over it all, scarcely comprehending. But he admired and respected Blackadder, and wished him well.

They came to the estuary of the Tiber, and turned therein, to sail the fifteen miles up to Rome, this through fertile and pleasing country, with much shipping to pass.

They found the renowned city, not quite so large as Naples but splendid indeed, placed on both sides of the wide river, set among seven small hills, and all within great walls said to be no fewer than twelve miles in circumference, these called the Aurelian, dating from the third century; and the Leonine somewhat later, this last including the Vatican City, in a sort of separate suburb. Because of stone bridges, they could not get their ships nearer than a mile from their destination. So the party had to disembark. They would leave the bishop to go and visit the Pope by himself, even though in theory all the envoys ought to do so; but Blackadder was highly capable and could do all that was necessary without their presence. Andrew, with Beth and the two earls and their countesses, would meantime explore the sights of this the most ancient city of Europe.

They were soon, in fact, all but lost in wonder and admiration for everything they saw: the Colosseum; the amphitheatres for gladiatorial combat; the triumphal arches commemorating various emperors; the great churches including the Basilica of St Peter, reputed to be the largest cathedral in the world, many of these built on the sites of ancient pagan temples; the aqueducts, no fewer than fourteen of these; the public squares, parks, formal gardens, even vineyards, all within these walls; an experience to leave the visitors all but speechless, however voluble some were when they started out. The ladies bought trinkets and keepsakes from the stalls in the paved streets, squares and even in the churches themselves, of which there were said to be one hundred in this city.

When eventually they got back to their ships, it was to find Blackadder already there. He was noticeably silent over his interview with the Pontiff, but admitted that he was now Archbishop of Glasgow, this with a deprecating shake of the head – a modest man.

Later he told Andrew that he had gained all the authority that King James had sought, Pope Alexander evidently interested mainly in the gifts James had sent him.

Their mission accomplished, to what value remained to be seen, the envoys set off on their return to Scotland. Whatever else, it had been a highly educative voyage, in more ways than one, Holy Church's situation in especial seen to be in grave need of reform, the new archbishop made the more aware of that. Andrew had come to recognise the power and spirit and initiative of the Portuguese, and what was to be learned from them in naval as in other matters. As for Beth, she said that she could now boast that she had travelled far and wide in the company of the Earl Marischal of Scotland, the Master of the Royal Household, the Archbishop of Glasgow and the Admiral of Scotland. The daughter of the Lundies had stepped up in the world!

17

King James, inspired by Andrew's initiatives and successes, indeed all but jealous of them, issued orders that every port in the land of sufficient size to build vessels should do so, not mere fishing-boats, and make these capable of acting in warlike fashion, with gunports for cannon, these to defend themselves against English privateers and to support merchant vessels. The great warship that he was building at Leith, the *Great Michael*, after long delays because of the monarch's over-enthusiastic changes in its planning, was now all but complete, having cost a vast sum, to the upset of the Lord Treasurer. This was to give a lead, and these others to be built were to support it, forming a large naval fleet. This fervour was scarcely shared by the nobility and magnates, nor the burghal leaders, and progress in obeying was slow and moderate indeed. So his admiral was commanded to forward the policy and to see to the completion of the *Michael*, and even though it was not entirely finished, to sail it round the ports of the land to give a lead in the matter.

Andrew was in fact distinctly doubtful about this huge and expensive vessel ordered by his monarch. It was, in his opinion, just too large and unwieldy for practical purposes, and required too many men to man it. And its draught was too great, deep, to allow it to enter shallower waters, so that it was much limited in entering estuaries and the like, wherein most ports were sited. But royal commands had to be obeyed; and, being made temporarily its captain and James Barton its lieutenant, he had duly to take James on an initial sail – it could not be termed a voyage – round the Fife ports and havens and up to those on the Tay, finding the great vessel awkward to manage indeed and unable to reach most of the havens desired. But the king was much elated over his creation despite this, and sought to show off the craft, if often only at a distance.

This enthusiasm for matters maritime was heightened by the word that was stirring all Europe in those years of the late fifteenth century, the exciting discoveries of new and distant lands beyond the seas, this over and above those already reached by the Portuguese. Two explorers in particular were making names for themselves in this, both as it happened from Genoa, one called Giovanni, or John, Cabot, who had come to settle in England, at Bristol, as more conveniently sited for his ventures; the other named Christopher Columbus. These rival seafarers were vying with each other, both believing that they could reach the all-but-fabled India by sailing westwards rather than eastwards through their own Mediterranean Sea. Cabot and his son Sebastian were claiming to have reached Labrador, naming it thus as meaning cultivable land, and its people Indians. Columbus, further south, had come to far-distant islands inhabited by strange, heathen folk called Caribs, that is their menfolk, the women speaking a different tongue called Arawak, this seeming scarcely believable. He claimed this land for Christ, naming it Salvador instead of the Indian Cusculan.

Andrew, to be sure, was interested in these resounding exploratory voyages, but had no real desire to emulate them, *his* concern to maintain Scotland's naval power in waters nearer home. King James, on the other hand, was talking about using his *Great Michael* to lead a crusade against the Turks who were occupying parts of the Holy Land. This Andrew strongly advised against.

There came word from Archbishop Robert Blackadder urging Andrew, whose influence with the monarch was well known, to use it to prevent James from appointing his brother, the Duke of Ross, aged twenty-one, to succeed William Scheves, who had died, as Archbishop of St Andrews, Primate of Holy Church in Scotland, that young man not even in holy orders. This admittedly would require papal acceptance, but after their recent experience with the present Pontiff and his pleasure over James's gifts, this would be apt to be forthcoming. Blackadder was much distressed over this, and declared that the good Bishop Elphinstone of Aberdeen would make the ideal Primate, not the young Ross.

Andrew had no wish to get involved in Church affairs, but recognised that this proposed appointment was unwise, and did speak to James on the matter. But the king brushed objections aside, saying that the churchmen had got altogether too powerful in the land, and this of his brother as Primate would help to keep them in order. He added that the archbishopric of St Andrews received the revenues of the wealthy abbeys of Holyrood, Dunfermline and Arbroath, which his brother would largely pass on to the crown, and which would be greatly appreciated by the treasurer. Also help to pay debts for the *Great Michael*.

James, for his part, desired his admiral's help. John, Lord of the Isles, had recently died, and had been succeeded by his grandson Donald. And this young man had promptly renewed his grandfather's league with Henry Tudor. James had forfeited him as Earl of Ross, as was suitable since there was now a royal duke thereof. But that had not worried the Islesman, and he was now encroaching further on the lands of Wester Ross, and this must be stopped. A naval expedition to the Isles was called for, Andrew to take him, the king, on it.

This demand could not be refused, however unlikely it was to result in any improvement in the situation. And it was pointed out to the monarch that the Islesmen's longships and birlinns, oared, narrow vessels by the hundred, were perhaps the most speedy and navigable craft on the seas, and although not equipped with cannon could be a menace indeed. Was such royal demonstration really necessary? After all, the Lords of the Isles had been acting independent princes for centuries. But James was determined. It was really a gesture against the English, a warning to Henry. James was planning to conclude a seven-year and possibly permanent peace with England, and this move through the Isles could well help with that.

So it was another sail around Scotland's mainland to the Isles, with the king aboard *Caravel*, Beth banned from accompanying them on this occasion on account of the danger from those longships – although the last thing that Andrew wanted was to get involved in battle with the Islesmen. It was to be hoped that this journey with the monarch would not produce that. It was only to be a gesture of the royal presence, even though he, Andrew, considered it unnecessary. It occurred to him that he might well make token cannonades of blank shot at various focal points, just as a demonstration and warning, since artillery-fire was the one thing that the longships could not match.

This, presently, they did, from *Caravel* and *Flower*, starting the noise off Stornoway on the Outer Isle of Lewis. They proceeded south to do the same off the two Uists, no challenge from longships nor galleys forthcoming. Then across to Skye, with three demonstrations off that large island. Here longships did put in an appearance, these from Dunvegan of the MacLeods, but kept their distance. James landed here, with Andrew and a party of his crewmen as escort, this to inform that important chief that he claimed the Isles as part of his Scotland, and expected no liaison with the English. But he was going to propose a pact with Henry Tudor, who was having trouble with his nobles, and might well be glad to be at peace with Scotland meantime. Their next call was at Armadale of Sleat, of the MacDonalds. Longships were in evidence again, but repeated blasts of gunfire served their purpose, and no actual contact was attempted.

They sailed over to Rhum, Eigg and Muick, to use the same tactics, then south again to pass Mull and head for Islay, the main base of the lordship, where they hoped to find the successor to John of the Isles, who had died the year before.

It was strange for Andrew to be taking the son of his late monarch to meet the grandson of the Lord of the Isles they had visited those years before. But at Loch Finlaggan they found this Donald to be very different from his dominant grandfather, a cheerful young man, as yet easy to deal with, hospitable and being guided by his mother, Mary Gunn, daughter of the chief of that Sutherland clan, and widow of Hugh who had died before his father John. She, not being an Isleswoman herself, was obviously impressed by being visited by the monarch, and proved entirely helpful, and would clearly guide her son to be likewise. Here was success for the entire expedition, to the king's elation, whatever else they achieved.

They remained two days and nights at Finlaggan, well entertained.

Then on down the west coast of the great Kintyre peninsula, this for long a source of dispute. Ever since the Norse King Magnus Barefoot had had his ship dragged over the mile of high ground between West Loch Tarbert on the Atlantic side and East Loch Tarbert on the sea loch of Fyne, this to claim that he could sail his ship round all Kintyre, and Robert the Bruce had emulated this later, the Islesmen had claimed it as theirs, although it was part of mainland Scotland – an old story. The Kings of Scots, of course, asserted that it was clearly theirs. It was a fertile and valuable seventy miles of country, nine miles wide of an average, and not to be lightly given up. The competition for it was still relevant, for the Campbell Earl of Argyll in theory lawfully owned it, whatever the Islesmen said, but had much difficulty in maintaining his overlordship. Since he was now Chancellor of the realm, and presided at parliaments, James felt that it was necessary that he should be supported. Some demonstration, therefore, was called for.

At the Mull of Kintyre, the very southern tip of the peninsula, Dunaverty Castle stood on its headland proclaiming, under its Campbell keeper, its dominance. Here James wanted to land, and support Campbell with the royal authority.

But Dunaverty was not the easiest place to reach, part of the reason for its being there, on a lofty cliff-top above the waves, facing across to Ulster. There was nowhere below to moor ships on the rocky shore lashed by the Atlantic rollers. But there was the small island of Sanda a couple of miles to the south, with a bay where vessels could anchor, the intervening channel having to be crossed in the ships' small boats.

So the king had to be ferried over, tossing in the waves, to land at a tiny shingly beach and climb the steep ascent, zigzagging up the cliff. James made no complaint. He was fit and active, and enjoyed all life's challenges.

At the castle the Campbell keeper and his family were astonished to be visited by the King of Scots, they apt to see little of strangers in their eagle's-nest of a hold, even Argyll himself but seldom there. James explained that he had come to emphasise that this peninsula was part of his mainland realm, not Isles territory. He was going to order Argyll to install a sizeable garrison here, to base itself not in the castle of course but nearby at Southend and Machrihanish. He would supply the hold with cannon to ward off longships, all of Kintyre to be patrolled. And to help pay for this, the Campbell was to be given the northern part, Knapdale, all but an island in itself created by those Lochs Tarbert, with the royal castle of Sween, forfeited by MacNeill of Gigha, one of the late John of the Isles supporters.

Approving of all this, and hoping that Argyll could maintain it, Andrew set sail northwards again, for Leith and home.

18

The great change from the fifteenth to the sixteenth century occurred that winter, and the king, if not the nation at large, celebrated it by making one of his pilgrimages to the shrine of St Duthac at Tain in Easter Ross. After the death of his father, for which he blamed himself, he had established the two shrines, south and north, at Isle of Whithorn in Galloway, and at Tain. Whithorn could be fairly readily reached, on horseback, but Tain was a different matter, three hundred and fifty miles from Stirling. So he was apt to visit the former more often. Now he would make a journey to Tain, and pay his respects. And, to be sure, his admiral could take him conveniently by ship.

There was no point in using the larger warships for this mission. The monarch was content to be taken north in the *Kestrel* that late February.

The site of St Duthac's, or Dubthach's shrine, that Celtic missionary who had been named the Chief Confessor of Ireland and Scotland, and who had died in 1065, had been marked in 1221 by the establishment of a small abbey by one of the Earls of Ross, to say prayers for his soul. This near to Edderton, almost three miles inland from the nearest anchorage at Shandwick Bay. Horses would have to be found thereabouts.

Andrew had never been to Fearn, where was the abbey, knew little about St Duthac and was not greatly interested. But Beth was, for she wanted to be taken also. So what started out as a royal pilgrimage of repentance developed into something of a holiday for the Woods and the *Kestrel*'s crew.

Shandwick Bay lay three miles south of Tain on the Moray Firth coast north of the Black Isle of Cromarty. Andrew's ships had passed here frequently of course but never halted. He recognised that there were innumerable placcs of interest along the coasts he skirted but of which he knew naught. Here was one small opportunity to learn, in the cause of duty.

James told them that Duthac, like Columba four centuries earlier, was an Irish bishop who felt the need to go as a missionary to Scotland, around the year 1050. His influence had been almost entirely in the north.

From Leith up to Shandwick Bay took two days and nights' sailing, and in the February weather the seas were distinctly rough. The king admitted that he normally rode all the way, calling in at Stobhall Castle near to Perth where he was friendly with the Lord Drummond's daughter Margaret; he admitted, grinning, that she indeed had a child by him. But she and her sisters were presently visiting their mother's family, that of the Earl of Montrose, near to Glasgow, and so this pilgrimage was being made by sea, with his admiral's favour.

At Shandwick they found a small fishing and crofting community where they were able to borrow six rough garrons to carry the monarch, Beth, Andrew, James Barton and two crewmen the three miles inland, rounding the Hill of Fearn, to the abbey. They found it pleasingly situated below the hill, no large establishment, consisting of an elderly abbot and a dozen monks of the Premonstratensian Order, a remote monkish fane now, but formerly quite important, Duthac having been highly thought of for his piety, missionary enthusiasm and founding of places of worship. Heathen Norse raiders had decimated the area later, sadly, and the abbey had been sacked more than once, but thankfully those days were over.

The brethren but seldom had visitors, pilgrimage place as it was; indeed this monarch was perhaps their most frequent as well as most distinguished pilgrim. Andrew and Beth were interested in this aspect of James Stewart's character. He could scarcely be called a holy young man, and his activities and interests, however enthusiastically pursued, did not tend to be religious. But his feelings of guilt over his father's death remained strong, possibly because James the Third *had* been that way inclined. Andrew rather wondered at it, for after all it was the Lord Gray who had stabbed that monarch to death after Sauchieburn, and the son ought not to blame himself, even though he had led the opposing army at that battle. Beth thought that his pilgrimages were partly to give him an excuse to visit his lady friends, not only Margaret Drummond, but Flaming Janet Kennedy, the daughter of the Lord Kennedy, at Dunure Castle in Ayrshire, conveniently on the way to and from the other pilgrimage destination of Whithorn in Galloway.

At any rate, they were all made welcome by the monks, however unusual it was to have a woman visitor. James made his devotions at the shrine, presented gifts to the abbot, and they returned to the *Kestrel*, duty done.

They arrived back at Leith to learn that envoys had arrived from England, sent by Henry Tudor. They brought proposals, highly important proposals. The King of England was beset by troubles, France's Charles becoming ever more aggressive, the English nobility restive and refusing to pay their feudal dues, the Portuguese assailing English privateers. Peace with Scotland would be of great advantage, perpetual peace. To this end he proposed marriage between his daughter, the Princess Margaret Tudor, and the King of Scots.

Astonished, James heard this. There had been talk for long, of course, of the monarch's desirable marriage to some European princess, despite his affections for Margaret Drummond and Janet Kennedy. Neither of these was of a rank to be queen; that position must be reserved for one of royal blood. Now, here was one suggested, young as Margaret Tudor might be. And peace with England. Henry was suggesting a meeting between representatives of the two monarchs at the borderline, to discuss the matter.

James considered. Bishop Elphinstone, former Chancellor and now Lord Privy Seal, advised it. Archbishop Blackadder, another respected adviser, recommended it. Peace with England was something to be sought for indeed, and this match ought to ensure it. No other princess would bring Scotland a like advantage. And Margaret Tudor, little more than a child, would not interfere with James's relationships with Margaret Drummond and Janet Kennedy. He came to the conclusion that this marriage was probably the best he could make.

So it was agreed to send emissaries to meet English ones, as suggested, at the border. He would not have his representatives to have to cross into England to make the arrangements; let the English come into *his* realm, he the monarch, she only the daughter of one, say at Coldinghame Priory or at Ayton, just into the Merse, across Tweed, and there meet with his representatives.

Andrew found himself appointed to be one of these, with the local Earl of Home, the Earl of Bothwell and Bishop Elphinstone. So it constituted a horseback journey for once, not a seaborne one.

At Ayton, on the Eye Water, seven miles north of Berwick-upon-Tweed, they awaited the arrival of the English. These proved to be Howard, Earl of Surrey, English Earl Marshal, and the Prince-Bishop of Durham, with a train of knights. The meeting was really only a formality, with little to discuss, save agreement on a betrothal, financial arrangements, and dowery lands for the new queen-to-be, the Pope apparently willing to agree that distant consanguinity, through the marriage of James the First and English Joan Beaufort, could be accepted. The date for the wedding was debated. A feast-day would be apt, in August the following year. The Name Day of

Our Lord would be suitable, but that, 7th August, was a Sunday. Make it the 8th, then, the bride by then just having passed her fourteenth birthday, the actual cere-mony to be at Holyrood Abbey.

Reporting back to James, all was approved.

Beth wondered how their royal friend, experienced as he was as to relationships with women, would deal with a child bride?

The eighth day of August 1503, duly dawned. The day before, a large party of notables awaited the princess at Berwick-upon-Tweed, the officers of state, including the admiral, seven earls, four prelates under Archbishop Blackadder – interested to be close to the river from which he took his name – numerous lords and magnates, with their womenfolk also, so that the girl would not be left without feminine company, Beth among these.

It was an English host that arrived, over four hundred lords and knights bringing the bride, under Surrey and the Prince-Bishop, Margaret Tudor, dressed in great finery as she was, seeming a very small focal point for all this display.

It was only midday, and it was decided to move on from Berwick. James was to await their arrival at Dalkeith, near to Edinburgh, to conduct her to Holyrood Abbey for the nuptials; but that was too far for so large a company to travel in one day. So, the Merse being Home country, the earl thereof for some reason decided that the queen-to-be's first night in Scotland should be spent, not at his castle of Ayton, too near Berwick, nor at Coldinghame Priory, but at his Fast Castle, none so far from St Abb's Head. This, in all probability, was a mischievous device to humble the proud English lords, especially those of Northumberland with whom he was constantly at feud, for Fast was not approachable on horseback, situated halfway down one of the mighty cliffs of that Merse coastline. They would have to walk, all but clamber, for almost a mile. That would teach them! Home was that sort of a man.

They were taught indeed. Protests, and not only from the English, were expressed when, at the large farmery of Dowlaw, all were told to dismount and leave their steeds and grooms there. The richly clad company left no doubt as to its disapproval, whatever young Margaret and her ladies thought. The lords were told that if they preferred to remain near their mounts, there was plenty of accommodation at the Dowlaw cottages, sheds, hay-barns and stables, there on Coldinghame Moor.

It did not take them all long thereafter to recognise why they had to leave their beasts behind. Abruptly they came to drama, the edge of enormous cliffs dropping sheerly hundreds of feet to the waves, with only a narrow winding track along the crest. Unprepared for this, all stared, Andrew and Beth with them, the clerics in particular shaken. What now? Where?

They learned. Along that dizzy cliff-top track they had to string out, for a few hundred yards, until they came to a dip, a descent, itself fairly steep. And beyond, there thrust a headland, tall and sheer; and halfway down its face a stack-like projection jutted out above the spray of the waves. Crowning this horn of rock rose a castle, its red-stone towers soaring up among the screaming clouds of seafowl, a sight to be seen indeed. All gazed.

At that sight, and Home's grinning onwards-waving, not a few decided that he had been helpful in recommending possible remaining at Dowlaw farm. They turned back, this including many of the women and clerics. Not Beth however. Grasping Andrew's arm, and chuckling, she headed on after Home and his Borders colleagues.

Down that dip they picked their way towards Fast Castle, amidst exclamations and cries, the which were drowned in the screechings of the seabirds that haunted these cliffs in their thousands.

How many would that extraordinary castle hold? she asked Andrew. He shrugged, and said that it was as well that not a few had turned back, whatever the accommodation might be like at the farm.

Some of the others did turn now, likewise. No doubt Home had relied on this reaction. But – what a place to bring the English princess for her first night in Scotland! What sort of a land had she come to? she must wonder. Home was clearly getting his own back on the English, after years of cross-border conflict.

When those who so elected got down close to the castle on its spur, they discovered that a yawning gap had to be crossed to reach it. A narrow drawbridge, presently lowered, spanned this, but with no handrail, even of rope, to comfort crossers. Andrew took Beth's arm as they edged over.

The fortalice, once entered through that dizzy gatehouse arch, proved to be larger than it had seemed at first sight, this because it occupied various levels of the cliff here, on narrow ledges and projections not obvious from a distance, so that there were possibly one hundred feet from the placing of the top towers to that of the lower ones. Even so, it was an astonishing site for a castle, and one to bring this company to.

Climbing up a rough stairway cut in the basic rock, the visitors reached a little yard, on which rose a tall square keep of four storeys and a garret within a parapeted wallhead, the main tower of the strength, although there were three others at different levels. They were led to a first-floor hall, up a winding turnpike stairway, Margaret Tudor being assisted up, the youngster's eyes round with continued astonishment and apprehension. Even with this thick walling, the high clamour of the circling birds was very evident; but as well now, there was a continual deep, pulsing booming, which seemed almost to shake the building. Lady Home explained that this was caused by a great cavern directly below into which the tides surged and waves broke. There was a stairway down into this cave cut through the rock entered from a trapdoor in the tower's basement, so that the hold, in case of siege, could be supplied by sea.

Even though most of the large company had remained on, or turned back to, the high ground, there was still a sufficiency to crowd the premises, plus the keeper's garrison. Only three other women than Beth had got thus far with the queen-to-be: Home's countess and two others of the same rank, the Ladies Bothwell and Keith-Marischal, who had more or less apparently appointed themselves ladies-in-waiting to Margaret Tudor. Now the five females found themselves allotted a second-floor chamber containing one large bed and a smaller one. But at least there was warm water awaiting them, and a maid to attend to their needs, or such as she might. None of course had been able to bring any baggage with them, all such left up at the farm with the horses. They would just have to roost here overnight as best they could, wagging their heads over it all as they attended to their toilets in the two garderobes.

Margaret Tudor asked if most Scottish castles were like this one?

There was a surprisingly excellent repast awaiting them in the great hall presently, fish and fowl and venison and sweetmeats, with wines and ale, which proved that the cavern below provided adequate access for supplies by boat. Home and his wife made worthy hosts, and there were even two minstrels, with lutes, to entertain them with sung Border ballads. Beth and Andrew had no complaints to make as to their hospitality, save that they were unable to spend the night together, the castle's accommodation being over-full; indeed they were bedded down in different towers.

It took some time for Andrew, for one, to sleep that night, not aided by one who shared a bed with him, an English lord, snoring. Beth did rather better.

In the morning, it was back up the steep ascent to the farm and their fellows and the horses, some of that company with their fine clothes creased and speckled with oat-husks and bits of straw after a night among the hay, however unsuitable for such folk. Thankful to be mounted again, all set off for Dalkeith, where King James was to await his bride.

They found him at the Douglas castle on the outskirts of that town, and he saw his bride for the first time, a strange meeting. For, in theory, they were already man and wife, this because they had been married by proxy at the Vatican. Their greetings were briefly formal, whatever each might think of the other. Without undue delay a move was made for the six miles to Edinburgh and Holyrood Abbey.

Bishop Elphinstone was to perform the nuptial ceremony, being Lord Privy Seal, although Archbishop Blackadder was present, this a somewhat unusual service since they were already wed, according to papal dispensation. The girl was presented to James at the chancel steps by Surrey, representing her father, amidst chorister-singing before a crowded church, the new queen looking nervous, the monarch seeming all out amused. Beth whispered that *she* judged it but play-acting, no real wedding. After the ring-bestowal, James's brother, the Duke of Ross who stood behind him, handed over hardly a crown but a gold circlet, which the king placed on the girl's head. And that was that. Scotland had a queen again, however unqueenly she seemed.

A benediction was pronounced upon them and all present, and the royal couple led the distinguished company out, and over to a banquet prepared by the Abbot of Holyrood, amidst speeches of congratulation and well-wishing.

Beth observed that although the Lords Drummond and Kennedy were both present, neither of their daughters was.

With all the visitors to be housed overnight, the abbey's accommodation was stretched to the limit, and some of the guests had to find lodgings in the nearby Canongate of the city.

For his part, Andrew took Beth down to Leith, where *Kestrel* was awaiting them. They would sleep comfortably in their cabin aboard, and be back over to Largo in the morning.

19

A dire tragedy shocked Scotland that next spring. Margaret Drummond and her two sisters died, poisoned — at least that had to be assumed, since all three suddenly died at the same time; and it could not be the food that they had eaten, for none of the servants who had eaten similarly was affected. The sisters had been at the new Drummond Castle in Strathearn, which their father had built from his older seat at Stobhall, and there, after eating and drinking, had collapsed. Most folk believed that this had been done by Henry Tudor's orders, he resentful that his daughter, now Queen Margaret, should have rivals for her husband's attentions, and somehow arranged for the young women to die thus.

James was devastated, and vowed that he would make the English pay for it, peace or no peace. And he sent urgent warning to Flaming Janet Kennedy, at Dunure in Ayrshire, to be aware lest she too became a target.

The new queen's popularity, never high, sank to a new low.

It was soon after this outrage that Andrew was sent by the monarch on a mission to aid his uncle, King John of Denmark, who was having trouble with his rebellious Swedish subjects. These were assailing Danish traders and ships sailing to Lübeck, and Andrew's familiarity with that area made him apt for the task. This young King John was a grandson of Christian the Second and brother of Scotland's late Queen Margaret, James's mother, who had married James the Third. Andrew was to demonstrate to the Swedes that the youthful monarch was not to be opposed.

In the circumstances, it was not an occasion for Beth to accompany her husband. But a brief trip up to Iceland, to collect more ivory to be sold at Lübeck, had to serve as compensation.

In due course, then, the *Caravel*, *Flower* and *Kestrel* sailed across the Norse Sea, well laden with powder and ball, to reach Danish and Swedish waters. Andrew was uncertain as to where to find King John, and where best to emphasise the Scots support. Sweden was a large country, with a great Baltic coastline as well as that facing the Skagerrak and Kattegat. Probably, then, a call at Gothenburg, off the latter, and then at Lübeck, before searching for him up the Baltic mainland of Sweden. It was all fairly familiar waters for Andrew.

Gothenburg, a large seaport, was situated up the estuary of the River Gota Alv. They sailed up this, passing a number of merchant-ships, which gave them a wide berth even in such narrow waters, none seeking any sort of confrontation with obvious warships flying the saltire cross of St Andrew, which would be well enough known and respected these days. At Gothenburg itself there was no sign of Danish royal presence, so Andrew contented himself with firing off salvoes of blank shot, to emphasise authority in John's name, before turning back and heading for Lübeck.

There he sold the ivory for a satisfactory price. They learned that King John had been there only five days before, and was sailing up the Baltic, hopefully to intimidate his Swedish rebels. Whether he was landing here and there was not known.

Andrew had sailed some way in Baltic waters, of course, but had never actually followed the Swedish coast up the reputed thousand miles to the Gulf of Bothnia. The Baltic was a strange landlocked sea, shallow, of brackish not actual salt water, subject to quite strong north-easterly winds but calm compared with the waters Andrew and his crews were used to, short, choppy waves very different from the swells and rollers of the oceans. In winter there was pack- and drift-ice to contend with, and some of the ports were apt to be closed for a month or two in deep winter. These waters demanded much tacking and sail management for a progress northwards.

How far north must they go seeking King John? Stockholm, the Swedish capital, was three hundred miles up, and it seemed likely that this would be the king's main objective. But there were towns, apparently, even cities, much further north, with unspellable names. They could grasp the names of the four main territories of the land. The southern, fertile area nearest Denmark was called Skane. Then the mountainous Smaland. The central low-lying belt, where was Stockholm, was called Svealand. And the vast northern tracts, largely forested, suitably named Norrland. What Andrew was expected to do to aid King John in all this remained to be seen.

Stockholm first, then.

Passing the ports of Malmö, Kristianstad and Karlskrona, they came to an extraordinarily lengthy but very narrow island which their pilot called Oland, over one hundred miles of it but a mere ten or a dozen miles wide. Nothing apparently to concern them here. But soon thereafter, to the north-east, was another large island called Gotland, this, unlike Oland, quite populous. They drew in at the southern port of Burgsvik to enquire, and learned that the king had been there, yes, but proceeded on for Stockholm.

So to the capital they headed, another one hundred and fifty miles, entailing much tacking in the strong northerly winds.

This proved to be a fine city, on a sort of sea loch named Lake Malaren, built, they were told, on no fewer than twenty-two islets, with a royal palace, a cathedral and many tall-steepled churches, and magnates' handsome houses. But King John was not there either, although he had been, and had hanged a number of rebel nobles and their supporters, before heading on further north still. Just to emphasise a presence, and help for John, Andrew fired off a blank cannonade at the extensive dockland before moving.

It seemed that there was another large group of islands, strategically situated in mid-sea about seventy miles on, called the Alands, and probably John was there. They lay where the Baltic changed into the long Gulf of Bothnia to the north and the Gulf of Finland to the east, this last leading to Russia and St Petersburg.

It was at the Aland isles group that they found King John and his ships. The rebels were especially strong in Finland and the north, and here he was seeking to demonstrate his rightful authority, although not with any great success, with the Swedes strong on land and not contesting him on the sea.

John of Denmark was a very boyish monarch, smiling, hearty and enthusiastic, reminding Andrew of a younger version of James Stewart. He greeted the Scots warmly, and proclaimed his links with their land, although he had never been there. He confessed that he was not making much headway against these rebels, they strong in numbers and land-based. But he was grateful to his fellow-monarch of Scotland for sending this aid, although what more seamen could do was questionable. Andrew said that they would see. Where were these rebellious folk apt to be based?

He was told that they were indeed fairly nearby, along the north shore of the Gulf of Finland, which he had come here to threaten. But unfortunately they could retire into the great pine forests; and seeking to fight them there was scarcely practical, with these in larger numbers and, knowing the ground, able to make the land fight for them.

Andrew said that his cannon might be helpful.

John admitted that he had little experience of cannon, his ships not equipped with them.

The combined squadron sailed up the Gulf of Finland.

It was not long before they perceived the blue smokes of campfires ahead of them. The gunners were readied.

As they neared the foe, they could see large numbers of men settled quite close to the shore, indeed the forest reaching nearly thereto. Now for confrontation.

The land-based host showed no signs of alarm or fear at the approach of the ships, for to be sure they much out-numbered the seamen. Apart from massing near the water-side and shaking swords and axes and fists, their reaction was all but scornful.

That is, until Andrew drew his three vessels ahead of the Danish to sail as close inshore as he dared risk the depth. And there he gave his waiting gunners the signal.

The cannon crashed out in thunderous bombardment, not blank shot this time, but ball.

The impact was devastating, even frightening Andrew, as the forty-pound balls smashed through the ranks of the Swedes, mowing down men by the score in bloody horror, carving grim columns through the masses of men. On and on the cannonade continued, with culver-ins, sakers, bombards and demi-cannon all hurling ball at the foe. And not only actual ball, for Andrew had purchased some of Poppenruyter's newest weaponry, case-shot, whereby, within a thin-skinned ball, many bullet-sized missiles would burst out on firing, and scatter widely, doing far-flung damage in place of direct hits.

Quickly the Swedes recognised that they could do nothing to counter this long-range slaughter and, whether by orders or just in individual self-preservation, they began to flee off into the shelter of the forest. Soon only the dead and wounded, with arms and baggage, remained by the shore.

Was it of any use to land men to go after the enemy, into that great woodland? Andrew doubted it, with the Swedes and Finns vastly outnumbering the seamen. But King John obviously thought differently. He began to have boats lowered from all his seven ships, and have people rowed ashore.

Whether this could be an effective move, Andrew felt that he could hardly retain his own men aboard. But he certainly did not want to have them dispersed into the forest, where they would have to face the hidden foe, these used to land-fighting.

He ordered about half of his crewmen to land, and take with them some of the light demi-cannon, which could be carried in the boats, to pose a further threat, he going with them.

Ashore, he joined King John, and expressed his doubts about proceeding on into the endless forest where it would be all but impossible to maintain any sort of control. The king agreed that this presented a problem, but felt that some offensive had to be mounted. A line abreast, he advocated, to push slowly but steadily after the host of Swedes. It was unfortunate, he said, that the wind was consistently northerly, or they could have set fire to this part of the woodland, these pine trees burning readily, and so endangered and driven back the opposition, but in fact this would only hamper themselves. Andrew renewed his assertion that he was not prepared to have his men go any distance into the dense greenwood, and strongly advised the eager young monarch to say the same. These were not the conditions in which to seek a land battle. Reluctantly John acceded.

There, among the dead, dying and wounded Swedes and Finns, they formed up a long line of men from the Danish ships, with a contingent from the Scots, making almost eight hundred men. Strict orders to keep in close order, despite the trees, and advance cautiously, were given, teams of Andrew's men dragging the demi-cannon and ammunition.

But once among the trees it became entirely evident that this was a pointless exercise. So dense was the growth, the uppermost roots forming surface obstruction for the cannon-dragging, that it became well nigh impossible. Whether it remained so thickly grown further inland was not known; but it was hopeless onward probing. Andrew sent word to John that he was for turning back. He would fire off a salvo or two of blank shot just to proclaim that they were there, ashore, but that was all. The king had to agree that this was all that was feasible.

So after a noisy expenditure of gunpowder, it was back to the ships.

John said that the capital town of this Finland, Turku, lay not up the gulf but on the Baltic coast some sixty miles, opposite the Aland Isles. A presence there would probably help his cause. Would Sir Andrew take his ships and artillery that far?

They sailed on up a coast that rivalled their own Scottish West Highlands, all sea lochs, or fjords as they called them here, islets, skerries and weed-hung rocks, demanding cautious navigation, rivers innumerable coming in from the east, flowing out of lakes apparently by the thousand, a country of mixed forest and water, which would be frozen for part of the year. These Finns must lead an odd life, active for six months and comparatively idle, save for fishing, for the rest.

They duly reached Turku, set among islets, no very large town, capital as it might be, and there Andrew sounded off one more of his salvoes, on the king's behalf. Then, well escorted, both went ashore.

No opposition was encountered, even if the Danish monarch was scarcely welcomed by the townsfolk. These would know, presumably, that the Swedish-Finnish host was none so far off, but would leave it to them to emphasise Sweden's enmity to Danish overlordship.

John paraded with his seamen through the streets, as a gesture; but there was not much more that he could do. He would act similarly at Raisio to the north, even perhaps go still further up. Andrew judging that he had done suffi-cient to represent James Stewart's support, and anyway running out of gunpowder, announced that he now intended to return to Scotland, where he might well be needed, unless King John had any especial tasks for him to perform? None was put forward.

So, one more duty accomplished, it was back from this Baltic to the Norse Sea, then to report to King James, and home to Beth. But he would divert sufficiently to call in at Veere, in Flanders, to see Poppenruyter and replenish his now scanty stocks of powder and ball, of which he seemed to get through great quantities. He wondered whether it would be possible to produce gunpowder in Scotland. He had heard that it was composed of saltpetre or brimstone, sulphur and charcoal. Saltpetre allegedly came from certain rocks, especially in caves. There were plenty of caves on his Fife coast. Sulphur was said to be part of coal. And charcoal was burned wood. So it might be locally made, which would be a great advantage. He must enquire into this.

Westwards, then, with much to tell and report on.

20

Another summons for Andrew came from his monarch in the spring of 1505, this to act much nearer home than the Baltic. King Henry was complaining of border troubles, admitting that the makers therof were as much on the English side as on the Scots. But they were endangering the somewhat precarious peace agreement between the two nations, and called for joint action. He was ordering Lord Dacre, the English Warden of the West March, to deal with this; but unfortunately the Scots Warden for the same March was not co-operating, this the Lord Maxwell of Caerlaverock, who indeed was one of the major offenders and disturbers of the peace. The King of Scots must take the necessary steps.

James was annoyed. This of peace with England, cobbled together with much difficulty, including the marriage with Margaret Tudor, was not to be invalidated by cross-border feuding. These Marchmen, of course, were always bickering, their Debateable Land ever the scene of raiding and dissension. But this seemed to be a worse outbreak than the normal, and Henry considerably upset. It put James in an awkward position, for the Lord Maxwell was a most powerful chieftain, and allied to other very important families, and he could, at need, provide a couple of thousand mosstroopers for the king's army.

James decided that he would have to deal with this himself, to try to ensure that the nation's best interests were not damaged, while not angering the Tudor. The main troubles seemed to be in Eskdale, this because the Armstrongs, Grahams, Johnstones and Maxwells were all represented there, and on both sides of the actual border-line, an awkward situation; so dealing with it, if possible at all, had to be done in co-operation with the English authorities. This Lord Dacre, at Carlisle, was complaining urgently.

So James Stewart was bound for Eskdale, and desired Andrew to assist. He could not get his ships very close to the actual dales, of course, but the Solway Firth ought to allow him to reach the estuary of the Esk, at Gretna, and a little way up it, near enough perhaps to pose a threat to the quarrelsome borderers, and so assist the royal efforts.

Andrew was doubtful, but agreed to do what he could.

It meant, of course, one more lengthy voyage around Scotland from the Forth, which would take time, and James agreed to delay his own activity for the few days necessary to allow the ships to reach the Solway. He would lead a horsed force from Edinburgh, by Peebles and Yarrow and Ettrick to Eskdale Muir, and so down the lengthy dale through the heights of the Wauchope Hills.

This mission had Andrew somewhat worried. It was the Solway that was the trouble. Of all Scotland's firths it was the most difficult, not only because its southern shores were in England. It was so shallow, and at low tide great expanses of it were but bare sand, with only a fairly narrow channel of the River Nith winding through. Not only that, but what was known as the Bore was notorious, and had to be watched out for. This was a strange tidal rise of waves of fully six feet, coming rolling in at great speed, the roar of which could be heard for a score of miles inland. Many were the wrecks and catastrophes caused by this alarming feature; and Andrew would have to be wary indeed not to get involved in such tide. In fact the time to sail the firth was probably at low water, however odd this might seem, carefully following the coiling route of the Nith itself through the exposed sand-plain, this reportedly deep enough for his ships. He was told that there were fully fifteen miles of this before, at Glencaple, the river began to present a normal course through recognisable banks. Obviously a local guide was needed, the place to pick up such being the fishing-haven of Southerness, at the point east of the Dalbeattie area.

This so awkward navigation, even so, would not bring him very near to the Esk's mouth at Gretna, well east of the Nith's estuary. But at least it would enable him to provide a presence, emphasised by cannon-fire, hopefully to distract the Marchmen as the king advanced southwards. James had judged that it would be worth it.

So the lengthy voyage to the Hebridean Sea and on southwards, this now becoming familiar, began. Past the Ayrshire and Galloway coasts they went until, with the tip of the Isle of Man none so far ahead, they entered the Solway, and caution became vital, with the state of the tide crucial.

Off Wigtown Bay the three ships lay to, as Andrew calculated conditions, and wondered how far the king had managed in his progress?

Next morning, the tidal situation discovered, they moved on to Southerness, where they had no difficulty in finding three experienced fishermen to pilot the ships, these anyway inimical towards the lawless mosstroopers of the Debateable Land.

When the tide had ebbed sufficiently to show the great sand-plain beginning to appear, their pilots urged slow onwards sailing, the south-west wind favourable as they headed as nearly north-by-east as the continually winding course allowed. It was, despite all his wide experience, almost the oddest navigation Andrew had known, roundabout and creeping their way, with the vast empty drying-out plain becoming ever more extensive on either side. It seemed almost unbelievable that ships could sail on through this tidal desert, but the Nith cut a fairly deep-water channel through it all, however coiling, and some of the bends tight enough to require *Caravel*, leading, to negotiate heedfully, however difficult the sail management. It was calculated that they could get the fifteen miles up to the Nith estuary before the Bore would herald in the new tide; and they could wait there until there was sufficient water to allow them to proceed, due eastwards now, making for Gretna and the Esk mouth.

In due course, off Sweetheart Abbey, famed as being built in 1275 by Devorgilla, daughter of the then Lord of Galloway, who married John de Balliol and was the mother of King John Balliol, the Toom Tabard, she who had also founded Balliol College, Oxford, strange situation for the like as this might be, they began to hear the roaring of the Bore, and were duly impressed. Here they did not actually see the great wave with its towering crest come surging in, this because of the headland behind which they advisedly sheltered, under the lofty hill of Criffel. But the additional depth of water that it brought was evident enough, swirling around them.

Now they could head for the Esk estuary at Gretna.

There, over a plain now become firth, presently they found their river-mouth, this quite quickly narrowing in and shallowing, so that Andrew dared not risk going any great distance up. With English soil only yards off, on the right, they anchored, and orders were given for the first cannonade, the thunder of it re-echoing from all the hills to the north. Lord Dacre, wherever he was, would at least hear it, and know that the Scots were near and playing their part. As would King James, however far south he had won.

Andrew wondered whether to land his men, or some of them, to emphasise the royal authority? But those mounted Marchmen could, if so they decided, cut the seamen in pieces with their swords, axes and lances. There seemed little point in it, the noise sufficient. Cannon-fire was a wonderfully effective symbol of threat and power.

At anchor, they saw no sign of any mosstroopers. Presumably these, if they were indeed seeking to counter the royal progress, would be up-dale and facing the monarch's force. So, a salvo say every half-hour to keep alarming these Border reivers. It seemed an odd sort of campaigning, but it was probably the most effective way of aiding the king.

For most of that day they lay there, the three ships taking it in turn to provide the gunfire, this without seeing any sign of activity on land, Scots or English, save for clusters of local folk staring. Carlisle was only a dozen miles to the south-east, and Lockerbie and Langholm a score northwards. So the noise would reach all, and be regarded variously.

When, towards evening, movement, apart from those staring folk, became evident, it was soon entirely clear who approached. It was a horsed company, with glittering steel and banners flying, these displaying the blue and white saltire of Scotland and the red on gold lion rampant of its monarch. Andrew had a boat lowered and was pulled ashore to greet the king.

James was exultant, actually clasping his friend to himself, and declaring that the day was his. All was well. The Marchmen had either fled or yielded. He had hanged a few of them as examples, Armstrongs, Johnstones, Jardines and the like. Lord Maxwell had come to him and professed loyal fealty, declaring that he would keep his folk in better order hereafter. This raid on the raiders of Eskdale had been a success, and his admiral's presence and demonstration had undoubtedly helped. It was all most excellent.

Andrew invited the king, and a few of his lords, to come aboard the *Caravel* to celebrate with wine and refreshment, this gladly accepted. And while they were doing so, they were informed that there had arrived on the English side of the river a quite large party, this also flying banners. So Andrew sent a boat thither to greet them, and, if Dacre was there, as was probable, bring him aboard also.

It proved indeed to be the English warden, with other Cumbrian magnates, including the Bishop of Carlisle. These were much interested to meet the King of Scots himself. They greatly commended the entire operation, declaring that King Henry would be suitably responsive.

All was well, then, everyone present satisfied. It was dispersal now, James to return to Edinburgh.

Andrew however had this of again dealing with the Solway ahead of him, the tides and the Bore to be negotiated. But now he was more aware of what was required. And he still had his three local pilots.

The passage was duly effected, however slowly, without any mishaps. Eventually the mouth of the firth and the Irish Sea was reached and the vessels could turn north. The king would be back in Edinburgh long before the ships could reach the Forth.

One more venture over, something to tell Beth, especially about the Solway Bore. She would no doubt be objecting that she had not been taken with him, would Beth Lundie.

21

In that year's February a son was born to seventeen-year-old Margaret Tudor, a weakly child, unfortunately. He was christened James, so that one day he could become James the Fifth. Sadly, he died within the year, to the king's great distress; after all, the monarch had numerous illegitimate offspring, all of whom had survived, and it seemed grievous that now his lawful son and heir should succumb. He and Margaret would have to try again – but wait for a year or two.

Meantime, he had another task for his admiral. The royal envoy, James, second Lord Hamilton, whom he had created Earl of Arran over his part in arranging the marriage to King Henry's daughter, had gone on a mission to the King of France. And on his way home, by land, with his brother Sir Patrick Hamilton, had been arrested and confined in the Tower of London. This allegedly because on his way south he had passed through England without royal assent – something hundreds could have been accused of, but in fact only an indication of Henry's jealousy over Scotland's links with France. Arran was still being detained. Andrew was to go and secure his release.

Was this an errand on which he could take Beth? Probably, yes, since of course he would be going by sea. There was to be no delay, with Arran and his brother in durance vile.

The sail southwards was uneventful, only the *Yellow Caravel* involved this time.

Andrew found Henry Tudor a very sick man, and his son, another Henry, very much taking control. He did not like this young man, tall, burly, arrogant, and acting as though he were already Henry the Eighth. Andrew gained the ailing monarch's presence however, and in King James's name protested at the detention of the Hamilton brothers, declaring that the King of Scots could equally well arrest and hold sundry Englishmen who had entered Scotland for whatever reasons, and there without his royal permission. Henry was vague about it all, Andrew gaining the impression that it was the Prince of Wales's doing, the son's. The king seemed more concerned, however, over the death of his new grandson.

He agreed to give orders for the release of Arran and his brother. Andrew suggested that he should take them back to Scotland in his ship, and the monarch said that he should see the Prince of Wales about that.

But that burly young man declared that Arran had been visiting the King of France, their enemy, and should not have thought that he could travel back through England without royal permission. *He* would decide if, and when, the Hamiltons were allowed to return home. Andrew pointed out that going north in his ship would be the obvious solution, but was pooh-poohed. These insolent Scots should be taught a lesson!

When Andrew declared that he had King Henry's agreement that they should be released, and King James would undoubtedly expect them to be brought back in the *Caravel*, he was told that the actual timing of the brothers' freeing was *his* business, seeing that he was seeing to affairs for his sick father, and he would interview this Arran over French matters and intentions before he let them go.

Andrew could do nothing to alter this attitude, and indeed wondered whether this domineering prince might elect to detain *him* as well, whatever his sire had said. When Henry the Seventh passed on, Scotland was going to have an awkward neighbour to deal with. The Tudor did not once mention his sister, queen in Scotland.

Seeing nothing to be gained by further waiting, and

thankful that they were not detained, he hastened Beth back to the ship in London's docks. He had meant to speak about English privateers operating on the seas, but decided that this was not the time for that.

Oddly enough it was Beth who had learned something of importance, this from the association with the Princess of Wales, Catherine of Aragon. It was that her husband was negotiating with her father, Ferdinand, King of Aragon, Castile and Navarre, to form an alliance against France; and was hoping to involve the Portuguese as well as these Spanish kingdoms.

Regretful that he was not able to take Arran and his brother back with him, Andrew set sail for Scotland once more. He would have much to tell James Stewart.

In the event, his liege-lord and friend was greatly concerned over all this of the second Henry Tudor, his own brother-in-law, and his increasing power and influence arising out of his father's decline. Particularly the matter of Aragon worried him. King Ferdinand was noted as aggressive and ambitious, and if he could persuade the other small Spanish and even Italian lesser kingdoms to unite with him against France, then Scotland could become involved on account of the mutual-support alliance with that realm. And that *could* mean war, war with England. Henry the Seventh was not warlike, but this son of his was clearly very different. And, a sick man, he was probably now not long for this life. Then . . . ?

Meanwhile, to be sure, James would in that situation have to send greetings and congratulations to the new monarch, absurd as this would be. Andrew hoped that he would not have to become involved in anything such, for his regard for the Prince of Wales was low. He suggested that, on Henry's death, James should send the strong Earls of Bothwell and Argyll, and possibly Bishop Elphinstone, and with instructions to be wary indeed. He felt somewhat guilty about not then taking these to the

Thames in his ship, wanting no further dealings with the next King of England, if he could help it. James noted this dislike and mistrust of his admiral for the Prince of Wales, and was warned.

Andrew had not forgotten his quest for gunpowder nearer at hand, and less costly than having to go to the Low Countries for it. After all, since it seemed that it was made out of saltpetre, sulphur and charcoal, two of these produced from rock, and the Netherlands were short indeed of stone, why have to go there for the substance of which he required so much? Scotland was built on rock of various sorts. Surely gunpowder could be made at home?

He went to see the master of the masons' trade guild in Edinburgh, to enquire as to possibilities. He found this man, by name of Gillies, a quarry-master and builder, quite interested in the possibilities of a new source of wealth. The charcoal was no problem. Andrew had learned that, of all things, saltpetre could be gained by boiling horse-dung in water; so that was simple, however unattractive. Sulphur, or brimstone as it was called in the Bible, was the difficult ingredient. But it seemed that this was one of the most abundant mineral products, and could be found in rock anywhere that had once been volcanic – which meant in much of Scotland. Edinburgh itself was largely built on such, Arthur's Seat its dominant mountain a source. So gunpowder ought to be produced locally. The quarry-master Gillies agreed to try to manufacture it.

In the midst of all this, Beth informed him that she actually believed herself to be pregnant, this to the astonishment and joy of them both. They had all but given up hope of having a family; but now, almost at the age when childbirth could be considered unlikely, here was a refutation, unless Beth was mistaken. The production of gunpowder was as nothing to this! When would it be?

She calculated in about seven months, say April of 1510. Andrew was elated, but at the same time anxious that his wife should not take any risks of a miscarriage, for instance by accompanying him on sea voyages, when stormy weather and a rolling ship might occasion such, this Beth dismissing as nonsense. He was set to go to Lübeck, and then to Flanders to get more gunpowder and ball, hopefully for the last time; and she was determined to go with him, and not to be denied. He had a very positive-minded wife.

Just before they set off, it was learned that Henry the Seventh had died. Now there was Henry the Eighth, and all that that might result in. Andrew was thankful to be on his way to the Continent, or he might well have been ordered to take James's ambassadors to London for the customary salutations and congratulations to the new monarch. He did not envy them their task.

Another royal interest that he feared he might not be able to escape involvement in was James's preoccupation with the huge and so far useless *Great Michael* vessel, this after its preliminary and scarcely successful brief voyage up to the Tay estuary and back, sitting idle at Leith. Now James was talking about making dramatic use of it, to take himself and lead a fleet with his admiral, to eject the infidel Turks from the Holy Land. Here was something he could do, in addition to his pilgrimages to the shrines of Saints Ninian and Duthac, to wipe out his guilt for his father's death. A crusade!

Andrew, it is to be feared, was discouraging over such godly enterprise, seeing it as romantic nonsense, with much more vital matters to see to nearer home, and indeed with grave doubts as to whether the *Great Michael* was sufficiently seaworthy to sail that far. He, like many another, felt that this James Stewart had to be restrained, if possible, from his more adventurous intentions. His own voyage to the Baltic and Flanders would at least take up enough time to preclude any such expedition before winter conditions made the like impossible.

Beth's pregnancy did not seem physically to upset her unduly, and did not spoil her enjoyment of the voyaging.

He had more ivory to take to Lübeck, this now one of Andrew's principal sources of income; and much needed, for the cost of keeping his ships manned and active was great, no help coming from the royal treasury. Fortunately the supply of walrus tusks from Iceland seemed to be endless.

On the way, he decided to call in at Copenhagen, King John of Denmark's capital. That young monarch had urged him to do so whenever he was in the vicinity; and King James was eager to keep in touch and form a valuable alliance. So that made a pleasant digression, and the Scots were most hospitably received, Beth observing that when she had married Andrew Wood she had not realised that she was going to become acquainted with kings, other than perhaps their own James.

From King John Andrew learned that there was great anxiety in much of Europe over Ferdinand of Aragon, Castile and Navarre, who was evidently trying to make himself almost an emperor over the Mediterranean lands, to the concern of the Vatican, and indeed more northern states, the German ones in especial, even Denmark also. Ferdinand's links with his son-in-law, the new King of England, added to the threat of him. Andrew would find men worried at Lübeck.

He did, the Hansa merchants much afraid that war on a large scale would develop, with trade an inevitable casualty.

The price of ivory and other goods did indeed fall, compared with Andrew's last visit, in consequence.

Beth had been told much about the Baltic, and, desiring to see something of it, was taken to visit the island of Bornholm, no great distance off. She enjoyed this, declaring it to be not unlike one of the Hebridean isles, with its sands and pine trees. She asked about Muscovy and the Russias, but Andrew confessed that that great land was beyond his ken, a world unto itself, even though its western shores were no great distance off.

As far as he was concerned, it was a disappointing voyage financially; he cursed Ferdinand – and, while he was at it, Henry of England. But Beth did enjoy it.

They arrived home to learn that the *Great Michael*, with James aboard, had run aground off the East Neuk of Fife, had been badly holed, and had to limp back to Leith, in danger of capsizing, so top-heavy was it, to the king's discountenance as well as danger. So much for royal enthusiasms. No more was heard of crusading to the Holy Land.

It became known that Ferdinand was now calling himself King of Sicily. And, to obtain the support of the new Pope, he had set up a body of bishops, abbots and priests to form what he called an Inquisition, to ensure what he described as religious orthodoxy. This was a man to watch, to be sure.

Beth was brought to bed in due course, and after a somewhat prolonged labour was delivered of a son, to much rejoicing. She insisted that he was to be named another Andrew Wood, but they would refer to him as Dand.

Largo resounded. King James himself attended the christening, brought over in the *Flower*. And he brought with him his latest fascination, a printed book. One William Caxton, an Englishman, had come home from Cologne where he had been inspired by this marvellous new invention, and thereafter produced the very first book printed in English, entitled *Dictes and Sayings of the Philosophers*. Henry, nobles and prelates were commissioning copies, and sought for others to be printed on chivalry, history and religion. James Stewart was determined to get involved in this exciting challenge, and sent his servant Walter Chapman south to learn of it, and bring back a sample. Now he, Chapman, was to set up printing in Scotland.

The ever-eager monarch had been smitten, also, by a new challenge: finding gold. He had learned that the precious metal was to be found in certain parts of his realm. The ancient Picts and Celts had golden ornaments buried with them, and where known such should be dug up to see if they had anything such, the remains thereafter blessed by priests with Christian ceremony. But these ancestral folk were said to have won their gold from quartz, this apt to be found in the gravels of certain rivers. The legend of the *Golden Fleece* told of gold being washed out of river sands with the help of sheepskins. Where was it to be found? All who had any knowledge or tales of this were to inform the monarch, especially the clergy, those most concerned with the accumulation of wealth. Parish priests were to be instructed to enquire far and wide of reports on the matter.

Andrew wondered what next his liege-lord would find to excite him. Hopefully this was not a quest in which his admiral was likely to be involved.

It proved, unfortunately, to be the taking of Queen Margaret to London to see her brother. She had not seen him for long; and the birth of a son to Queen Catherine of Aragon called for this visit. James, however, who greatly disliked his brother-in-law, decided that this was time for one of his pilgrimages, to St Ninian's at Whithorn. He would go on horseback, so Andrew should take Margaret south, she no great horsewoman.

Beth was called upon to go, as extra lady-in-waiting, along with the Countess of Angus, the queen's favourite attendant. And the Douglas Earl of Angus accompanied his wife. Thereafter Andrew was astonished to find the rather stodgy and, in his assessment, unattractive queen actually flirting with this earl on their voyage, apparent as this must have been to the countess. It seemed strange, but possibly the queen was in need of some masculine association, for it was no secret that James Stewart found her of little allure. It was reported that they slept apart.

Now the queen and Angus spent much of the time in each other's company, while the countess, a much more comely female, associated with Beth and Andrew, who had their little son with them in the charge of a nursemaid. The Woods wondered why the earl was accepting Margaret's attentions, since it was unlikely over physical desire.

At Whitehall they learned that King Henry was at Windsor, up-Thames. So they had to hire a barge to take them there, bridges preventing the ship's passage. And at that great castle they found the monarch wholly absorbed in the charms of a very beautiful but low-born young woman, indeed chasing her naked about the stairs and corridors of the establishment, to squeals of laughter. In the circumstances, with Queen Catherine apparently being down-river at Greenwich Palace with her infant son, who had indeed been born there, Henry was not particularly pleased at his sister's arrival, all but the reverse. Andrew and Beth he ignored.

They did meet one interesting character there, however, Thomas Howard, Earl of Surrey, son of the Duke of Norfolk, the Earl Marshal of England. He was a fine-looking man, and easy to get on with. He told Andrew that his father, Norfolk, was Lord High Admiral as well as Marshal, although he probably did not know the bows of a ship from the stern. It was, unlike the Scots one, merely an empty title, which he deplored.

Margaret, offended at her brother's neglect of her and interest in the raffish female, decided to cut short her visit and go down to Greenwich to see Queen Catherine and the baby, which was really the object of the journey. So they quite quickly rejoined the *Caravel* at London's docks, and sailed the five miles back downriver, to the not very large Tudor palace where King Henry also had been born. There Catherine of Aragon received them more kindly. She confessed that she was in despair over her husband's preoccupation with what she called street-women. He had always been promiscuous, as were so many monarchs, as his sister would realise – this with a knowing look – her own father that way inclined, something that princesses had to put up with.

She was, however, desperately worried over her little son, the baby Prince of Wales, whom she declared weighed less than when he was born, at six months. To the visitors, this small Henry did not look like surviving. They could only sympathise, in this as in Catherine's other troubles.

It was home for them, then, and in stormy weather, which made the voyage unpleasant indeed. The gales, driving rain and cold grew worse as they neared Scotland.

22

That grim weather lasted until harvest-time and beyond, and with dire results. Never in living memory had Scotland seen the like. And the effect on grain-growing, like so much else, was disastrous, the farmers, and not only them, in despair. All the arable land was waterlogged. Folk were depressed and, worse, hungry. For there was in fact little grain to harvest. Starvation loomed.

King James sent for Andrew. His people were in grievous straits. Somehow they must be fed. The bad weather was affecting England also, although not quite so sorely. But it seemed that France and the Continent were not suffering. Costly as it would be, they must import grain from France and the Netherlands. And to make any real impression, a great many shiploads would be required. The admiral must see to it.

So Andrew was faced with an unusual duty, the assembling of what would amount to a vast fleet of vessels of all kinds and sizes, to take to France to purchase and bring back the grain, and this as quickly as was possible.

He had to send out his own ships to all the ports and harbours of the land, west coast as well as east, seeking crewed craft to try to meet the enormous demand of a whole nation facing hunger. Payment therefor? The national treasury, never full, would be stretched to the limit. But fortunately Andrew's own credit was good. He would, somehow, some time, be reimbursed.

The marshalling of such fleet, or fleets, in the Firths of Forth and Clyde was itself a formidable task. Fortunately, the need for food being so widespread and general, co-operation was reasonably effective, and the extraordinary assemblage of vessels did eventuate. But the needs of hungry people were such that no waiting for the more distant arrivers and late-comers was to be considered. James Barton, in his *Lion*, was sent over to the Clyde to take charge there, while Andrew Wood superintended in Forth and Tay.

As groups of vessels gathered, they were sent off southwards for France, under the oversight of one or other of Andrew's own captains. He was greatly concerned over the English privateers, for they represented hungry folk also. Going, the empty vessels would be in little danger probably; but coming back, laden with continental grain, they might well be liable to capture and robbery. So his cannon-bearing ships would have to act as shepherds, as far as was possible, for this straggling armada, as it went to and fro.

And how long would French and Netherlands supplies last? Even Portugal and the Spanish kingdoms might have to be tapped.

James's concern for his people was very real, and he went so far as to join the *Caravel* and go in it round the Fife harbours to urge that every possible vessel, even the larger fishing-craft, contributed to these squadrons.

The task for *Caravel*, *Flower*, *Kestrel*, *Goshawk* and others was clear, and proven. For, only the third day out, Andrew himself came across a privateer escorting three captured Scots grain-ships towards Sunderland. Attacked and putting up a fight, he had his vessel holed at the waterline by the Scots cannon sufficiently for it to begin to sink. Not seeking to have the crew drowned, Andrew had them lifted off on to the grain-ships, and leaving the enemy craft to founder, he led the rescued vessels to the nearest harbour, which happened to be Seaham, just south of Sunderland. There he fired off a salvo, just to indicate effective presence, put the Englishmen ashore, telling them that they could be better employed than as privateer crews. Then he escorted the grain-ships northwards to beyond Berwick-upon-Tweed, whereafter they ought to be safe.

He returned southwards again.

This incident represented Andrew's tactics for many days and into weeks that followed, with a continuous procession of vessels carrying the much-needed provender northwards to be guarded. The privateers fairly quickly learned their lesson and the dangers of these so dreaded cannon, and limited their activities, although some of the grain-ships were undoubtedly captured. On the whole, however, the great majority of the Scots vessels got safely to their home ports, to unload, and then to return south for more.

This procedure took up the entire autumn and early winter, and Andrew and his people were thankful when it tailed off, with the stormy weather getting still worse. It was to be hoped that 1511 would be a better year. Scotland deserved it.

Sadly for Andrew and his friends the spring started out badly. James Barton, returning from Portugal in his *Lion*, with a smaller vessel, was set upon by a very superior sort of privateers, commanded by the Lords Thomas and Edward Howard, sons of the Duke of Norfolk and brothers of the Earl of Surrey. And their ships, unlike most of the English ones, were equipped with cannon. In the battle, Barton was first wounded by an arrow and then killed by a cannonball. The *Lion* was captured, and taken to the Thames as a prize. King Henry greatly praised the Howards.

Andrew was told by James to increase his unofficial campaign against the privateers.

He was not averse to doing so, although he recognised that this could possibly lead to full-scale war between the two nations, Henry being the man he was.

Fortunately the general run of privateers were *not* equipped with artillery, unlike the Howards' vessels, and so were none so difficult prey for Andrew's craft. Fairly quickly the Englishmen recognised their handicap, and took to sailing in groups of three or four. Even so, they were at a grave disadvantage and lost many of their ships to the Scots. Andrew wondered when these would recognise that they must invest in cannon if they were to continue to compete.

He was no killer, however successful a battler, and he made a point of always trying to rescue the crews of the vessels he managed to sink. He preferred, of course, to capture rather than sink these predators of the seas, and got into the habit of marooning his captives on islands and remote headlands, such as Lindisfarne and the other Farnes, Spurn Head and similar inaccessible reaches of the English coastline – which must have been a humiliating process for the enemy.

But his anti-privateer campaign came to an abrupt end, for with the start of the martial season in early 1514 all Henry's ships were required for more official hostilities. His father-in-law King Ferdinand, with the support of the corrupt Pope Julius the Second, declared war on Louis of France, and an alliance called the Holy League was founded by the Vatican to summon all the faithful to arms against him. Henry, who had always hated the French and coveted former Plantagenet lands there, promptly announced his association with the Holy League and enmity to France. He did not actually declare war but clearly that was envisaged. He began to mass troops and assemble transport.

The arrival of a new French ambassador to Scotland, a soldier of standing named De la Motte, further emphasised that war was likely, he quickly making an impact on James. Impetuous as ever, the king threw himself into preparations for hostilities, all nobles, provosts of burghs and masters of trade guilds to rally and train men, la Motte advising.

Andrew, needless to say, was involved in all this, readying ships for conflict on a major scale. He had now sixteen large war-vessels in addition to many smaller craft, all allegedly headed by the *Great Michael*, although that top-heavy figurehead was no more than a symbol of royal authority, too unwieldy for real action.

James brought to him one Robert Borthwick, a kinsman of the third lord of that name, who had set up a small foundry at Ballencrieff in Haddingtonshire, and whom the monarch wanted Andrew to take to see Poppenruyter at Antwerp, to learn more of cannon-founding. Also a German called Urnebrig from Hamburg, who was son of a maker of gunpowder, and who could set up a manufactory for it in Scotland. Poppenruyter could instruct him also.

So there had to be a hasty voyage to the Low Countries with these two passengers, to leave them there to learn more, and bring back additional cannon.

Just before he left for the Continent, to the delight of the king, and indeed the nation, Queen Margaret was delivered of a son, at Linlithgow, safely this time, and the infant healthy, to be named one more James, an heir to the throne.

After delivering the pair at Antwerp, Andrew was to go on to France, taking documents, duly signed, renewing the alliance with King Louis, this in his role of Admiral of Scotland. So he considered that it ought to be a safe enough voyage for Beth and little Dand to accompany them, since so she was ever eager. There might well not be another opportunity for some time.

Despite the tension prevailing among the nations, that journey of the four vessels proved uneventful, the absence of privateers very noticeable, these presumably assembling in the Thames to convey the English army to France.

At Antwerp Andrew learned that it was too late to deliver James's message to King Louis. Henry Tudor had in person crossed the Channel at the head of a great army, and was now camped at Rouen, eighty miles up the Seine.

It was back to Scotland as soon as was possible, then, in these circumstances. It looked as though there would indeed be no more voyaging for Beth for some time to come.

At Leith he heard what he had feared: the king had declared war on England. He had, apparently, received a letter and a scented glove from Anne, Queen of France, who obviously knew of the King of Scots' romantic tendencies, requesting him to advance at least a yard into England, in force, for her sake. Now he was assembling a great army on the Burgh Muir of Edinburgh.

Sending back Beth and the child to Largo in the *Caravel*, he made his way up to the capital, to discover what his part in the hostilities was to be.

Up on the level common land just south of the city, he found an enormous concourse of men, mounted and foot, camped, and being added to by the hour, with contingents from the Highlands and the Isles still arriving.

James, magnificent in gold-inlaid black armour but bare of head, his hair held in place by a gold circlet, was glad to see him. He was in a state of great excitement, announcing that he had already eighty thousand mustered, with more expected. He would show Henry Tudor that the Auld Alliance with France was still to be reckoned with.

As to what help Andrew could offer, the monarch said that he could not see that ships could be of any assistance at this stage. He was going to advance over the east-central borderline, to cross Tweed at Coldstream. That was a score of miles from the nearest ships could be got, at Berwick-upon-Tweed. And then to head down into Northumberland on a wide front. It was armed men that were required, in even greater numbers, for once they were over the border they would have to spread out in a long front to make a lengthy advance, their flanks well guarded. Best for Andrew to bring up most of his crewmen to join this host. His shipmen were skilled fighters and would all help. How many could he thus field?

Andrew reckoned three hundred. He would return to Leith to fetch them. Even as he left the moor he heard the wailing of bagpipes of another Highland contingent coming from the west to join the king.

His seamen, of course, were unused to fighting on land, but they would do their best.

On the Eve of St Bernard's Day, 19th August, the host set off, James now claiming it one hundred thousand strong, with fourteen thousand horse, the greatest army Scotland had ever fielded, he asserted. Henry Tudor had better come back from France forthwith if he wanted to try to save his realm.

At this stage the vast array marched in a miles-long column, progress inevitably slow, the nobles, knights and mounted men well ahead. Coldstream was about forty-five miles from Edinburgh through the Lammermuir Hills and the Whiteadder Water, by Duns and Swinton. This host could not cover more than a dozen miles a day, at most, so five days, food to be gathered on the way. The Earl of Dunbar's sheep stock in those hills was going to suffer, but in a good cause he was told. The monarch, at least, was in high spirits throughout.

On the fifth day they reached the Tweed, at Coldstream, the first stretch, some fifteen miles from Berwick, where the river could be forded, there the king not alone in shaking a fist at the land beyond.

Getting the multitude across that quite fast-running ford took hours, even though on this occasion there was no opposition. They camped for the night on both sides, those on the English side scouring the neighbourhood for cattle to provide roasted beef.

Ahead of them now rose the long line of the Cheviot Hills, with their escarpments of Monylaws, Branxton, Flodden, Barmoor, Etal and Duddo, these known to be defended against border raiders by their castles and towers. But so far no conflict, although so great a force could not have remained unobserved by the ever-watchful Borderers.

Marching through the Northumbrian countryside, Andrew Wood with his men was put in charge of the rearguard, as seemed to James suitable for seamen. And as well as the long lines of ox-drawn carts laden with gear, they had others to see to, these carrying a strange gift sent by King Louis, thousands of eighteen-foot pikes, which he declared were the most valuable weapons against enemy cavalry. By forming circular groups of standing and kneeling men thrusting out these lengthy spears, like giant hedgehogs, horsemen could be kept at bay. James was doubtful about their use, implying, as it did, defensive tactics, whereas he was no defensive fighter. They must find a better use for them. This was to be a gesture of support for France, to bring Henry back from his French invasion, if possible.

The great army spread out now on a wide front. And quite soon they recognised, in the rearguard, that there was trouble ahead — not battle but upset, this as smoke clouds began to rise right and left. The advancing Scots, or some of them, were evidently setting alight houses and farmsteads, even villages by the size of the smokes, this not the king's wishes, indeed the reverse. He was not here to damage the English land, but to indicate to Henry, or his advisers, that France should not be assailed. He sent out messengers to his scattered leaders that this must stop, no ravaging of the land, no attacks on communities and manors and castles.

Passing Cornhill and Pallinsburn and Crookham, the Scots centre came to Ford Castle, so named after a ford on the swift-running River Till. It was evening, and James decided to camp his people here in the castle's parkland. In fact he knew Sir William Heron, the squire here, one of the English March Wardens, and indeed had lodged in his house on one occasion in a dispute over border raiding, and had admired his good-looking wife. So, typically James, he would seek to pass the night in pleasant company.

Andrew found himself, along with others of the leadership, invited into the castle for an evening meal, and duly admired this Lady Heron. It seemed that Sir William was elsewhere. The king was obviously very appreciative of their hostess, emphasising that he was not invading, only making a demonstration which might affect King Henry. He was giving orders for the evident burning activities to be stopped.

Andrew spent the night with his men in the great encampment. But James did not, Angus and sundry other nobles remarking upon it.

The next day was spent, partly in making the Scots' presence felt in the Cheviot foothill country, but also in ensuring that there was to be no more sacking and ravaging, as indicated by those smokes. Andrew, mounted, was one of those sent off to announce the royal commands. Sadly, he found signs of much burning and devastation. He recognised that armies were apt so to act on what they saw as enemy territory. Troops from all over Scotland saw the position rather differently from the monarch. James's present emissaries were less than popular on their missions.

The king's aim was to make an unhurried progress down through Northumberland, skirting the Cheviots, perhaps as far as Alnwick, the seat of the Percy earl thereof, to Whittingham, Netherton, Rothbury and Otterburn, there to meet up with the far right flanking wing, under Bothwell, who would have come down Redesdale from Jedburgh. Actually they met with no organised resistance, although groups of the local folk, under some landowners, did make defiant gestures before escaping into the hills, vastly outnumbered. Of course this area, like the rest of England, would have many of its menfolk off supporting Henry Tudor in France. There was still some burning, mainly of hay-barns and the like, such easily set alight, to James's anger.

They got as far as Wooler and Chatton that day, and on to Whittingham and Alnmouth and Alnwick the next.

James made no attempt to assail that great castle, any more than he had done at Bamburgh. This was enough, he decided, and it was back with them all to near the border-line. He suggested that another night at Ford Castle would be pleasant, especially, no doubt, if Sir William Heron had not returned.

Andrew was, as ever, amused at his liege-lord's great interest and fondness for the ladies. He himself was appreciative of the creatures, but not quite so actively, for of course he had a highly attractive and spirited wife, whereas James had only Margaret Tudor!

It was on their fifth day over the border when their forward scouts sent to inform the king that a large force was approaching from the south, from the Ashington direction, many thousands it was assessed. Widespread and scattered now as James's host was, he recognised the danger of it being penetrated and cut up into sections apart, and so unable to form a united front. He had better concentrate his people. He asked the Earl of Home, who knew this country best, just across from his own Merse lands, where he should order his people to make for, a good and strategic assembly-point? Home said that Branxton would be best, about four miles west of this Ford, where there was high ground, Branxton Edge, which would give them security. Home's men were sent out so to order.

One more night was spent at Ford, as men assembled in its parkland. Then the move was made westward for Branxton Edge.

That hill, no great height, proved to have a partner summit not so far off, this named Flodden Edge. They both had flat tops. This one would be the place to halt and face any foe, a difficult site to assail.

So up there the host climbed. The east-facing slope was steep and rocky, but the west side was more gentle and grass-grown, this for the mounted men to climb, and there were the thousands of them.

Almost a plateau, it was extensive enough to take all the

array of men and horses. James was gratified for Home's advice. There they settled, meantime, to await events. No battle was sought, only a presence shown.

He had his scouts out, of course, to keep him informed of the changing position, these mainly Home's men, knowledgeable and ideal for the task. It was presently reported that there were actually three forces advancing northwards, the main one reputedly under the Earl of Surrey, marching up the Heiton Burn towards Lowick; another nearer the coast; and the third up Till itself. *They* of course, also had their scouts, and must know well of the Scots, in great strength, on this Branxton hill. So far, none of the foe was nearer than five miles.

It was evening, and beginning to rain, with low cloud. There could be no action for many hours.

The host settled down for a wet and uncomfortable night, sentries on the alert.

In the morning, still raining, the first word brought to James was that the enemy forces were on the move again, but all marching due northwards, not towards this hill, but directly towards the Tweed. This seemed strange. What were Surrey's tactics? To get over the great river and so try to prevent the Scots getting back on to their own land? His main force appeared to have spent the night at Barmoor, this some five miles east of Branxton, and still about ten from Tweed. Only the Till grouping was nearer.

The king was the recipient of varied advice. Angus wanted an immediate move, and he was an experienced campaigner, this to get back over Tweed before the English could do so, if that was their objective, and so use the great river to aid them. Others urged a descent at once, to separate Surrey's three forces from each other. Some recommended a continued presence on this height until the main enemy strategy was clear – this Andrew urging also. James agreed. Getting the main English groups across the narrow fords of Tweed would take much time, whichever they might choose, at Coldstream, or Norham or

Wark. And they would be vulnerable as they had to wait. A descent upon them then?

Home said that it was possible that Surrey would turn westwards before Tweed, and so seek to form a barrier on the low ground, to try to cut off the Scots from their own land, which could well be bad for their morale. James told him to take his mounted mosstroopers down that western slope and seek to guard against any enemy move from there.

The host waited there on the hilltop.

Presently they saw, through the rain, that Home had been right. A horsed enemy company was indeed riding round the northern base of the hill to get behind to the gentler slopes. The mosstroopers would have to deal with this.

Then they were able to see the main English forces coming together, from Barmoor and the Till valley, and marching directly towards this Branxton. It was to be confrontation, apparently.

All on the hilltop tensed themselves, ready for whatever developed. At any rate, they had the strong position and almost certainly much outnumbered the foe. On the face of it, they were all but impregnable.

But they had reckoned, most of them, without their romantic and chivalrously minded monarch. As Surrey's host settled itself at the steep eastern hillfoot in great ranks, with Home and other border mosstroopers preventing them from reaching round to the gentler flanks, James saw it as unsuitable, even humiliating, to wait up here, secure, inactive, while the enemy were faced with having to climb this difficult hill to get at them. This was not for such as himself, the King of Scots. Surrey was offering fight. He must be met, challenged, not tamely waited for. They would go down to meet him.

Angus Bell-the-Cat was not the only one who loudly protested. That would be folly. To yield their strong position, and descend in an inevitably unruly rush to a ranked and waiting mass of English spearmen, archers and swordsmen, was not to be considered.

But James was adamant. He was not going to wait up here, safe, like some faint-heart while the English either attacked, attempted to climb up to reach them, or besieged them as though they were in some sort of great castle, to starve them out. That was not how a monarch should behave. They would go down to meet them, even so, not on equal terms, for the Scots would much outnumber Surrey's men. Down with them!

His people, almost reluctantly, obeyed.

Thereafter, quickly it was realised that that hillside was a disaster for hordes of men, especially those burdened with unwieldy and overlong French pikes, this with rocks and outcrops and screes to stumble over. And stumble they did, literally in their hundreds, pressed on by the masses behind. Swiftly those pikes made a chaos of it all, tripping men, catching on obstacles, their shafts a menace in the close-packed headlong ranks. James himself slithered and fell more than once, as did Andrew and most others. It was not any advance, more of an avalanche of uncontrolled humanity.

And, as the hordes hurtled down near to the waiting foe, the English bowmen were offered their opportunity. The arrows, the dreaded clothyard shafts, came at them in unending streams; and although many of the Scots had helmets, breast-plates and half-armour, some with padded leather tunics, the slaughter was devastating, men by the score falling, and others tripping over them, even on that steep braeside the heaps piling up into limb-lashing bloody mounds, which had to be clambered over by the mass behind.

Andrew, close to James, his lion rampant standard fallen in the fray, was struck on the breast of his half-armour, and the shaft, deflected upwards, pierced the gap at the shoulder. He was scarcely aware of the pain of it, in the excitement and ferment. Tossing the sword to his other hand, he plucked the arrow out, it not having penetrated deeply.

The king fell, in front of him, but only over a body, and rose again to plunge on. His standard-bearer was less fortunate, and crashed to the ground, not to rise again, the precious banner being grasped by a successor. So it went on, a shambles indeed.

Then, nearing the level ground, there was some relief for the Scots. Home and his horsemen arrived from around the hillfoot to the west, and assailed the flank of the enemy. This distraction largely turned the English to face it, with hasty mounting of steeds at the rear to confront the challenge. James and his people, such as were still able, reached the foot of the slope, and there came to actual blows with the foe, in a smiting, thrusting, slashing turmoil, the Scots front pushed on from behind.

Andrew saw James go down, with an arrow into his throat, but seeking to rise, and then the charging mass behind poured over the monarch, unable to avoid it. There were perhaps six hundred yards of that slope, which produced unstoppable impetus, this admittedly having an inevitable impact on the enemy. Few of those pikes reached the foot.

Then, with Home's borderers attacking in flank, the English ranks wavered and crumpled. But on the levels the fighting continued and it was difficult, for Andrew at least, to judge who was winning. To and fro the struggle went, with the English gradually moving back and back.

But the Scots had lost, as well as their thousands slain and wounded, much of the will to continue to battle. Their monarch had fallen, and with him unnumbered nobles, knights and fighting men. Only Home's mosstroopers, seconded by Huntly's cavalry, remained more or less unbeaten on their left wing, the northern and western sides of that hill, indeed pursuing Lord Dacre's mosstroopers, their own traditional foe. *They* would fight another day.

In all the confusion and disarray at the sorry end of the three hours of confrontation, Andrew, wounded slightly but nowise incapacitated, saw that there was no more to be done at Flodden other than to escape with as many of his men as had survived. Actually, being seamen, they had not been in the forefront of the charging masses, and apart from four dead and a few with minor wounds, their company was more or less intact.

Andrew had had plenty of time, up on that hilltop, waiting, to survey the surrounding scene. He recognised that down the north-western slopes to East and West Learmouth villages would bring them fairly quickly to the Wark ford of Tweed, three miles west from that of Coldstream. Get across there, and they would be able to make their way north-eastwards to the coast. There they would find fishing-boats to take them north across the mouth of the Forth estuary to the safe Fife coast.

That must be their design, then: Learmouth, Wark and then head for the large fishing-harbour of Eyemouth where, at the admiral's authority, they would gain the craft to get them home.

It was a sorry day for them, as for all Scotland, their eager king dead, along with thousands of his subjects, and a seventeen-month-old child, with a Tudor mother, to succeed as James the Fifth. And no doubt further English attempts to take over the northern kingdom likely to follow. But that was for the future. Here and now, it was somehow to get home.

23

Scotland mourned. Twelve thousand dead, including the popular monarch, this including no fewer than ten earls, innumerable lords and knights, and James's young illegitimate son Alexander, whom he had had appointed Archbishop of St Andrews at the age of twelve. What would happen now?

In fact, nothing dramatic immediately followed. The Earl of Surrey, the victor, had himself lost a great many men. And Henry the Eighth, in France, was calling for reinforcements, and needing them badly. This was no time for any large-scale invasion of Scotland. And with his sister the queen and his little nephew now on the throne, and Margaret Tudor's friend Archibald Douglas, Earl of Angus, known to be pro-English, matters there could wait. Surrey and his brothers and what was left of his army marched south.

Andrew had been expecting calls for his warships to play their part in efforts to keep the English at bay, but none such arrived, Henry's problems in France increasing. Who was to rule in the northern kingdom, in the name of the infant James? His mother was pregnant again – and there were whispers that this was by Angus, with whom she was over-friendly, her late husband having been but little interested in her.

A parliament was hastily called, to meet at Perth, Andrew of course to be present. It was but poorly attended, with so many of its regular members suddenly dead, and their successors frequently young and unsure of their positions in this cataclysm. So it was largely clerics who dominated the scene.

The first and vital decision was the identity of a regent who would govern in the name of the child monarch. Queen Margaret was not to be considered as such, being the sister of King Henry, and consorting with pro-English Angus. The heir presumptive to young James was in fact a far-out kinsman, John Stewart, Duke of Albany, son of James the Third's brother, who had married a French-woman and had gone to live in France, where the present duke had been born and brought up, he too now married to a Frenchwoman. He could not be ignored, but what sort of a man was he, and would he desire to come to Scotland?

The lack of experienced earls and lords and magnates left this parliament notably unsure of itself. Andrew, as admiral, indeed found himself, in some of the debates, taking the lead. Angus had fled to England, and it was feared that Margaret Tudor would follow him, and might well seek to take her little son with her. This had to be prevented at all costs. Lord Borthwick, one of the few veteran nobles surviving, was appointed keeper of the royal citadel of Stirling Castle, and guardian of the infant king.

But first, James must go through the coronation cere-mony, this of course at Scone – largely why the parliament was being held at Perth, only a few miles from that abbey. So the entire company had to go up Tay to attend that brief solemnity. At least there were plenty of prelates to conduct it, however unhappy the queen mother looked, she return-ing to the resumed parliament, to listen to all from a gallery.

Among the distinctly noisy proceedings, Andrew found himself deputed to go to France in his ship, and persuade, if necessary, the Frenchified Duke of Albany to come back with him as regent.

A peculiar development preoccupied that parliament, this the state of the prelacy in the land now. The primacy, that of the archbishopric of St Andrews, had become vacant on the death of James's son the young Alexander, aged sixteen. And the senior bishops of Caithness and the Isles had also fallen at Flodden. The most prominent and venerable prelate was William Elphinstone, Bishop of Aberdeen, who had founded that university. He was proposed for the primacy; but he courteously declined it. Bishop Andrew Forman of Moray was recommended for the Pope to raise to the dignity of Archbishop of St Andrews, but this was contested by Gavin Douglas, uncle of Angus and provost of the capital church of St Giles in Edinburgh, a notable divine. It was left for the Pope to decide on this.

The realm was in a state of disorder, owing to the disaster of Flodden and the deaths of so many of the magnates. So it was decided that the Earl of Crawford, who had survived, should be Justiciar North of the Forth, and the Lord Home to the south thereof, both with full powers and maximum authority. It was to be hoped that these two strong men might be able to keep order until the Duke of Albany arrived.

Andrew was commanded to go in his ship and bring the new regent to Scotland.

He judged it a difficult task indeed, and found it so, when he got to Paris. For Albany was all but a Frenchman, with a French mother and French wife, and spoke French better than English. And he proved to have no desire to move to Scotland, however close he might be to the throne as heir presumptive. He was a handsome and stylish young man, well content with his position at King Louis's court. He said that he would consider the situation, but meanwhile would remain in France. To him Scotland was a far-away and reputedly disorderly country, which he could do without. When Andrew sought to convince him otherwise in the name of parliament, he was informed that King Louis did not want to lose him at this stage. Meantime, he would send his close friend Antoine de la Bastie, a noted soldier, courtier and also poet, the admiral to take him north for the time being to act in his name.

Very uneasy about this, Andrew could not change the young man's mind. He had to take the Sieur de la Bastie aboard *Caravel*, together with James Hamilton, Earl of Arran, who had some royal blood and was a friend of la Bastie, to act as Albany's envoys. What the Scots parliament would make of this was anybody's guess.

On the voyage he got on well with de la Bastie, a cheerful, competent and spirited character, who was obviously a man of wide experience. The latter was somewhat unsure of what his duties were to be in Scotland, as representing the hoped-for regent. Andrew was unable to advise him, but declared that the Lord Home, Justiciar for the South, would no doubt guide him, and hopefully co-operate. It seemed strange to be bringing a Frenchman to act as deputy for a regent who was also French-born and still based on France. The Auld Alliance seemed to be asserting itself. But Scotland, after the yawning gap left in its leadership by the calamity of Flodden, did require some such lead. When asked where the newcomer should base himself, Andrew thought that it might be best to be near the Home country of the Merse, to act with the justiciar. Possibly Dunbar Castle, midway between there and the capital, Edinburgh, rather than at far-from-the-border Stirling, where the infant monarch was being guarded. Arran, who seemed vague about the entire situation, did not disagree. He seemed more concerned with replacing Lord Borthwick as keeper of Stirling Castle and guardian of the child king.

Arrived back in Scotland, it was to discover that Queen Margaret had actually married the Earl of Angus, this only a matter of months after her husband's death. It seemed highly unsuitable, to Andrew as to others. This attitude was emphasised by the unexpected calling of another parliament, with the perturbed commissioners deciding that she should not be allowed to have custody of young James, nor of her younger son Alexander, Duke of Ross, especially as she was now rumoured to be pregnant again, and by none other than Angus. Margaret Tudor was an awkward character to be so closely linked to the Scottish throne.

Andrew found himself to be very doubtful about James Hamilton of Arran, whether as Albany's envoy or otherwise. He judged him to be a self-seeker, but scarcely an efficient one, using his far-out connection with the royal house to his personal advantage, but not otherwise contributing to the well-being of the nation. Even de la Bastie treated him with a sort of amused patience.

It seemed that the best course was to introduce the Frenchman to Home, the justiciar. Between them, they could decide what role the former was to play on Albany's behalf. Where, then, was that great lord to be found? It seemed that he was not at Edinburgh nor Stirling nor Perth, so presumably he was back in his own Borderland. Leaving Arran at the capital, Andrew turned his ship back, to sail down to Eyemouth, the nearest large harbour to the Home lands, Berwick-upon-Tweed being in English hands. On the way, he explained to de la Bastie the rather extraordinary position of the Home chief, quite apart from his rank as justiciar and Chief Warden of the Marches. The fact was that the family, or clan, of Home more or less dominated not only the Merse but all the eastern Borderland, there being no fewer than eighteen quite sizeable Home lairdships in the area; indeed it was hard to find any large properties thereabouts owned otherwise.

On the way south, Andrew was able to point out Fast Castle, halfway down a great cliff on a spur of rock, where Margaret Tudor had been taken for her first night in Scotland, the Frenchman shaking his head over it. This was not the lord's main seat, of course, which was at Home Castle near to Kelso, almost thirty miles to the south-west, so large was that lordship.

Docking at Eyemouth, and asking if it was known where the Lord Home was at this present, they were told that he had been at Home Castle four days before and was probably still there. So there was nothing for it but to hire horses for the quite lengthy ride up the Blackadder Water to Greenlaw, all through Home territory, and then the four miles south. Home Castle was very evident long before they reached it, rising high on an isolated ridge out of the level and fertile cattle country. Banners flying from its towers seemed to indicate that its lord was in residence.

Alexander, fourth lord, was there, a stern-faced man of middle years, who was just civil but hardly welcoming towards de la Bastie, whom he seemed to look upon as some sort of French interloper, whatever he thought of Andrew. Lady Home was more friendly. It became evident that it was the Frenchman's position as deputy for the new Regent Albany that he rather resented, seeing it possibly conflicting with his own status as Justiciar South of the Forth. De la Bastie, whose command of English was excellent, sought to reassure him that there need be no dispute.

Home was also Warden of the East March, and as such very much aware of, indeed involved in, border raiding activities, his fellow-Homes not averse to join the like. De la Bastie declared that the Duke of Albany had spoken to him on this, and indicated that it could escalate into more general hostilities.

Home produced his first and only guffaw of laughter at this, even Andrew shaking his head. This cross-border mosstrooping had existed since there had *been* a borderline.

But De la Bastie was neither amused nor convinced. He was, in effect, now ruling Scotland in the name of the regent. This of the border would have to be better ordered. He himself would see to it. He would appoint himself *Chief* Warden of the Marches, and so could ensure that Albany's will prevailed.

Home looked sceptical but also frowning. But he was not in a position to do more than glare at the Frenchman. For a Home, in the Borderland, it was almost an unheard-of situation.

Andrew was much diverted. Scotland might have an infant monarch and many ambitious lords seeking the power, but it looked as though it was going to be ruled effectively, even although by a foreigner. He admired de la Bastie, and could work with him. Parliament might well be doubtful about all this; but parliaments could only be called by the representative of the child king, the regent. De la Bastie was Albany's friend. In effect, Scotland was going to be governed from France. The Auld Alliance was very much in the ascendant.

Andrew wondered what de la Bastie would order him to do next, as admiral?

He soon learned. Home was proving obdurate, and ordering his people to oppose a Frenchman as Chief Warden; and not only his own people. Other Borderers found the situation objectionable.

De la Bastie, a hardened commander, declared that he could deal with the Home lands, even Home Castle itself, with a sufficiency of troops mustered in the king's and regent's names. But Fast Castle was different. Situated as it was, no amount of siegery could bring it down, for it could be supplied by sea, this via the cavern beneath it and the shaft up into the hold. And even a watch by ships would be unlikely to prevent small boats entering the cave by night with provender for the Home garrison. The admiral was to attempt to reduce Fast Castle.

Andrew thought long on this mission, how to ensure that the Homes were starved out? Assault was not possible. And his cannon, at sea level, could not have their muzzles elevated sufficiently to bombard the hold. Nor could they be got down the adjoining cliffs to fire effectively from land. That cavern, and the shaft from it, were the only weaknesses, and that could be guarded day and night. But there *must* be some method of countering the defences.

Suppose that he contrived an unbroken chain, as it were,

of ships and boats, with cables and ropes, to bar entry to the cave, even in darkness. Was that possible? These cliffs, facing the fierce tides of the Norse Sea, with reefs and rocks, would make such barriers difficult indeed. But surely it could be done?

He made an exploratory sail down that savage coast. The folk in Fast Castle would see it, and wonder, of course, but that did not signify. He would have to be very careful about manoeuvring his vessels in close, because of the reefs, but he judged that it could work. He and de la Bastie could then make their assaults on the two castles at the same time – although *his* could not be termed an assault, only a threatening presence.

One week later, then, the moves were made, the Frenchman having mustered his quite large force. Andrew led his ships, towing the small boats, from Leith, quite a squadron, out of the Forth and down past Dunbar Castle, which he was advising de la Bastie to make his headquarters, to just below Fast.

Up there the Home garrison undoubtedly would recognise what was being attempted; but there was nothing they could do about it.

Heedfully marshalling his craft into the desired position, in a small boat himself, he organised the formation of the semicircular barrier of ropes and chains linking the vessels, this taking much time and effort because of the heaving waters, the great rollers striking the cliff-foots and then surging back, tossing the small craft this way and that, oar-work tricky.

But at length it was done. However upheaved and erratic, the cordon was formed. Nothing could get in or out of that cave-mouth without Andrew's agreement. For how long would the folk above survive without further supplies of food? De la Bastie would see that none reached them by land.

Andrew left one of his shipmasters in charge of the barricade, and sailed *Caravel* to Eyemouth, to discover how de la Bastie fared in the Merse inland besieging Home Castle.

He found all satisfactory there. How lengthy would this siege be? It was a large stronghold, and undoubtedly had a numerous garrison. Supplies for such, with no siege anticipated, would not last indefinitely. De la Bastie was fairly hopeful of a fairly early capitulation. What was to be done with Alexander Home, who was presumably still within? Lady Home had been pleasant; it was a pity that she had to suffer all this.

They settled to wait. Andrew wondered whether all the many Home lairds in the area would assemble their men to come and try to relieve their lord?

Three days later a white flag was run up to the masthead on one of the castle towers. Surrender. Riding uphill towards the gatehouse on the ridge, de la Bastie demanded Lord Home's presence. He was told that he was no longer present. He had slipped away, alone, in the darkness of the night before. It was Lady Home who was yielding up the stronghold.

What now? In this Home country the missing lord could be anywhere, safely hidden.

De la Bastie said that somehow this situation must be resolved and bettered. Come to terms with Home? Offer him pardon for any misdeeds if he would cease from further offences? He being still Justiciar South of the Forth complicated matters. How to reach an agreement? A meeting, a compromise. Could such be arranged? He, Albany's representative, had more to do here in Scotland than try to bring Home to order.

Andrew suggested that they might get the rebel lord to meet them if he was promised his safety from arrest. Why not in some assured place, hallowed ground? A church? And in Home country. Say Dunglass? There was a Home castle there, near the junction of Lothian and the Merse, not far from Colbrandspath, but also a fine cruciform collegiate church, built in the fourteenth century by a

Home lord. The awkward lord would almost certainly meet them there, secure.

De la Bastie agreed. They would inform Lady Home, who would, no doubt, be able to get the word to him, wherever he was. Say, in three days' time. Meanwhile they would go and view this Dunbar Castle, which Andrew had advised would make a worthy seat for himself, convenient for both the Borderland and Edinburgh, the capital. It had been forfeited by the ancient line of Earls of Dunbar and March, and sequestered by the crown some fifty years earlier.

Lady Home was given the word, and Andrew took de la Bastie to examine Dunbar and its castle. Here was a thriving fishing-haven, the harbour dominated by the fine fortalice set on a series of rock-stacks rising from the sea, between which access for the boats had to be gained, this providing the hold with the ability to close the haven to vessels if so desired, thus enabling its lord to levy a toll on all catches of the fishermen. De la Bastie did not contemplate anything such, but did approve of the castle, and said that he would use it.

Thither Lady Home presently sent word. Her husband would meet the regent's deputy at Dunglass church – although that did not imply recognition of Albany as rightful governor of Scotland.

So they returned to Dunglass, where they found Alexander Home with a large train of his people, and looking haughtily unhelpful. In the handsome sanctuary they held their meeting, de la Bastie intimating that Home's behaviour in the past would be overlooked by the regent, and his justiciarship supported if he would agree to accept the regency situation and maintain the peace in the Borderland. Home emphasised that he did not recognise Albany's right to call himself regent for the infant king; but he would ensure peace south of Forth and thus display his fealty to young James the Fifth.

That was as fair an arrangement as they could hope for. They left the matter thus.

Thankfully Andrew went back to the *Caravel* at Eye-mouth, and took de la Bastie north to Leith, then sailed for Largo and Beth. He had learned at Leith that Fast Castle had indeed been starved into submission and his ship-master had taken over.

24

That summer passed seemingly fairly uneventfully for Scotland and its admiral. But, in October, it was proved that this was only a superficial peace. And once more it was Lord Home who was the culprit – he and Arran, who had become allies. And the alliance extended further, indeed to include cross-border affiliations, with none other than Margaret Tudor and her husband Angus. These two, with their new infant daughter, had been living in Northumberland, with the support of Lord Dacre, the English Chief Warden of the Marches. Now Home had joined that grouping, extraordinary as it seemed for the Scots and English Chief Wardens to ally themselves against the regent of the Scots king. De la Bastie called it treason, and Andrew had to admit that it was not far off it.

That curious character, James Hamilton, Earl of Arran, had now joined this odd confederacy, and all were now contesting the regency of the absent Duke of Albany, Arran demanding replacement of Lord Borthwick as keeper of Stirling Castle and guardian of the child king.

De la Bastie was still ably governing Scotland for Albany, although his rule scarcely included the Merse and eastern Borderland. He felt it necessary to show a presence there now and again, however. He would march an armed force of loyal lords and Highland chiefs down through that difficult territory again, not this time to besiege Home Castle but to demonstrate and give warning to the pro-English party. The admiral should make his support evident by sailing his ships up Forth to as near to Stirling as was possible, and back down the hundred miles of coastline to Berwick-upon-Tweed, and even some distance further along the Northumbrian shores, possibly as far as Alnwick, where he should fire a cannonade to remind the opposition that the regent was still very much in command.

This Andrew did readily enough, and hoped that his gestures would serve their purpose. He did not know just where in Northumberland Margaret, Angus and possibly Arran were based; but by firing blank shot off Berwick, the Farne islands, Bamburgh, Dunstanburgh and Alnwick, there could be no doubt as to his and de la Bastie's concern.

But the other confederacy could make its presence felt also, it proved.

Home and Dacre, in alliance, made a concerted attack on the West and Middle Marches of the border, on the Scottish side, burning, slaying and devastating the land, from Hawick, Selkirk, Jedburgh and Kelso. This was an inland area where Andrew could not usefully help with his ships. De la Bastie had to cope without his aid. With Albany's authority he declared Home guilty of high treason once more, and put a price on his head. He could not do the same over Dacre, of course, but protested to the English envoy, Dr West. His priority now was somehow to arrest Alexander Home and have him tried and disposed of. Andrew did not see how he could aid him in this, unfortunately. He still held Fast Castle, under his shipmaster, but that was no major help.

At least de la Bastie had the loyal support of parliament and the Privy Council, plus the great majority of the Scots lords and churchmen. And this proved to be of vital importance ultimately, when the West March chiefs, the Scotts, Turnbulls, Johnstones, Maxwells and Armstrongs, perceived that Home and Dacre, in alliance, were threatening their Debateable Land, and for once united against their depredations. That wild country of the dales of Nith and Esk, Annan and Liddel, right to the headwaters of Middle March Teviot, was home territory for the mosstrooping clans, where they were in their element and could make the land fight for them in ambushes and the like. Home was at a disadvantage thereabouts, especially in having Dacre as an ally, that individual the man the Scots Marchmen most hated. They decided that they had to act in unison for once; and at Teviothead, none so far from Hermitage Castle, a seat of the Chief Warden, they ambushed Home and Dacre, defeated their force, slaughtered many, and took their leaders prisoner.

Dacre, their long-time foe, was however something of a problem. As Chief English Warden he represented Henry Tudor in the Debateable Land, and holding him captive could cause major upset between the two nations, with who knew what repercussions. They judged in the end that he had learned his lesson, and taking him to the head of Redesdale, at the Carter Bar, traditional meeting-place of the opposing Wardens, they set him free, unmounted and alone, to find his way to Carlisle as best he could. But Lord Home, and his brother who was with him, they held on to, and would hand over to de la Bastie, the governor, who was known to be anxious to have him, the declared traitor.

When Andrew heard of this, he was satisfied. The biggest troublemaker in Lowland Scotland was taken.

De la Bastie did not hesitate nor delay. He ordered an immediate trial, for high treason, at Edinburgh. And, High Justiciar South of the Forth as Home was, the Privy Council ordered the three judges to find him guilty.

This was done, and sentence of death was to be implemented forthwith.

Alexander Home was duly executed, this before a great crowd in the city's Canongate, and his severed head set on a spike on the Tolbooth.

So the chief of all the Homes passed on to another realm where, it was to be hoped, his capacity for mischief would be severely limited if not ended once and for all.

Much of the nation sighed with relief, Andrew Wood included.

But the Homes of the Merse were otherwise minded – and there were plenty of them. From the castle of Dunbar, where he had chosen to reside, de la Bastie sought to establish order on the Borderland, with constant appearances, in strength, from one end of the hundred-mile March to the other.

The Homes bided their time. Then they staged a play-acting. A small group of them made a gesture of assailing the modest castle of Langton, on the Blackadder near Duns, in the northern Merse, this less than a score of miles through the Lammermuir Hills from Dunbar itself, belonging to a branch of the Cockburn family. One of the Homes, pretending to be a Cockburn, hastened to Dunbar to inform de la Bastie of the attack – it could scarcely be called a siege; and the Frenchman, ever concerned for law and order, with only a small company of his men, rode the eighteen miles to Langton to sort matters out. There he found only a little group of Homes under the sons of the Laird of Wedderburn, one of the more important leaders of the clan. These fled on the arrival of the governor, but there was a large company of their father's mosstroopers hidden nearby in the narrow enclosed valley of the Langton Burn. As the Frenchman was assuring the Cockburns of his concern for them should there be any further assaults upon them, Wedderburn and his hundreds of horsemen appeared and surrounded de la Bastie's group, greatly outnumbering them. And they knew the territory, whereas the newcomers did not. In the conflict that followed, the Frenchman's people were forced to scatter, to head back for Dunbar and safety.

Concentrating on de la Bastie himself, Wedderburn managed to force his quarry into the common-land approach to the village of Gavinton. Not known to strangers to the district, this grazing ground was partly marsh. De la Bastie and others, fleeing, rode into this, and quickly their steeds were up to their houghs in the mire, and floundering. Well aware of this, the Homes promptly dismounted and went leaping after the bogged-down governor, ignoring the rest, and thus, lighter-footed than the horses, reached him and dragged him from his saddle and stabbed him to death there and then.

Letting the rest of de la Bastie's men make their escape, the Homes dragged the corpse to Wedderburn, who with his own sword cut off the governor's head. He tied the bloody trophy to his saddle-bow, and rode with it to the nearby town of Duns. There, in triumph, he set the head, tied by the long hair to the top of the market-cross, as a public spectacle of Home power in the Merse.

So ingloriously died Scotland's French governor, Albany's representative, a most able and distinguished man.

When Andrew was told of it, he grieved indeed, appalled, for they had become good friends.

What now?

25

The murder of his friend and representative brought the Duke of Albany hastening from France. He called a parliament, in the name of the king, to be held at Perth. James himself, now aged five years, was to be present with his regent. Andrew attended.

The Chancellor, Archbishop Beaton of Glasgow, conducted the business. Great regret was expressed by almost all over the death of de la Bastie; and the assembly passed a motion, unopposed, for the forfeiture of the new Lord Home and all his supporters, Wedderburn especially named. None of these was present, needless to say. Nor were the Douglases, Angus and the pro-English party keeping their distance. Who was to enforce the Homes' forfeiture?

A new Chief Warden of the Marches had to be appointed, and this was an obvious task for him. James Hamilton, Earl of Arran, was given that position, Andrew doubtful, for he considered him weak, but could not say so. He would be no match for the Homes, but parliament ordered him to proceed against them.

When the session was over, Arran came to Andrew and sought his help in this matter of the Homes. His cannon were famous, and could be a great help in this. If they could be got inland, they would constitute an enormous advantage. To get them there, could they be carried on carts? Against Wedderburn. The new Lord Home was young, and no great danger as yet.

Andrew thought that sleds would be the best means to transport the artillery, these drawn by oxen. He would seek to have this organised, little as he relished working with Arran. Beth told him that, as admiral, he should insist that his activities ought to be confined to shipboard.

Arran said that there was nothing for it but to drag the sleds overland, however far, Andrew pointing out that this would be more easily said than done. There were not only the cannon themselves, but the necessary balls and sacks of gunpowder to transport. The earl seemed to think that this could be done behind an armed force from Edinburgh's Burgh Muir itself, so impractical a strategist was he. It would take many days for the slow-moving oxen to reach Wedderburn, in mid-Merse, and meanwhile the Homes would be well warned, and, knowing the terrain, able to ambush the great train of men and beasts and cannon. That was just not to be considered.

Andrew judged that the nearest he could get his ships to Wedderburn was probably Cove, a small fishing haven near Colbrandspath. Even that would be fully fifteen miles. Oxen could be collected from the local farmers, but the entire operation would take time. A week, then, to meet near Wedderburn, Arran to send forward a party to keep the Homes from any attempt to ambush and capture the artillery. Undoubtedly, in their own country, they would get to hear of the approach.

Cove harbour was tidal, so one of the smaller ships was given the task of carrying in the cannon at high water. Four pieces would be sufficient for their purpose, he judged, with ball and powder. So say eight slipes or sleds. Farmers used the like, so there was no difficulty in borrowing both them and the oxen to pull them.

How long would it take to get them over the fifteen or so miles of undulating, watery and wooded country? Four hours at least. He sent word for Arran to have his force thereabouts in good time.

As far as Andrew was concerned, all went according to plan, and he reached the upper Blackadder tributary, the Langton Burn, with his four cannon and some one hundred and fifty men at the given time. But there was no sign of Arran's people. He did not want to get too close to Wedderburn Castle without the protection of much larger numbers. So he waited in large woodland some way north of Duns. Waited and waited.

When, after five days, no word reached him from Arran, he sent a messenger to ride to Edinburgh's Burgh Muir to discover the situation. And when that young man returned, after two days of hard riding, it was to reveal that Arran had proved his unreliability in major fashion, presumably forgetting all about Andrew and the cannon. Wedderburn, having learned of the strength of the earl's army, had sent messengers to Edinburgh offering to present to the justiciar the keys of both Wedderburn and Home castles, at, say, Lauder, and full co-operation hereafter with the regent's government, if he and Lord Home were promised entire freedom from any punitive measures. To this Arran had readily and weakly agreed, and marched back from Lauderdale to Edinburgh and dispersed his army.

This news had Andrew shaking his greying head in angry frustration. What was to become of Scotland, with its king a child, its regent preferring to live in France, and its Justiciar South of Forth, and Chief Warden of the Marches, acting thus?

He turned back for Cove, with his cannon, a man exasperated.

Astonishing news reached Largo shortly thereafter. Albany, in France, had decided that this of being regent for his young kinsman of Scotland was proving to be an unwelcome task, and interfering with his preferred life on the Continent. He had written to the queen mother urging her to take over as representative of her son, and to act regent. And the Tudor woman had declared that she was willing to return to Scotland, but did not desire the responsibility of government as regent. She had become reconciled with Angus and had got him to discard the mistress with whom he had been living for some time, and urged that he should be given the position of regent. Arran, and indeed almost all the nobility, rejected this. So, reluctant or otherwise, Albany remained regent meantime, but in France, a highly unsatisfactory situation, which all but asked for power-hungry lords to grasp at control.

And not only Lowland lords but Highland and Isles chiefs. Sir Alexander MacDonald of Lochalsh decided that here was opportunity for him to try to regain the forfeited lordship of the Isles. He rose in arms. MacIan of Ardnamurchan, with whom the MacDonalds were ever at feud, feared that his interests could suffer, and allied himself to nearby Maclean of Duart, in Mull, formerly another enemy, to counter this move. War broke out in the Isles and West Highland coasts.

Albany appointed the Campbell Earl of Argyll to be Lieutenant-General of Scotland, with instructions to restore peace in the Isles. And Argyll sent for the admiral to help see to this.

Andrew had no desire to do anything of the sort. The Isles were awkward indeed for navigation, among all the currents, downdraughts, skerries and overfalls, as he knew from past experience; and the feuding chiefs were best left to their own activities. But this was, in effect, a royal command, and he had to obey. He would at least make a gesture of it.

So, taking just *Caravel* and *Flower*, he set off northwards.

Rounding the land, he called in at Lochalsh of Skye, but found that MacDonald was down assailing his traditional foe, the said MacIan. What would Argyll expect of him in this? To go and seek to separate the two clans in their battle? Was this any task for him? Doubtfully he sailed on.

This of being admiral was becoming a trial and trouble for him. Or was it just that he was getting old? He was now of fifty-eight years. He found himself beginning to seek a quieter life, at home at Largo with Beth, and leaving national affairs to others.

Reaching the most westerly headland of all the Scottish mainland, Ardnamurchan Point, he called at Mingary Castle on its cliff above the sound of Mull, a seat of MacIan, where he learned that MacDonald had sailed his galleys fleet past here and on up Loch Sunart, where he must have heard that MacIan was presently basing himself at Strontian, at the loch-head. There could be battle there, for certain.

So the two warhips sailed thither, cannon loaded.

About a dozen miles up the long, winding sea loch, they came upon a scene new to Andrew, a sea battle being fought between longships and birlinns and galleys, not full-rigged ships. Fully fifty of these craft, with their scores of long oars, or sweeps, and square painted sails on a single mast, with their helmeted crews part-sheltered behind ranked shields, were assailing each other in mid-loch, with swords and battle-axes and spears, each vessel seeking to damage the opposing craft by rowing alongside close enough to smash the other's long oars aside and over, this causing havoc among the rowers with smashed and splintering wood. The yells and shouts and screams resounded from the flanking hillsides. It was impossible to tell, in that mêlée, which side, if either, was winning, although the galley of the Isles and the black swooping sea eagle of MacIan were emblazoned boldly on the sails.

Andrew had been sent here to seek to enforce peace. To do so in the present situation was no simple task. Would cannon-fire be the answer in these circumstances? Blank shot be effective with these fierce combatants? He could not assail them with ball. But he might have a few fired into the water near the ships, to form great spouts. Would that be sufficient to convey the message?

Whether, in all the battling, the crews were fully aware

of the approach of the warships was not to be known. Certainly, if so, it did not affect their combat.

Andrew ordered a salvo of blanks to be fired.

The noise, re-echoed from all around, may have penetrated to some of the contestants, but, if so, combat went on uninterrupted. He ordered ball to be fired, but only two or three, for these were not to be wasted. The spouts and splashes created in the water nearby produced no evident impact on the clansmen.

He decided that there was nothing for it but to drive his two large ships right into the mass of struggling low-sided vessels and scatter them thus. It made a strange experience, deliberately to ram their way through the smaller craft, this occasioning still further chaos among the oars and their oarsmen, actually capsizing some of the galleys. But it did have the effect of much lessening the battle.

As they went in, Andrew was seeking to identify the leaders' vessels. How to do this? They all had painted sails of one clan or the other. Then he thought of feathers, eagle's feathers. Chieftains ever sported these in their bonnets, one for lesser commanders, two for heads of families, three for high chiefs.

It made a difficult search in all that confusion, peer as he would. There were not a few feathers to be discerned, these quite tall rising above heads. But three? Would his shipmaster on *Flower* think of this?

Presently he spotted what he was looking for, in the stern of one birlinn, this under the galley of the Isles sail. That would be MacDonald. How to reach and if possible collect him? Andrew shouted to his crew. Lower rope-ladders down to that vessel, many of them. Mainly towards its stern. Descend to it, himself with them. Grasp that feathered man. Get him up to the *Caravel*, somehow. Blank shot to continue to be fired.

That developed into a wild and far from disciplined venture, amidst shouting, battling men, abandoned and broken oars, and the continuing thunder of cannon just above, keeping the large ship alongside the galley itself no light task for the helmsman. Three times Andrew sought, from a dangling ladder, to land himself on the quite small stern platform of MacDonald's birlinn, but the heavings of the two craft made it difficult, the dagger he grasped in one fist no help. But at the fourth try, along with three of his men, he set foot on the lesser craft, where MacDonald was preoccupied in directing his fighting men, ordering his helmsman, watching for those ladders and those descending by them, and concerned with an attacking longship on the other flank, all the while deafened by the gunfire.

Andrew managed to grasp the chief's shoulder, and flourished that dirk in the other's face.

"MacDonald!" he shouted. "I am Wood, the admiral. Hear me. Sent by Argyll to halt you. And MacIan. This is to cease. Your fighting. Have you aboard my ship! Up with you!"

The other, more used to the Gaelic speech than to English, and hearing only partially because of the cannonade, shook his head. He was a man of later middle age, and in a state of turmoil, physical and mental.

Yelling in the other's ear, Andrew demanded, "MacIan? Where is MacIan? Which his craft? MacIan's?"

That hated name penetrated, at least. The other gestured to the galley alongside, the two crews still struggling with each other, although because of *Caravel*'s bumping at the opposite flank the MacDonalds were distracted. The two chiefs would single out each other, to be sure. How, then, to capture MacIan as well as this MacDonald?

His people were still descending by their many ladders. At least he had large numbers of crewmen to assist. How many to deal with on these galleys? But they were fighting each other, scarcely heeding the descending newcomers. His shipmaster, on *Flower*? If only he would see the need, and steer round to assist, in all this stramash and affray, on the other flank . . .

But at least, that name MacIan had registered positively

with MacDonald. He grabbed at Andrew's arm and pointed, this over at the stern of the attacking galley. Of course. There stood another eagle-feathered character beside the helmsman, sword in hand.

If only *Flower* would come round.

Andrew changed his orders to MacDonald. "MacIan! Capture MacIan. *Your* men, and mine. Get him, I say! All board that craft. He is your foe. And mine, meantime. Get MacIan."

No doubt MacDonald saw advantage in this, for himself, whatever the overall position. His shoutings and pointings would not be very evident in this noise; but Andrew's men were now descending into the galley in numbers, and the MacDonald clansmen, seeing their chief gesticulating towards MacIan with fist-shakings, would realise that the newcomers were not foes to be opposed but allies against the enemy. A sort of united front evolved.

Then, in the confusion of battling vessels and din, the positive development was demonstrated. The *Flower* did manage to steer round from the far side of *Caravel*, to push through the mêlée to reach the MacIan galley on the further flank, no easy task. His shipmaster and Dand had seen the need. Thankfully Andrew pointed and waved and pointed.

What was now required was obvious, MacIan's vessel wedged between the two large ships. When the other was in approximate position, Andrew led the assault, hampered as it was by all those oars cluttering and obstructing, to board the trapped galley, men descending on ladders and ropes from *Flower* also. The assault was accomplished, the defenders hopelessly outnumbered. MacIan cast his sword from him, and stood, in defeat, but proud defeat.

Andrew picked his way to the man's side and raised a hand high, in all but salute.

"MacIan!" he cried. "I am Wood, the admiral. Sent to bring you to Argyll, the regent's lieutenant-general, together with MacDonald. To end this fighting. Peace to prevail. Come aboard my ship. Good will come of this, whatever *you* think! Come, you."

The other shrugged, grimacing, a hawk-featured, dark-haired man.

Andrew led him to a ladder against *Caravel*'s side, and gestured to him to climb. He followed him up.

Whether or not the rival clansmen in all the other galleys saw what had transpired, the fighting went on. Would the capture of the two chiefs, once it was known, end the struggle? Probably not. And in all the noise, no commands from these would be heard or evident, even if such were made. Andrew decided to leave them all to it.

There was nothing more that he could do here. He would take the two chiefs to Argyll's main seat at Inveraray, on the sea loch of Fyne, whether the earl was there or not, and leave them. Then sail home, duty done. He himself was getting past all this of campaigning and battle, not the actual doing of it all, but the challenge. Should he resign his admiralship? *Could* he? And who would succeed him? Dand was too young.

He knew what Beth would say.

26

Andrew's return to the Forth informed him of news of dramatic happenings on the wider front of national affairs. That strange man, Arran, was allying himself with the queen mother and the pro-English party, and claiming that Albany, still in France, was no suitable regent, the inference being that he himself would make a better one. He was even consorting with Dacre, claiming that peace along the border could thus be established, whatever the Homes might say to that. Young King James was now just old enough, and beginning to assert himself, and Arran was bowing to this, flattering the boy, obviously seeking the regency.

While Andrew recognised that a regent domiciled abroad was no apt ruler for a nation, he judged that Arran would be no great improvement. In the circumstances he thought that a council of regency would be the answer, not any one individual. Could this be brought about?

Beth said that, as admiral, he was in a position to help to achieve this.

How? Whom to approach? Arran certainly would not be in favour of it, and he was Justiciar South of the Forth. But the Lindsay Earl of Crawford was the Justiciar *North* of the Forth. And he was an able and reliable man. If he, and Argyll, were to co-operate, such regency council might be established, and Albany probably quite prepared to accept and join it, allowing him to remain in France. That would put a spoke in Arran's wheel.

As it happened, although the Crawford earldom took its name from Lanarkshire, the present earl normally lived at

Pitcorthie, only some six miles east of Largo, more convenient for his duties as justiciar. And he was married to
Isabel Lundy, a kinswoman of Beth's. Andrew would go
and see him.

Crawford was not at home but gone to Dundee to hold
one of his justice courts. So Andrew had to sail thither. He
found the earl glad to see him, and, like himself, worried
about the state of the realm, and no admirer of Arran. The
idea of a council of regency appealed to him; and he
thought that, between them, they could convince Albany
to agree to it. Also persuade sundry substantial lords, in
addition to Argyll, to join it. Parliamentary sanction would
be required, of course; but many of the magnates, spiritual
as well as temporal, worried about the situation, would
almost certainly see that it was passed. Albany would have
to call such, as regent. And be present.

So Andrew had one more voyage to make, to France, to
put it to him. Beth and Dand could accompany him on this
mission.

They reached Paris to find Albany at his favourite
activity, hawking in the Bois de Boulogne. When he
returned, he took them to his chateau of Mirefleur in
Auvergne, quite a lengthy journey, where they met and
were excellently entertained by his duchess, Anne de la
Tour. The duke was a friendly character, and they enjoyed
their visit. He was pleased with the idea of a council of
regency, which would relieve him of some of his respon-
sibilities. He agreed that the other members, which must
of course include the Earl of Arran, should be the Earls of
Argyll and Crawford, with the prelates, the Archbishop of
Glasgow and the Bishop of Moray. And Andrew found his
own name being added to the number, as admiral. He,
Albany, would call the necessary parliament, giving the
required forty days' notice, and would return to Scotland
for the sitting.

The visitors spent three days sightseeing in the Auvergne area, and then returned to the *Caravel* on the Seine,

taking the document which called the parliament, this to be held again at Perth.

Andrew was surprised to be heading for home nominated by Albany to be a member of the regency council; but Beth was not.

It was strange to consider, as they sailed back down the Seine, that this land was at war with England, and that Henry Tudor was presumably fighting somewhere none so far off. And that the Continent was in some sort of turmoil over a humbly born German monk and scholar named Martin Luther, who was leading a movement for the reform of Holy Church, and an attack on the many ecclesiastical abuses being perpetrated by the leading clerics in the name of the papacy. It all seemed somewhat remote from Scotland, but Andrew recognised that the repercussions could reach them in due course. He himself was not a great churchman, although he worshipped sincerely in his own fashion; but he was well aware that this Lutheran campaign could have a major impact on Scotland. He would try not to get involved in that, at least, regency councillor or none.

On return home he learned that there had been a great clan battle at some place called Craig-an-Airgid in Morvern, with the MacDonalds being supported by MacLeod of Dunvegan, while his former ally, Maclean of Duart, had changed sides and fought for MacIan – but to no great effect, it seemed, for MacIan and his two sons were slain. All the Isles and West Highlands were in a ferment.

Andrew hoped that he would not be called upon to help settle this upheaval; but with Argyll's Campbell clan lands so nearby, he might well be.

Meantime there was a parliament, to appoint the regency council.

That session passed off without any real controversy, with the young monarch present, and Albany sitting beside his throne. The members of the council were duly accepted, with a representative added from the north, Keith, the Earl Marischal, as was suitable. Dand and Beth watched all from the gallery, with Isabel Lundy, Countess of Crawford.

As Andrew had rather feared, Argyll, sitting beside him at the first meeting of the council, asked him to go and show a presence through the Hebrides, which were still in a state of unrest following the deaths of the MacIans, who had had their major influence. The MacDonalds were now very much in the ascendant, which was not unsuitable as they were in direct descent from the ancient Lords of the Isles. But they must be guided not to overdo their author- ity and arouse conflict with the other clans which had favoured the MacIans. A visit by the admiral's ships would be a wise move.

They made a quite pleasant voyage of it, the presence of Lady Wood an added symbol of goodwill on the part of the admiral. They were well received at Lochalsh by Sir Alexander MacDonald, and at Dunvegan by the Ma- cLeod; and in the Outer Isles MacNeill of Barra and Clanranald at Benbecula welcomed them, the latter escort- ing them to remote St Kilda, the extreme limit of Scottish soil, or rather rock, ever a spot to visit.

Beth declared it was high time that she and Andrew started having a normal husband-and-wife home life. There was ample to keep him occupied at Largo. If the Duke of Albany could act regent from France, Andrew could surely do the like from Fife? Beth had never been very enthusiastic over this regency situation.

Actually, Andrew had an activity in prospect for his hoped-for more leisured life at Largo, but he did not mention it as yet to Beth.

The notion of retirement received a blow that spring of 1521. Albany arrived from France with orders from King Francis to invade England in force, this under the Auld Alliance, in order to get Henry of England to return to his own country to repel the threat. It was admittedly only to be a token sally, but in sufficient numbers to make the danger seem real to the Tudor.

So a great muster was ordered for Edinburgh's Burgh Muir; and the admiral was to make his mark once more down the Northumbrian coast.

This, to be sure, was no great task for Andrew, much less so than for most lords and magnates, who had to assemble their fullest strength for the army. He would make a demonstration coincident with Albany's advance.

Actually the duke's move was also only a demonstration. After raising some sixty thousand men, he divided the host into three. One force was sent to cross the borderline at Gretna, but not to go on to assail Carlisle; another he led himself to the Tweed at Coldstream; and the third, under the late Lord Home's brother, now with his title restored, to make an assault on Berwick. Its castle was much too powerful for successful assault, but a gesture against the town could be effective. Andrew was to show a naval presence, with gunfire.

That presented no problem. Off the Tweed's mouth he used up much gunpowder. But he saw no signs of Scots invaders. He went on to perform similarly off Alnwick. Then returning to Berwick, he waited there for a couple of days, firing occasional salvoes; but still there was no indication of a Home attack. One more day he lingered, to the distress of the Berwick fishermen, but with no development evident, he sailed back for Leith.

There he learned that Albany had made only the briefest of gestures, and then disbanded his army with scarcely a blow struck.

Whether this would be sufficient to bring Henry Tudor back from France was highly doubtful. Andrew at least could go home to Largo.

He had hardly rejoined Beth when a further demand came for his services. King Christian of Denmark, who had a treaty of alliance with Scotland, sent an envoy urgently to request the use of one thousand Highland clansmen to assist him in the putting down of Norwegian revolt; it was interesting to Andrew that he wanted Highlanders, some reflection of the old Viking–Scots days in the Isles? The regency council was not disposed to send such a contingent, declaring that the English threat was too great for the like; but that they would despatch some two hundred and fifty clansmen, provided hopefully by Mac-Donald and MacLeod, and these to be under a seasoned commander, Stewart of Ardgowan.

So as well as delivering these, Andrew had to go and collect them first. He was beginning to feel that he ought to be making his base somewhere in the Isles, instead of at Leith, so often did he have to travel there these days.

Once again, then, Skye was his principal destination, for, despite all the hundreds of islands this, the greatest one, held the main seats of both Sir Alexander MacDonald and Alastair Crotach MacLeod, the eighth chief, although almost sixty miles apart, Lochalsh on the south-east and Dunvegan on the north-west. He had no difficulty in persuading MacDonald to supply one hundred and twenty-five men, but when MacLeod heard of it, he had to double that number. He was a big, hump-backed and determined man, these aspects of him emphasised by the fact that, when he wanted to wed one of Cameron of Lochiel's daughters, the first nine of them refused him, because of the hump, but the tenth accepted. So Andrew found himself transporting nearer five hundred clansmen. He had to sail down to the Clyde estuary to pick up the veteran Stewart of Ardgowan to command them all in Denmark, he descended from Robert the Third, and living at Renfrew.

Then back with them all, in four ships, round the Pentland Firth and across the Norse Sea to the Skagerrak and the Kattegat. Christian's envoy had not said where he was to deposit Stewart and the men, so he went on to the Danish capital at Copenhagen.

He had been quite prepared for that monarch to require him to involve his vessels in the Norwegian–Swedish situation again, and sail up the Baltic. But Christian was holding a conference of commanders of various sorts for his campaign, and although glad to receive the Scots reinforcements, did not call for any naval assistance.

Quite thankful, Andrew disembarked his many passengers, wishing them well in their further activities. He gained the king's assurance that he would have them ferried back to Scotland in due course.

While he was so comparatively near, he proceeded on to Lübeck. He wanted to know whether more ivory was sought. He also wanted to talk with some of the Hansa merchant-princes as to his long-considered project for Largo, this ever at the back of his mind. These would know whom he should consult, probably some master artisan at Hamburg.

All this he did, to his satisfaction, especially over the rising price of ivory. Iceland was now providing the greater part of the revenues required to pay for the cost of ships and crews.

Home, then.

27

A meeting of the regency council was called, before Albany returned once again to France, to appoint a new member to succeed the Earl Marischal, who had died leaving only a son too young to be considered for such position. By general consent, John, third Earl of Lennox, was chosen, he of the royal line of Stewart and an able and reliable character, his brother, Stewart of Aubigny, in fact a Marshal of France. His mother was a Hamilton, aunt to Arran, but the cousins did not get on together – the which commended Lennox to Andrew. He was married to a daughter of the Earl of Atholl, and seemed likely to become a useful member of the regency.

And a strong regency quickly became necessary in Scotland. Through the weakness of Arran, Angus and the queen mother, their differences patched up and talk of divorce dismissed, took over the guardianship of the young monarch at Stirling Castle. So that, in effect, Angus and his Douglases became in a position largely to dominate, Margaret Tudor supporting. And in this situation, young James, even though only in his twelfth year, proved to be of independent mind; he managed to get a royal secretary, one David Paniter, a cleric and Commendator of Cambuskenneth Abbey, to come and contact the Earl of Lennox, whom the boy trusted, to endeavour to get him out of the clutches of his mother and Angus.

This, of course, created an awkward situation. Albany was overseas, Arran was a regent and was in league with Margaret Tudor and Angus, so the regency council, as such, was not in a position to rescue the young king.

Lennox approached Andrew. What could be done? Argyll, the lieutenant-general, would be favourable to helping the boy. But the Marischal was dead. That left only Crawford and the two prelates of the council, and these last were hardly of the sort usefully to aid their monarch. Yet Lennox looked upon it all as a royal command. James must be freed from his mother and Angus, however it was achieved.

Lennox said that he could raise a quite large force to help challenge the Douglases and Hamiltons, with Argyll's and the admiral's help.

Andrew was doubtful about this, in effect getting involved in civil war. Yet James was his liege-lord and he had sworn fealty to him. He urged that, with the other members of the regency council, they should require Angus and the queen mother to release the king to them, as he was desiring, or a large force would be sent to aid him in arms.

The answer to that was a challenge from Angus to attempt it.

So it seemed that there was nothing for it but battle, the regency divided. The lieutenant-general, the admiral, Lennox and Crawford against Angus and Arran; in effect the Stewarts, Campbells and Lindsays against the Douglases and Hamiltons – back to clan warfare. What part could Andrew usefully play, he who had been contemplating retirement from the national scene?

Since the king was held at Stirling, as was usual, it seemed that one more approach with his ships to as near there as possible was indicated. It was to be hoped that his cannon would not have to be used on this occasion, save perhaps as demonstration.

Lennox, Argyll and Crawford assembled their people, their thousands, at Edinburgh, for no one underestimated the strength of the Douglases in especial, probably the most powerful clan in all southern Scotland. The march for Stirling commenced on a September day when, the harvesting over, the manpower could be free for action, always an important consideration, and for both sides. Andrew sailed five ships up Forth. Argyll and the other two earls would keep in touch with him by sending mounted scouts down to the riverside as they advanced westwards.

The ships sailed a deal more swiftly than men marched, of course, so pauses had to be made frequently to ensure fair contact.

They were off Boroughstoneness, the harbour for Linlithgow, halfway to Stirling, when horsemen flying the Stewart banner hailed to them that scouts ahead reported a great army of Douglases and Hamiltons advancing just short of Linlithgow. There would be battle undoubtedly, and all leal men required to rally to James's cause. Could the admiral bring as many of his crewmen as was possible? And somehow carry his artillery with him?

This last Andrew was not prepared to do. Firing ball or grapeshot at his fellow-Scots, however mistaken their allegiances, was not for him. Perhaps this was nit-picking, but that was how he felt. Fair fight, yes – but not that.

It was landing, then, of about four hundred men. How far inland must they march? There was a bridge over the River Almond less than a mile west of Linlithgow town. Lennox would seek to use it against the enemy, almost certainly. That would be about four miles from the coast, just over an hour's march.

Well before they reached the river they heard the noise of battle, the shouts and screams of men and neighing of horses and the clash of steel. Hastening the more, Andrew led his people. Lennox had come from Stirling, of course, to the west, so the Douglases and Hamiltons would be on the east side, coming from Edinburgh. They had to ford one of the many bends of the river at a mill and its dam, and quickly thereafter, from a modest height, they saw the struggling forces at another of the bends none so far ahead. Swords drawn, they advanced at the run.

The fighting appeared to be on both sides of the Almond, so some of the foe must have forded it, if Lennox was still holding the bridge itself. Which side to descend upon? The east would probably be most effective, since that would tend to get them behind the enemy.

The four hundred hurled themselves into the fray, yelling.

Because of the narrow bridge and the steepish small banks down to it, horses were only a handicap, and both sides had dismounted to fight on foot. Andrew thought that he saw an opportunity here, to drive those waiting animals on the east side down upon their struggling owners.

Leading the way, he reached the mass of the steeds, and recognising that he could best control his people from the saddle, where all could see him, he hoisted himself up on a beast, and waved the men on right and left.

It was thus that he entered the fray, shouting to his men to beat the horses' flanks rather than mounting them, urging them all down upon the rear of their former riders in pounding menace, Andrew more or less carried onward in the rush.

Reaching the steepish bank the animals, seeing the river ahead of them, sought to avoid plunging into it, in rampant, tossing chaos. And, cannoned into by other beasts, Andrew's animal reared high, jerking aside, and he was thrown from the saddle to crash down among the kicking, stamping hooves. He was aware of crashes against head and legs, and knew no more.

When consciousness returned, he found himself lying on grass at the bank-head, in grievous pain, men bending over him anxiously. When he tried to move he all but passed out again, so great was the agony in his shoulder, but worse at his lower left leg and ankle. He groaned. He could only lie there in racking torment.

Heeding his suffering, his men between them carefully lifted him into a sitting position. They contrived a sort of stretcher out of lance-shafts thrust through the sleeves of doublets, and hoisted him thereon, to his gasps of agony. Further movement, and he lost consciousness again.

Thereafter he was only vaguely aware of what was happening, physical suffering his preoccupation when he was in any state to know anything at all.

Eventually he found himself actually lying on his bunk on *Caravel*, with others seeking to raise him sufficiently to get some whisky into his mouth, this but adding to his pains, because one side of his head and face was also bruised by hoof-stampings.

Scotland's admiral was in a sorry state.

When he could take it in, he learned the results of the Battle of Linlithgow Bridge. Lennox was dead and his army defeated. Actually, injured, he had been standing in reeling shock when Hamilton of Finnart, a bastard son of Arran's, slew him, unprotected as he was. So now the Douglases and the Hamiltons, under Angus and Arran, would rule the land; and with the former much the stronger character, and married to the queen mother, he would undoubtedly show who was master.

Andrew, when he could get on his feet, found himself to be a lame man now, his left ankle grievously smashed and bent. All the more reason to seek retirement from his admiral's duties. Could he also resign from the council of regency? Angus had more or less appointed himself to it, and Albany, not liking the way things were developing, remained in France.

In this situation King James, from Stirling Castle, took a young but very positive hand, whether with his stepfather's, Angus's approval or otherwise. He announced that he was, in fact, now assuming the rule of his people, not just reigning; and was going to remove himself from Stirling to Edinburgh Castle, at his capital city, and was calling a parliament to confirm this change. Albany's regency was therefore at an end, as indeed was that of all the other members of the council, including Andrew. James the Fifth would henceforth act the monarch.

No one was in a position to deny this royal announcement, whatever Angus and Arran thought about it.

The parliament, held at Edinburgh Castle, with James Beaton, now Archbishop of St Andrews, the Chancellor, conducting the proceedings and James his liege-lord very much present, accepted the young king's announcement with acclaim. Most attending feared the Douglas and Hamilton ascendancy.

The youngster then made a demonstration of his resolve. He ordered and led a procession down from the citadel to Holyrood Abbey, ordering Angus and his own mother to ride behind him in supportive role, with Arran and the Chancellor and Argyll and a long train of magnates including the admiral, there all either to take part or to watch a lively spectacle, of tournament-jousting, he himself competing, racing, archery and wrestling contests and tugs-of-war, youthful enthusiasm at its height, most, including the capital's citizenry much appreciative and diverted. Their young monarch was going to be popular.

The limping Andrew was accorded royal sympathy.

Thereafter, that ankle injury actually enhanced and brought forward the project that had been simmering in the victim's mind for some time, as it happened, and which he had enquired about in some measure at Hamburg. The German gunpowder manufacturer there had introduced him to a friend, a master artisan named Dirk Schroder, who had constructed subsidiary canals linked with the great Hamburg–Lübeck one. Now his notion was to make a canal at Largo, only a very modified version of the German ones, but an artificial waterway of his own. He had always felt that it was a great pity that his home was almost a mile inland from the sea, his element. Now, part disabled as he was, this was the more challenging. He would have one constructed. It would demand steps and stairs of a sort, of course, because of the differing levels. He would go and fetch that expert from Hamburg, and so, one day, be able to sail his barge from his home to salt water.

Beth encouraged him in this undertaking, which she saw as keeping him near her. If he could route it by Largo Kirk, that would be a help of a Sunday.

So it was to Lübeck and Hamburg with the latest load of ivory. He had some difficulty in persuading the man Dirk Schroder to come back with him to Scotland, but a sufficiency of financial inducement overcame reluctance.

A survey of Largo was made, and difficulties pointed out, mainly as to levels, no problem about water, the Boghill Burn providing ample. The German said that it would demand much physical labour, but Andrew reminded him that he had plenty of crewmen who could exercise different muscles from those used on shipboard. The route, by the church, was decided upon, this requiring quite a bend eastwards; and it was agreed that, at this stage, no actual descent to the seashore need be attempted. They would see how the first and highest part went, from one hundred and sixty feet at the upper village to one hundred at the lower, with the kirk at the former. How many weirs, locks and water-gates would be necessary was problematical, with their sluices. And of course there should be two paths at the sides for horses to draw the barges, with much manhandling through the locks, with windlasses to raise the boats to the new levels. Schroder said that, a century before, the Stecknitz Canal, twenty-one miles long, from Lake Möllner to Lübeck, fell forty feet. He would go back to Hamburg and prepare plans. The *Kestrel* would take him and bring him back in due course.

28

While Schroder's return was awaited, a new call upon Andrew's services was received. It came from the monarch himself, and for an especial mission. James was to wed, now that he had reached marriageable age. There had been talk of this for some time, of course. And almost inevitably it must be to some princess of France, to support the Auld Alliance, and help to keep Henry Tudor on his toes, since royal marriages were, sadly, seldom concerned with attraction and affection, but with dynastic alliance and advantage. Now it was proposed that he should wed the Princess Marie de Bourbon, daughter of the Duke of Vendôme, kin to the King Francis of France.

So the monarch had to be taken for a wedding to someone whom he had never seen, and taken in style, with a great train of notables, Andrew to transport them all.

With a new bride to bring back, that man thought it suitable that Beth should accompany them as assistant to her kinswoman, the Countess of Crawford, that earl one of the royal party. With so many going, Dand in *Flower* and his shipmaster in *Kestrel*, Andrew had to join the *Caravel* for this great occasion.

All was meticulously planned. The dauphin, heir to the French throne, would meet them at Dieppe and conduct them to Paris. Andrew would conveniently have sailed his ships up the Seine, but that was not what had been arranged by King Francis.

A splendid company of French nobles would ride with the Scots party through the Normandy provinces of Seine-

Maritime and Seine-Inférieure, populous and fertile lands, the almost one hundred miles to Paris.

Prince Henry duly met them at Dieppe, with much display and flourish. By the chosen route, to visit various important magnates, they rode through this Normandy, passing the first night at Neufchâtel-en-Bray where they were handsomely entertained, despite the great numbers, Andrew and Beth having to admit that they fared better than they would have done aboard the ships.

Next day the lordly company got only so far as Gournay, haste of no concern, with calls at chateaux and great houses on the way, for almost overmuch hospitality. The following night they slept in the castle of Gisors, built by Henry the First of England, and where Richard Lionheart cried out the words "*Dieu et mon droit!*" which thereafter became the motto of the English royal arms. Pontoise, on that great river, made the next stop; and on the fifth day they at last reached Paris – where Andrew could have had them up Seine in less than half that time.

King Francis awaited them at the outskirts of the city. The large company was installed in various palaces and establishments, at this stage Andrew and Beth, with Crawford and his Isabel, separated from their monarch.

The day following they discovered that a distinctly extraordinary situation had suddenly developed. At the palace of the Duke of Vendôme, James had met his proposed bride, Marie de Bourbon, who had seemed impressed by the good-looking and gallant monarch. However, also present in the distinguished company was the Princess Madeleine, daughter of King Francis himself, a young woman of but sixteen years, but beautious if somewhat frail-seeming. And James had found *her* much more to his taste. It did not take long for the impetuous King of Scots to declare that he desired to wed this young female, not Marie. Whatever the effect on the rejected princess, King Francis could not dissuade his fellow-monarch.

This all created a major upset, needless to say, but James was determined, and all plans had to be altered, the court in considerable fluster, poor Marie much despondent.

But the bridegroom-to-be was in a position to have his way, by royal command, Diana of Poitiers, Francis's mistress, a masterful woman, much more so than the queen, manipulating the matter for James.

So, in due course, the King of Scots was married, with much pomp and ceremony despite the change in brides, in the Church of Nôtre Dame, to the Princess Madeleine, before an assembly of two other kings, Francis and Charles of Navarre, and no fewer than seven cardinals sent by the Pope, this to help strengthen Holy Church against the machinations of the reforming Martin Luther. Thereafter the celebrations continued for several days and nights, before James was able to conduct Scotland's new queen to the ships at Dieppe, for home. He had been away from his realm for long, and was concerned over the possible activities of Angus and the queen mother with the Douglas faction. But his delight in his Madeleine was such as to ensure that he sailed a happy man indeed. Seldom was it granted for a monarch to attain to a love-match. The young woman was obviously equally enchanted with her husband.

Andrew and Beth were glad for their liege-lord. On board *Caravel* they looked with interest and some amusement as James described his land to his new queen, his fondness for his people, concern for their welfare, and the scenes and conditions she was going to discover when she set foot on his northern kingdom. It was to be hoped that she would not be gravely disappointed.

With James's agreement, from Dieppe the *Caravel* sailed eastwards to Hamburg, to pick up the man Schroder for the canal-building, the royal pair seeing it all as an interesting honeymoon trip.

In fact, when the young woman did eventually land at Leith, she promptly got down on her knees to kiss the soil of her new country, with a little prayer of blessing.

It made an encouraging start, even though it had been noted on the journey and voyaging that Madeleine did cough a great deal, amidst not a few weakly turns.

James decided that the stern citadels of Edinburgh and Stirling Castles were not the places to install his bride. She would have her own dower-house of Linlithgow Palace, of course, but for much of the time they would occupy the abbot's house of Holyrood Abbey, the hunting-seat of Falkland in Fife, and the palace of Scone, near Perth.

Back at Largo, Dirk Schroder and Andrew's ships' crewmen got busy tree-felling, digging, and banking up earth, no complaints forthcoming.

They had landed the king and his bride at Leith on 17th May; and it was only seven weeks later that they heard the tragic news. Madeleine was dead. She had taken one of her fits of coughing, more violent than usual, and bringing up blood and vomit she had choked and died.

New queen as she was, the nation mourned. James was devastated.

Madeleine was buried at Dunfermline Abbey, beside James's palace, amid scenes of grief remarkable. Andrew and Beth attended the funeral.

The canal construction progressed. How long before they would have to start digging to redirect the water, or some of it, of the Boghall Burn, to supply it? Quite a task also, for the nearest the stream came to the line of the canal was some five hundred yards.

Despite the king's desolation over the death of his Madeleine, the Auld Alliance still required to be evidenced and maintained by marriage to a French queen. So only a matter of months later, David Beaton, a nephew of the Archbishop of St Andrews, was sent back to France to find another bride for James, less than eager as the monarch was to replace his beloved. What choice was there? The king had not greatly liked that Marie of Vendôme; and it would look very strange for the rejected one now to be accepted, as it were, in lieu. So young Bishop Beaton had a somewhat delicate quest.

He came back, after no very lengthy interval, with a recommendation. While there was no other royal French princess available, the de Guise family was highly influential, and descended from the Bourbons, the Princess Antoinette having married the Duke Claude. They had produced two sons and a daughter, Marie. She, at the age of nineteen, had been wed to the Duke de Longueville, but he had died. By him she had a son, Francis. So now this Marie was a widow aged twenty-two, and had shown her capability for child-bearing, which was important. Beaton reported that she was tall, well-built, not exactly beautiful but comely, spirited, vigorous and intelligent. James had met her, among so many others at the court of King Francis and, ever aware of feminine allures, had not failed to note possibilities, although not in any marked way. Now he considered. Scotland could do with an heir to the throne. The admiral was sent for, to conduct the king to France again, in quest of someone who would make an effective queen, this a purely practical mission, while the monarch still grieved for the loss of Madeleine.

Andrew, canal-building, could have done without this duty. But he felt it unsuitable to use Dand as his deputy. And Beth said that she enjoyed these trips to France.

This time there was no nonsense about being met at Dieppe, so *Caravel* was sailed up the Seine to Paris with no delays.

They found that the duchess was not at court now but at her Longueville, with her little son. This was quite a large duchy in the Loire valley, some sixty miles east of Tours, but all of two hundred and fifty south-west of Paris. Andrew declared that he could reach there by ship, although quite a lengthy voyage; but James said that he would ride. He would be glad, however, if Andrew and Beth would accompany him.

It was indeed a lengthy ride, by Chartres and Bonneval,

Cloyes, Montoire and Baugé, to reach a huge chateau, which made their Scottish castles seem modest, apart from the great citadels like Stirling and Edinburgh. In fact, James began to worry a little that he should have come on this quest when he could offer no similar establishment, other than the dower-house at Linlithgow. Was the Scots monarchy remiss in not seeking finer palaces than these fortresses?

What the Duchess Marie thought of the so unexpected arrival of King James was not to be known; but she greeted her visitors kindly, assuming that they were on their way somewhere further. James, embarrassed over the reason for his coming, asked Andrew to, as it were, prepare the way for him, while he and Beth went off with the small duke to admire the gardens and orchards and vineyard, something they could not show in Scotland.

Marie de Guise was a young woman to salute and pay respects to in more than her rank, connections and already quite notable experiences. Andrew, even more struck by her looks and personality than when he had seen her among so many others previously, was somewhat worried about broaching the subject of this visit. But her friendliness helped him. Fortunately, his French was good, his much travelling having made him something of a linguist.

"Madam Duchess," he said, "His Grace, King James, has asked me to approach you on his behalf, in the first place, on an important matter, but . . . delicate, shall we say? He, in fact, was much admiring of you, in person and manner and position, when he first met you. And now, on due consideration, has come to the conclusion that he should seek your further goodwill. So great is his esteem that he has told me to ask you if you would deem it possible to contemplate a closer relationship with him? This before he makes any more personal approach?" This speech had been rehearsed.

She looked at him quizzically from those fine eyes. "Indeed, Sir Andrew. Is the King of Scotland so unsure of himself that he must use you as spokesman, whatever his intentions and wishes?"

"His Grace, Duchess, would not wish to occasion you any upset should you feel disinclined to proceed further."

"Proceed? Has he further interests in mind?"

"He has, yes. Much further."

"And he would have you test the water, my friend?"

"In some measure, yes. Best if there is no embarrassment between you and himself should you, er, dismiss the matter as not for consideration."

"It must be a very serious issue, Sir Andrew, from the way you speak? And I am no ogress, to be approached with great caution!"

"Serious, yes, lady. For it concerns . . . marriage."

"Ha! Is that it? Do not tell me that the King of Scotland has come all this way to propose marriage to my humble self? And that he now lacks courage so to do!"

"No. It is just that he does not wish to disconcert you. Should the notion be . . . distasteful."

"He is most . . . careful, no? If I am to consider marriage to any, I would expect to have it put to me by the man himself!"

"It is a matter of some complexity, lady. You have a duchy to control, for an infant son. Marriage would mean you going to live in Scotland, at least for most of the time. You would become queen there."

"So I would! That would be a notable rise in the world for me, would it not! *Could* I rise to it?"

"You would consider it then, Duchess?"

"Say that if King James comes to put it to me himself, I would have to heed and ponder the matter."

"But not dismiss it, out of hand?"

"We shall see, Sir Andrew . . ."

They left it at that.

When James and Beth and the child returned, Andrew gave his liege-lord a significant nod, hoping that this was a

243

fairly evident indication. Taking Beth's hand, he led her from the room.

They learned in due course, first by the smiles on the king's face, that the situation was at least moving in the right direction. They judged that it would all be to the monarch's personal advantage, and possibly his realm's also.

It was just under one year since Madeleine had died, and it was felt proper that the new wedding should not take place before a decent interval had elapsed, especially as this was not exactly a love-match, however much the couple found each other acceptable. So unlike the previous nuptials, there would be some delay. And this wedding would take place in Scotland. Andrew would take the king home, and come back for the bride fairly soon thereafter.

29

An especial parliament was held on James's return, to announce to the nation the forthcoming marriage and the arrival in Scotland of a new queen-to-be, to the enhancement of the traditional links with France. But at the same time it was to be a very notable occasion for Andrew Wood, although he was not informed of this beforehand.

After the monarch was led in to the throne, to the usual flourish of the Lord Lyon King of Arms' trumpets, the Chancellor, Gavin Dunbar, Archbishop of Glasgow, announced that His Grace would make a personal statement before proceedings commenced.

James rose, so all present must stand also, but he waved them down.

"Two matters of importance I put before you, my lords spiritual and temporal, commissioners of the shires and representatives of the royal burghs," he declared. "One is my intention to wed the Duchess de Longueville, the Lady Marie, sister of the Duke de Guise and the Cardinal of Lorraine, and thus to strengthen the relations between this realm and France, as is meet. This marriage to be celebrated shortly, at St Andrews." And he inclined his head towards Cardinal Beaton, that archbishop.

He went on. "Second to announce to you the resignation from office of one of my most valued and effective officers of state, the Admiral Sir Andrew Wood of Largo, here present. Here is an occasion for great and very sincere expressions of gratitude on behalf of the entire nation. Never before has this realm been so advantaged by having a fleet of ships to act in its interests, in so many ways. And these ships the property not of the kingdom but of Sir Andrew himself. Yet always available for the state's needs, and these most effectively and courageously met and carried out. No King of Scots has ever before seen and been able to rely upon the like, and I hereby declare Scotland's indebtedness and praise . . ."

Although it was unsuitable and indeed *lèse majesté* to interrupt the monarch, James would have been the last to complain of the cheers that arose from all over the assembly to drown his words.

He went on when these died down. "Scotland owes Sir Andrew more than I can here state, as all know well. But I can, and do, thank him on behalf of all my realm. He has served this nation well beyond the calls of duty. On behalf of all I thank him. I hereby promote him to not just admiral but to be Lord *High* Admiral. And he . . ."

The royal voice was lost in the shouts of acclaim.

Andrew, from his place among the officers of state, bowed deeply, much moved by the royal tribute. He did not risk words.

"His retirement to his own Largo is well earned. But he will, I hope and trust, still be available to advise and instruct. And it is my pleasure to appoint as admiral in his place, his son, another Andrew, whom I intend to raise to knighthood also, assured that he will continue his father's great services."

In the gallery, beside Beth and other watchers of the scene, Dand stood. He bowed to the throne, and to all.

"Furthermore," James continued, "I hereby confer on Sir Andrew the lands of Balbraikie, formerly belonging to the abbey of Dunfermline; the baronies of Fawfield and Frostleys and Briwnlands; and the island of Inchkeith, with all fortalices, mills, fishings and rights of tenure, held direct of the crown, this as some token of the realm's appreciation and admiration. May he live long to enjoy them! And, I say, to be the subject of my personal esteem. I name him my adviser and my friend." And waving to the Chancellor to proceed with the parliament's business, James sat down, to further loud applause.

Andrew knew not whether any acknowledgement or personal reaction to this extraordinary royal favour was appropriate. He could only stand and bow again, biting his lip, as the cheers went on. He might now be Lord High Admiral, but that did not make him the more eloquent.

He was glad of this of knighthood for Dand.

He had his opportunity to thank his liege-lord that evening, when he and Beth and Dand dined with the king.

Epilogue

Andrew Wood, although retired, still contributed much to Scotland's causes, with his men and ships. He saw much of James, and his new wife, Marie de Guise; and was a frequent visitor at Falkland Palace, none so far from Largo, the favourite royal hunting-seat, often using his ship to convey the court to Dysart, the nearest haven thereto, and sometimes from the Tay at Newburgh.

He lived to the great age of eighty-eight, Dand dying before him; but he was blessed with Beth's good company to the end, a man fulfilled. He was able to hail and rejoice in the birth and survival of Marie de Guise's daughter, after the death of two little sons by King James, the girl who would one day, on her father's death, become Mary, Queen of Scots at the age of only a few days.

NIGEL TRANTER

COURTING FAVOUR

Younger son of the ninth Earl of Dunbar and March, John Cospatrick expected to inherit neither title nor estate. But when his mother, the formidable Black Agnes, bequeathed him the earldom of Moray in the far north of Scotland, John was to find himself unexpectedly elevated to become the King's lieutenant and arbiter up in those unruly parts.

At the age of twenty-two, with no experience in such matters, John was to prove himself a skilled diplomat. But his greatest test as envoy and negotiator came when the new King, Robert the Second, sent him to England to win over John of Gaunt and attempt to end years of cross-border warfare by entering into a formal treaty of peace and accord with England and an alliance with France.

'Tranter's research is impeccable and his historical notes at the end a fine complement to this extremely readable book.'
The Times

HODDER AND STOUGHTON PAPERBACKS